The Marriage of

THE MARRIAGE OF INNIS WILKINSON

LAUREN H. BRANDENBURG

Illustrations by Sarah J. Coleman

LION FICTION

Published by
Lion Hudson Limited
Wilkinson House, Jordan Hill Business Park
Banbury Road, Oxford OX2 8DR, England
www.lionhudson.com

ISBN 978 1 78264 299 2
eISBN 978 1 78264 300 5

First edition 2020

A catalogue record for this book is available from the British Library

Printed and bound in the UK, July 2020, LH26

To my parents
For leaving a legacy of faith, marriage,
and memories of a perfectly magical childhood.

"I loved her against reason, against promise, against peace, against hope, against happiness, against all discouragement that could be."

Charles Dickens, *Great Expectations*

CHAPTER 1

Margarette Toft had no reason to wonder why Norvel Poteet was cartwheeling down the middle of the stone inlaid street. Nor did she find it odd that Lawrence Hennigan, the mayor, was up before the sun, standing alone in the center of town, watching the minutes tick by on the municipal building clock.

At the base of the hill, in the morning shadows cast by the old shoe factory, the town of Coraloo stood still, waiting patiently for the rest of its citizens to wake as the rising of the sun brought with it a gift, a moment, an event so grand it was the perfect fit for the citizens of Coraloo. The Heaken Beaver Festival.

It is said something happens during the festival, something obscure and curious that magically relieves the residents from the minutiae of day-to-day life. It is a time when tradition is king and superstition his queen, crowning Coraloo in a canopy of red-and-white bunting.

The others would come. The citizens of Coraloo never quite knew how many or who would stumble upon the month-long tribute to a legendary antlered beaver, but they would certainly come. They always did, even without advertisements, elaborate commercials, or brilliantly colored flyers displaying images of fire jugglers, sugared popcorn vendors, and a tartan-clad cast of reenactors.

It was as if *the others* simply appeared, strolling into town as curious spectators, wondering how their timing was so impeccable that they'd found themselves active participants in this local custom. They would arrive shortly after the artisans, who anticipated their coming, practiced in peddling their tonics, poultices, and jewelry uncovered from the depths of the Baltic Sea.

"It will cure whatever ails you!" one would claim.

"Nothing else like it in all the world!" another would vow.

"I can do it with one hand tied behind my back!" would come the promise of a performance the citizens had all seen before but would happily entertain once again.

Margarette peeked out through the cottage window into the dimly lit streets of Coraloo, her grandmother's quilt draped around her shoulders. She had received offers from tourists to purchase her place on more than one occasion, mostly because of its proximity to the river – more of a shallow stream, exactly thirty-one feet from the center of town. Multiple potential buyers had wanted to turn the cedar-shingled cottage into a nail parlor or day spa for pets. Thankfully, her cottage was on the historical registry of Coraloo as the original home of the first pastor of the Coraloo church. However, a few years ago the town historian had revealed that the landmark was more likely to have been home to an admiral of the Spanish navy who fled his country after being accused of piracy. Margarette had no idea how the self-appointed historian had come to that conclusion, as she'd never seen any evidence that a pirate had once lived in her home. Either way, the cottage's status did not stop people asking if she had torn up all the floorboards. And if she had not, they would do it for her, as a small fortune in pirate bounty was rumored hidden somewhere beneath.

She glanced over her shoulder at the time on the twin-bell alarm clock resting on the bedside table, catching sight of the black velvet ring box sitting open in front of it. The box was right where she had left it… not as if it was likely to grow legs, wake in the middle of the night, and run off to the city or even the next town over.

Margarette… Blackwell. She was going to be a Blackwell.

She grinned, feeling the sudden urge to take off for a morning jog, barefoot in her floral pajamas. No one would question her choice of athletic wear because today was May 1st – officially the first day of the festival. One could get away with just about anything during the month of May by virtue of the festival. Want to wear your clothes backwards? Blame it on the festival. Decided to die your hair magenta, which her cousin Sylvia had already done at least twice this year without needing an excuse? Blame it on the festival. Run shoeless through town in your sleepwear? The festival. Every year Margarette had a student or two who attempted to attribute their missing homework to the ravenous appetite of the Heaken beaver.

"The beaver ate my homework, Miss Toft."

She had been teaching long enough to have an arsenal of witty comebacks at her disposal: *"Then clearly it's hungry and you need to do twice as much so you can feed it and have some left to hand in."* To which she would receive an eyeroll and then the homework the following day.

Margarette was proud of her wit, and truth be told she would rather not do her own homework during the month of May – lesson planning, grading end-of-year projects, and so on. Alas, there would always be homework. But there would not be field trips, especially during the festival – absolutely none. Ever. No matter how educational, affordable, or fantastic. She refused. The incident at the art museum five years ago was reason enough. It was the sudden outburst of raucous laughter that had let her know something was amiss.

The disturbance broke through the quiet of the museum. Margarette pushed toward the Degas, through a cluster of congregating sixth-graders to find the sneaky blighter – trousers hanging down around his ankles and a little white bottom pointed up in the air toward the security camera.

She had never yelled at a student, but in that moment an anger rose inside her that could not be contained by museum decorum or common sense, let alone the quivering lips of sheer mortification.

"Charles Michael! Cover yourself! Have you not an ounce of common decency? You're in a public place! You're in a museum! No one came to see your backside! They came for the art! Your behind is not art!" She took a minute to catch her breath. "For the rest of the day you are to be by my side. You will be my shadow. You will walk where I walk. You won't say so much as

9

a single word. And if you do, so help me if you blink wrong, I'll make sure you never see the inside of my classroom again."

She'd meant a lot of what she said, but not that. Charles Michael was smart, a good student. He needed to be in school.

His face red, and clumsily pulling at his khaki trousers to the giggles of his entertained classmates, Charles Michael bumbled, "I'm sorry, Miss Toft."

"Not another word!"

Margarette turned around and bit her lip, imagining what they were saying at the other end of the camera. She covered her mouth. Her insides shook as she fought to hold back the laughter churning inside her chest. Charles Michael had mooned the museum.

The gentle rumble of wheels on cobblestone drew her attention back to the window. She stared, momentarily puzzled at the sight of Innis Wilkinson pushing a cleaning cart toward the hill that would take her up to her employment at the Coraloo Flea Market.

"The festival strikes again." Margarette laughed in the quiet coolness of her cottage room. Innis Wilkinson had an air of mystery about her. She was quiet and, along with her husband Wilkin, rather elusive. Margarette was unable to recall a time in her life, in all thirty-seven years of it, that she had ever seen Innis or Wilkin Wilkinson away from the market. And had Norvel Poteet not cartwheeled into a rubbish bin outside Margarette's cottage she might still be in bed, missing this rare public sighting.

She had the urge to tell someone. But who could she call at five thirty-one in the morning? Her mom? A cousin? Roy? She grinned again. *Roy.*

Suddenly, the cart stopped, seemingly caught on a loose stone. Margarette pulled shut the vintage blue linen curtain she had procured from a flea market vendor in such a way as to hide herself should Innis glance in her direction. Innis, with her blonde hair piled loose atop her head and a pair of old scissors hanging long around her neck, bent down, slowly and gracefully, dislodged the obstruction, and then proceeded on her way.

When Margarette could no longer see the market cleaning lady she glanced back at the antique alarm clock, weighing up the idea of an impromptu jog with another hour in bed. A jog before school would be something new. In fact, it would be a first. She had always wanted to be a jogger, pumping her arms back and forth, lost in her thoughts as her feet pounded the sidewalk. She frowned. Did she *actually* want to pump and pound? Not really. Not today. But she could use the exercise. After all, there was a wedding dress in her near future.

Maybe I'll jog tomorrow...

The clock's tiny hammer banged back and forth on the silver bells. She turned and flopped across her bed so as to flip the lever on the back of the timepiece, silencing the gentle clanging.

"I guess the jog will have to wait."

Margarette reached over, removed the delicate diamond ring from its velvety hold, and slipped it onto her finger as she had done for the past three mornings. She smiled, holding her left hand out in front of her, admiring how the light of the rising sun captured the glisten of the ring. Then, she slid it off and returned it to its usual home. An unwelcome uneasiness came over her. As far as she knew – and she would know – the family hadn't heard about the proposal.

She inhaled slowly, then exhaled.

"I am going to marry Roy Blackwell," she declared.

The couple's first "official" date had been on a Saturday, when she had decided to stop in at the station.

"I brought you lunch to say thank you. I don't cook much, with it being just me and all. But I clipped a new recipe from the paper the other day. And I'm trying to make a point of actually cooking the recipes I clip... I have notebooks full of them." Full was an understatement. *"Do you like spice? I thought you'd said you did."*

He looked at her, not responding. Oh no... Had he said he didn't like hot food? Maybe she should have gone with just a simple sandwich and not the spicy recipe. Or maybe she had misread the subtle intent of the stakeout – their unofficial first date, as she had liked to think of it. Maybe he really had wanted to catch Father Milligan in the act of disfiguring her flowerbeds. They'd laughed a lot at the time and had delicately exchanged a few comments about doing it again sometime… only without the priest.

This was a mistake. She should have thought it through a little more carefully. He hadn't asked her to bring him lunch, and she hadn't offered. What if he was one of those people who didn't appreciate surprises? She adored surprises in every shape and form: gift boxes, special events, unexpected moments. Like when Roy had asked her to join the stakeout. She had spent the rest of that evening trying to convince herself the flutters in her tummy were nothing other than hunger. But the truth was that Roy Blackwell was the best, most perfectly wrapped and unexpected surprise she had experienced in a long time.

And now here she stood, having potentially read into the moment much more than she should have. He was the constable. Constables go on stakeouts. They don't eat spicy grilled cheese sandwiches with frantic townspeople who are worried about the state of their dahlias. Embarrassed, she instantly regretted her decision to surprise this man, who most likely did not appreciate surprises. It was definitely a mistake.

"I'll just leave the basket here and you can return it, or I'll swing by and pick it up later."

A basket? Really, Margarette? Just because he's older does not mean he eats his picnic lunches from a basket. You've offended him before you even had a chance to date him! Date him? Is that what she wanted, to date Roy Blackwell?

She set the basket down on the desk, smiled, and turned to walk away.

"Aren't you going to stay?"

Before turning to face him, she grinned, then composed herself and spun around.

"Well, I did make enough for two."

Well done, Margarette, she thought. Well done.

Margarette Toft had said yes to Roy Blackwell with every ounce of certitude she possessed. She had never been surer of anything in her entire life.

Had her grandmother still been alive the news of Margarette's engagement would probably have sent her to the grave. Her family had been at odds with the Blackwells longer than she had been alive – longer than anyone in Coraloo had been alive, for that matter. Margarette had a plan, and if she was lucky the family would either look past the last name or blame it all on the festival.

"Mrs Roy Blackwell." *Blackwell. I'm going to be a Blackwell.* "Blackwell. Bla-ck-well."

She took another look at the ring, hidden from her family in its little box – it wasn't just a symbol of her commitment to Roy but to the Blackwells. And a betrayal to the Tofts.

CHAPTER 2

Roy Blackwell refolded the newly laundered waffle-weave blanket at the end of the prison cell bed, inhaling the aroma of soapy lavender and making a mental note to pick up more laundry detergent at the hardware store.

He proceeded to wipe settled dust away from the iron bars and sweep the stone floor, then removed a small stack of books from the wooden beside table. He'd already read them, so he would return them to the flea market's bookshop and replace them with three new ones.

Roy stepped back to examine his progress. The three brick-walled cells looked exactly as they had the week before, and the week before that, and the month before that. Tidy. Disinfected. It had been months since anyone had occupied these cells, but he wanted to be ready. The festival's peculiar effect on the citizens of Coraloo did not tend to disappoint.

He plopped himself down in the slat-backed wheeled chair, pulled himself up to the desk, and placed his father's rectangular reading spectacles on the bridge of his nose. His grandmother's edition of *The Complete Medical Handbook for Home Diagnosis* said the blurred vision he was experiencing could be neurological. His doctor had gently suggested he try glasses. Roy had considered buying a new pair, but Margarette said the black-rimmed frames were *classic* and *masculine*. She always had the right words to say.

The chair beneath him creaked. *The station could use a few new things.* He sucked in his mid-section, noting that he could lose a few things as well.

The ring and jangle of the station's rotary desk phone startled him out of his musing. He exhaled, releasing his stomach, and glanced at the clock: 11:45. *Right on time.*

"Coraloo Police," he said, lifting the receiver. "Oh, hey Bert. You doing all right today?"

Bert Thompson called at least once a day, claiming he had either forgotten, once again, whom he was trying to call or that he had dialed the wrong number. But Roy knew the truth: Bert was lonely. His wife Mildred had passed peacefully, but unexpectedly, a year ago. As far as Roy knew, Bert did only two things these days – call Roy and pick his newspaper up off the doorstep.

Roy glanced up at the clock again. There was no reason to rush the conversation. Whatever festival shenanigans were going on outside could most likely wait, and the market would remain open for another five or six hours. He could pretty much recite Bert's daily monologue by heart, but he listened attentively as he always did.

"I'm sorry to hear that, Bert. If I can ever do anything you know where to find me." Roy meant it. He'd have welcomed the company himself. "I'm about to walk up to the market for lunch. Want to join me?"

Every time Bert called, Roy invited him to lunch. And every time, Bert declined. Since Mildred's death he preferred not to stray too far from home.

"Well, I'll be up there for an hour or so if you change your mind."

All of a sudden, Bert's familiar patter took an unexpected turn.

"A wedding present?" For a moment Roy wanted to ask how Bert had heard about his recent engagement, but it was Coraloo and news traveled fast. "That's real nice of you, Bert. We'll appreciate whatever it is."

Roy couldn't help but smile. He was getting married. After eight months of seeing one another, Margarette Toft had agreed to marry him. He had proposed the previous Sunday, but they'd decided to wait a week before telling the town, thinking it a good idea to share the news with close family members before word spread between the Tofts and Blackwells that two of their family members had forgotten their last names and decided to wed, further fanning the feuding flame that had burned through Coraloo for longer than anyone could remember. Last night, after three blissful days of holding the secret between them, Roy and Margarette had braved telling the families and gotten the worst of it out of the way.

Margarette had told Roy she had a plan. She would bring them together with food. The Blackwells and the Tofts.

Roy and his Aunt Sorcha had been the first to arrive.

A woman, tall and thin with dark hair quaffed into a neat shoulder-length bob, answered the door. "Peter! He's come for you!"

"No, ma'am," Roy said, attempting to play along. "I'm here for your daughter."

He'd met Margarette's mother, Anna Sue Toft, once before when Margarette had brought her down to the station to meet him. Anna Sue had laughed back then, assuming it a clever yet distasteful joke that the two might be romantically involved. From that moment on, Roy and Margarette had decided to keep their courtship discrete – not a secret, just low-key – enough to not rouse suspicion, but not enough to quell the worries – or the gossip – of either side.

"My Meggy?" Anna Sue gasped, clutching her chest. "There must be some mistake, Officer. She's a saint, an angel! She makes the communion wine for the morning service. She didn't go and get herself drunk, did she? Her grandmother – on her father's side, of course – had a little issue with the communion wine. That's why they passed the recipe down to my Meggy."

Roy didn't know if she legitimately thought he was there to arrest Margarette or if she was revealing a hidden talent for acting.

A tiny voice piped up from the doorstep behind Roy. "That's not the only thing Rose had issues with!"

Anna Sue's face turned scarlet, her disposition changing from surprise to annoyance. "Coming with your nephew to make house calls, Sorcha? I thought they buried you in a barn or something."

The small woman stepped out from behind her nephew, walking cane extended and eyebrows raised. "Heads will roll, Toft! Heads will –"

Roy cleared his throat. "You agreed…"

Sorcha Blackwell and Anna Sue Toft locked eyes.

The elderly woman lowered her cane. "I agreed to hear you out, Roy, but I had no idea I would be dining with Tofts."

"Dining with us?" Anna Sue's voice was raised, however clearly fighting to maintain decorum. "Margarette didn't tell us our 'special' guests were Blackwells. I thought Meggy'd given up on this embarrassing jaunt of hers. She was engaged to a doctor once, you know."

Roy knew.

Margarette appeared at the door. "Come on in." She stood up on the balls of her red heels and whispered into Roy's ear, "We could always elope, you know. Move to Delhi. What do you think?"

She smelled of vanilla, rich and warm. "I think that's a great idea." He meant it – the eloping, though not necessarily the move to Delhi. "But is it safe to leave them alone with each other? I bet your mother's got a good right hook."

"Good point."

Dinner was a quiet affair. Margarette attempted to make small talk with Roy until she could stand the awkwardness no more, at which point she just came out with it.

"Roy and I are engaged."

Aunt Sorcha choked on her water.

Margarette's father started laughing.

Her mother tossed her napkin onto her plate and tried to storm out of the room, only she tripped over the chair leg and found herself sprawled in Roy's lap.

Other than the joint accusation from Anna Sue and Aunt Sorcha that the festival had gotten the better of the two – the first time Roy had ever heard a Blackwell and a Toft woman agree on anything – and if they would "wait it out" until June the couple would see this whole debacle for the mirage it was, Margarette's plan had gone off better than they'd expected. No food fights had ensued, no injuries sustained – just awkward silences and the occasional malicious stare.

As Roy hung up the phone after his call with Bert the station door burst open. A woman garbed in a pink velvet robe with cotton balls stuck between each of her freshly painted toes ran up to him, waving her umbrella around the room and sloshing water droplets across the floor.

He'd clean the safety hazard up later. For now he was quite concerned with the sudden appearance of Ms Brimble in her bathrobe.

"Ms Brimble! Is everything all right? Would you like to have a seat? Can I get you a cup of Darjeeling?" *Or some proper clothing?*

"How could I possibly drink tea at a time like this? We have to go! Now! Their lives depend upon it!"

Lives?

Ms Brimble rushed back out the door. Feeling a surge of adrenaline in response to her urgency, Roy hurriedly followed the widow around the corner to her cottage on Odenbon. He knew the street well. The Prices had moved in last year, and Mrs Price was due any day now.

The baby!

Roy picked up his pace to a run. He wasn't qualified for this. They'd need the doctor... a surgeon... anybody but him!

"You have to save them! You have to save them!" Ms Brimble wailed, pulling her robe tighter with one hand and steadying the umbrella over her hair with the other.

"Is it the baby?" he called to her. "Is Velveteen all right?"

As far as he knew, Ms Brimble wasn't the dramatic type. She was highly educated and had been a professor of botany at a university in another state. She now provided herbal remedies to the townspeople free of charge. He had a whole cabinet of her blends at home.

"My babies! My babies!" She turned down her drive and ran toward the back of the cottage.

Roy's heart raced. *Her babies?* As far as he knew her children were fully grown and lived in the city. *Grandchildren, maybe?*

He should call for backup... He'd been in much better shape during his younger years. He paused to catch his breath, hands on hips. Then he swallowed and took another breath.

"This way!" She led him over to the herb garden at the back of her cottage. "Oh, I do hope they're all right!"

Roy stopped short, looking for some sign of danger or ailing persons as another gentle sprinkle fell from the sky. A ferocious squeal rent the air from behind the shrub. A dog barked and then the howl of another animal emanated from the undergrowth.

The robed woman wailed louder, burying her head in her hands. "I can't watch them die. Not my babies!"

Roy crept closer toward the source of the pained screeching, dropping to his knees to navigate through the greenery. A furred paw batted at his eye as a dog that looked, to all intents and purposes, like a cuddly toy, growled at the cat once again.

Roy pulled back, shaking his head, frustrated to have exhausted himself for a domestic dispute between her grouchy pets.

"Ma'am, cats and dogs have been fighting for years. How about we let them work it out between them?"

He turned, damp and disappointed, to stare out at the well-manicured garden beds, noticing her meticulous attention to detail. It was then he caught sight of a bicycle painted turquoise and employed as a decorative garden planter.

Ms Brimble grabbed him by the shoulders and shook him. "They're trapped in there – you have to help them! Before something… like a wolf! Yes, before a wolf eats them and it's all my fault!"

Despair setting in, her head dropped down onto his uniformed shoulder. He had never seen her like this before – so frantic, so out of her mind. He hoped she had not taken to misusing the herbs she claimed were for medicinal purposes only.

He patted her on the back and laughed to himself. It was highly unlikely they would be eaten by a wolf in Coraloo. A coyote, perhaps, but he'd never tell her that.

"Don't you worry about the wolves, Ms Brimble. We'll get them out."

"Thank you, Roy, thank you! Oh, I hope he won't lose too much fur."

"I'm sure…" Roy started to respond but realized he had no idea what she meant by "lose too much fur". "What's the dog's name?"

"King Alfred III. But call him Alfie. He prefers it." She cupped her hands over her mouth. "Hang on, Alfie! Roy's going to get you out!"

Alfie. Roy exhaled, and, praying either of the two weren't carriers of some zoonotic disease, he stuck his head back inside the bush and called, "Come on, boy. Come on, Alfie."

The dog refused to budge. It howled again.

The cat shrieked.

Roy felt the sting of a frantic hand smack at the back of his wet head.

"I tried that! Can't you see they're stuck!"

He glanced over his shoulder at the woman. "Stuck?"

"Yes! All three of them!"

Three?

Roy took hold of the bichon frise's rear end.

Alfie howled, the cat cried, the sky opened, and the rain fell hard.

"You're hurting them! You're hurting them all!" The woman stomped in circles behind Roy, her arms swimming backwards and her hands swatting at the wind.

Roy shone his light inside the shrubbery to further assess the situation. On closer inspection his eyes widened. He backed out slowly and faced the woman, stunned.

"I'm terribly sorry, Ms Brimble, but I don't think I can handle this one. I believe we may need to bring in animal control."

"Oh no. Please no! They'll have me locked up in an institution! I didn't mean to torture the poor creature… I really didn't. You know me, Roy. You've known me for years. I wouldn't so much as hurt a rabbit – even though I'm quite certain they're the ones who've been nibbling at my daisies. But the glue trap… It was all I had; you have to believe me. I usually just scoop the little mice up and set them free, but not this one. He just kept coming back. That's when I decided to set the trap. I didn't want to kill it, just startle it a bit. Catch it and move it somewhere safe. I swear that trap was all I had. And when I caught it, I tried to take it off, but its tail was stuck tight, so I took it outside."

Roy stood upright for a moment, puzzled and dripping wet, as he tried to put together the pieces of her unexpected rant. "Ms Brimble, were you trying to catch a mouse?"

"Didn't you hear a word I just said?"

He had heard, but hadn't made a bit of sense of it. "You didn't want to torture it, so you tossed it out in the garden?"

"I couldn't just throw it in the rubbish alive. Can you imagine the smell? How exactly was I supposed to put it out of its misery? I thought if he fell asleep hypothermia would set in and the little one would die peacefully. I never imagined Muffins would try to eat it! Oh, poor Muffins! Her face is stuck tight!"

Roy sat down on the damp ground, mentally questioning for the second time what else Ms Brimble might be growing in the herb garden. She might have intended the mouse to be left to the mercy of the elements, but she clearly had not expected Muffins and Alfie to experience the same sticky ending.

"I'm going to have to call animal control. They'll know what's best for Muffins and Alfie. And, minus the tail, they might even be able to save your mouse." Ms Brimble started to cry. Roy handed her his handkerchief, allowing her to blow her nose and wipe the tears away from her swollen eyes. "I'll explain what happened."

"You'll tell them I didn't mean to hurt it, won't you? You'll tell them, Roy?"

"I'll sure do my best. And if they try to take you away, I'll tell them they have to take me too."

"You're a good man, Roy Blackwell."

On his way out of the garden he took a second look at the poor paint job on the old Schwinn bike. "Where did you find it?"

"What?" she sniffled from under her umbrella.

"The bicycle."

"Oh, down at the market. I bought it from a vendor. Didn't I do a good job fixing it up?"

Roy couldn't lie to her, so he just smiled. Truth be told, he wished he'd found it first. It looked... pretty, he'd give her that, but bikes were made for the open road, and it saddened him to see this one chocked with ivy.

He waved goodbye and moved quickly through the rain back to the municipal building. Once there, he put in a call to animal control, gathered the stack of books and his rain jacket – something he wished he had taken with him to Ms Brimble's cottage – and headed up the hill toward the market.

Paperwork awaited him back at the station – a detailed recount of the sticky trap fiasco. At least it was something to do. But Roy craved more, something along the lines of the golden days of Coraloo when the constables kept the cells rotating like a hotel for the town's undesirables. When banks were robbed and bootleggers tried setting up shop in the back of the laundromat. He didn't really want the bank to be robbed, especially since the Second Bank of Coraloo held his entire life savings. He planned to use a portion of the savings to take Margarette somewhere exotic after their wedding – Bali, perhaps, or Bora Bora. It wasn't his idea of a perfect getaway, but Margarette was young and adventurous. She had traveled overseas for university, spent a summer hiking the Camino de Santiago, and gotten a tattoo in Thailand that she had yet to show him. She wasn't afraid to sample exotic foods… or any food for that matter. He, however, was content to eat pot roast every day, and the farthest he had been from Coraloo was only a two-hour bus ride for his own stint at university.

His mind wandered to far-flung honeymoon destinations. He'd need to research vaccinations. There were some highly infectious diseases out there, like dengue fever with its blood-boiling temperatures, nausea, nosebleeds, and the excruciating pain that gave it the nickname "break-bone fever", among other things. He had stumbled across it the other day in his grandmother's book. *The Complete Medical Handbook for Home Diagnosis* had been in the family for years. His grandmother had referenced it to diagnose everything from ear infections to scarlet fever.

On several occasions he considered packing the book up and mailing the fearmongering thing to the library in the next town over with a note that said: "WARNING! MAY CAUSE EXTREME CASES OF HYPOCHONDRIA!"

As a single man of a certain age he'd found it handy at times. However, on a few occasions it had cost him an embarrassing trip to the infirmary, like the time when he had suddenly developed a strong distaste for corned beef. As it turned out, he did not have liver disease as the book had led him to believe. But, according to his doctor, he did have seasonal allergies, which made sense given he could barely breathe twice a year. He made another mental note to grab a bottle of Blackwell honey from the market. It was not only highly medicinal but delicious on croissants.

Roy made his way up the hill with the stack of books protected under his raincoat, passing the same buildings he saw every day, including the one next door, which was the only vacant store front. Previously a fishmonger, it was now owned by his soon-to-be in-laws, who were holding out for both the highest and most unique bidder. The Tofts had made a fortune over the past few years, helping to bring Coraloo back to its former glory.

As he reached the top of the hill, with the newly reopened Coraloo Flea Market before him, Roy glanced back down at the town. His hometown. He was the only Blackwell to live in the Toft territory below. All the other Blackwells lived behind the market. But the police station was in the valley, and so was Margarette. He coughed and pulled his hood tight around his ears. He'd drink some elderberry tea when he got back to the cottage, just as a precaution.

It was only the second day of the festival. He had seen more action with Ms Brimble's pets than he'd seen the past five months – since the day he'd had to hand his second cousin Shug Blackwell over to the city authorities for embezzling funds from the family business. There was no telling what the coming month would bring. No doubt there would be tavern brawls, late-night disturbances, and *the others*... the randoms who strolled into town, drawn in by the festival's mystical lure. *The others* were always good for a bit of commotion.

But then what? At the festival's end? Everything would go back to the way it had always been.

He shook his head, suppressing the discontentment that had haunted him over the past year.

I'll still have Margarette.

CHAPTER 3

Margarette tried to ignore the prattle of prying Tofts seated around her, allowing the ritual fuss taking place outside the shop to act as a distraction. It's what she and Roy would need to make it to the wedding – distractions. On the other side of the salon window a scattering of industrious hands orchestrated the precise placement of the stage's construction in the town's center square, while another team contemplated the most artful way to hang strings of lights from the hickory trees.

She had her own part to play in the town's merriment, and it came in the form of a six-foot, weather-resistant Heaken-beaver-honoring parade float thought up and assembled by twenty-three overly excited and emotionally confused sixth-grade students. She loved it! She relished the challenge of bringing them together via a common idea and watching them whine their way through the physical labor, only to ride the thing with unabashed pride for exactly thirty-three minutes… unless the car holding the former year's Heaken Beaver Queen got a flat tire, backing up the line of floats, high school band members, and reenactors as it had three years ago. Float construction was usually the highlight of her year, but this year she had something else on her mind… Something bigger. Something… perfect.

Margarette turned sharply at the sound of her name, furrowing her brow and casting her glare over the assembly of cousins and aunts, their hair in rollers as they sat beneath the dryers in the steady and ambitious hands of Sylvia Toft. Any sane person would have thought it ridiculous to sit among the hecklers, but Margarette had to face them sometime and her hair was in drastic need of a trim. She didn't know what most of the ladies in the room did with their days, or their money. As far as she knew they spent it all at Sylvia's. Maybe one day Sylvia – single and an entrepreneur – would turn out to be the wealthiest Toft in town.

She swiveled back round, returning to watch the works of tradition unfolding outside. Food and artisan vendors stood proudly beside their wares within the shelter of blue-and-white-striped canvas tents, while umbrella-carrying patrons took their daily pass for a bite to eat or a quick purchase before moving on with the rest of their day.

It always rained during the festival. For years the townspeople had debated postponing the festival by a month or two to avoid the predictable spring rain, but the Tofts had declared such a move bad luck. Margarette wondered what unfortunate event could possibly be worse luck than the inevitable torrents of rain.

Truth told, she loved the occasion more than anyone else in town. The festival itself was a Coraloo tradition. *Tradition*. Roy's family was steeped in tradition. There were so many traditions Margarette could barely keep up with them all. That's why she had organized, alphabetized, and categorized them by name, date, and occasion into separate notebooks. There was nothing the Blackwells could put in front of her that she was not ready to experience.

Pulling together the snippits she remembered hearing during her childhood, she had gone so far as to research the Blackwell customs at university, finding them absolutely intriguing and the perfect topic for her senior thesis. She'd been fascinated by the Blackwell stories since she was a little girl, despite being warned more than once that Blackwells were no-good land-stealing traitors who, among other strange customs, like to celebrate their deaths while still living. The bizarre custom was of particular interest to Margarette, and although she had not quite settled on having a funeral before she died, she thought the opportunity to learn what one might have missed in life – and then have the chance to do it before it was too late – had its merits.

The Blackwells had founded the town, holding claim to the land, and as their history told, the Tofts had tried to take it for themselves in a duel to the death. In the end, no lives were lost, only pride, as the legendary Mungo Blackwell won the right to keep his land on the hill.

The valley at the bottom of the hill had mercifully been bestowed upon the Tofts.

The Tofts, however, had a slightly different history, one which claimed the Blackwells were no-good, land-stealing beaver worshippers. Margarette knew every corner of the town's *true* history, according to the Tofts, and at this time of year it was her job to teach it. No sixth-grade student escaped Coraloo Elementary without hearing it. As far as she could tell, the Blackwell version was historically accurate, though she would never dare tell her family.

Coraloo Elementary wasn't just her place of employment; it was an outpost for her daily pilgrimage to educate the town's future generations of Coraloo. The building itself was not as old as the market; however, it had suffered its fair share of renovations over the years, becoming the subject of many controversies:

"Keep the hardwood floor!"

"Tiles are easier to clean!"

"Chalkboards are old-fashioned."

"The next town over uses whiteboards."

"I say we knock it down and start over."

Margarette liked the building the way it was. There was plenty of room and it always smelled the same... like chalk dust and lemon cleaner. She hoped it would never change.

She fidgeted with the one-karat diamond ring on her hand. It had been Roy's mother's, passed down through the Blackwell family for centuries. It was vintage, delicate, ornate, different. Perfect. It just needed the perfect dress to go with it. She grinned at the thought. There was going to be a Blackwell wedding. Her Blackwell wedding!

Roy had warned her the list of Blackwell wedding traditions was twice as long as the one for funerals, but she had reassured him there was nothing to worry about. She had done her research; she could handle anything they threw at her, even one of their infamous pickled eggs.

The history, the family, and all the peculiarity that was Blackwell was partly what had drawn her to Roy. It was what made him different from other men.

Margarette watched as passers-by took refuge from the increasing rain beneath awninged storefronts. She turned away from the window and peeked over at her mother sitting in the padded swivel chair beside her, reading this month's novel for the newly formed Ladies of Lower Coraloo Book Club. There was no getting around it. Blackwell wedding or not, her mother would add a smattering of Toft here and there whether Margarette liked it or not.

Her heart beat faster with a twinge of anxiety. Could they actually pull this off? Could a Toft really marry a Blackwell? She picked at her nail polish, glanced over at her mother again, then inhaled, attempting to calm her apprehension.

She coughed. The faint hint of artificial mango from the ammonia-based perming solution was doing a poor job of masking the pungent aroma rising from the hair rollers attached to her aunt Clara's head.

Aunt Clara caught her stare and smiled pleasantly, as if Margarette were someone to be pitied. Then returned to her not-so-private conversation with the other aunts: "Well, I feel sorry for her."

The salon's patrons craned their necks, curious, to catch a peek at Margarette. She held a magazine up to her face, hoping they would take notice of the Junoesque bride on the front.

They didn't seem to care, continuing their public conversation:

"She's way past her prime."

"Maybe if she dressed more her age she could have kept Thomas around. He was the one."

The aunts bobbed their foiled, roller-laden heads in unison.

Margarette frowned. What was wrong with her button-up cardigans and full, colorful, tea-length skirts? Her mother had offered to take her shopping on more than one occasion, but she had declined. Margarette enjoyed the thrill of finding something spectacular and in great condition at a second-hand store, selecting each piece for its detail – embroidery on the shoulder or pearl buttons at the wrist – and for its history. She had always loved history, and when she wore something preowned by another she fantasized about what life must have been like for the person wearing it. Did the former owner have hobbies? Play in a band? Go to the movies? Work as a nurse? A writer, maybe?

Besides, it had been her decision to "not keep Thomas around". Her sense of style had nothing to do with the broken engagement and had never kept her from dating. She'd had plenty of suitors over the years. It was just that none of them had been… the right fit.

Margarette licked her finger and turned another page of the magazine in front of her, pretending her hecklers were heckling someone else. The image of a bouquet, Scottish thistle and pink heather, caught her attention. Unity meets good luck. Perfect. She'd clip it and add the bouquet to her wedding notebook when she got home.

She lifted her Wedgwood blue, hexagon-shaped handbag onto her lap – a recent purchase from a thrift store in the next town over – unclasped the lock, dug inside to find a pair of small brass scissors she used specifically for her magazine clippings, then set the bag back down beside her.

Her mother leaned over. "Did you check the back?"

Margarette quickly turned the page over – an advertisement for a wedding venue in Spain. Spain would be nice. She looked closer, making sure her tiny scissors were not about to mar the face of some poor unexpectant soul. It was a silly superstition; but regardless, one must never cut across another's face. The superstition was so imbedded in her that she sporadically prayed forgiveness for accidentally snipping people she'd never met. She had no idea what was supposed to happen to the venue model on the other side of the page, but whatever it was, it wasn't worth adding the bouquet to her notebook.

The Toft superstitions were as ingrained in her as the Blackwell traditions were in Roy; for the most part, Margarette rationalized that these superstitions were coincidental nonsense, dwindling down to mindless habits. Besides, if stepping on sidewalk cracks actually broke a mother's back, there would clearly be millions of mothers walking around with broken backs.

She would take the age-old quirky Blackwell traditions over the fear-inspiring Toft superstitions any day. She'd spent half her childhood afraid to look at a graveyard, let alone breathe near one. It was a wonder she hadn't passed out walking to and from school each day.

Margarette turned the page and groaned at the image of yet another wedding gown. They all looked the same: white, boring. Same, same. Same-ity same. She'd started setting aside money for a gown exactly a month after she and Roy started dating. Because she knew. This time she knew. There was no doubt in her mind that she and Roy Blackwell were the right fit for one another. She only wished she could be as certain that she would find a dress that fit the occasion.

"Ugh!" She closed the magazine, pulling it close to her cardigan, catching the concerned looks of Clara, Sylvia, a few cousins, and a tourist who had decided experiencing the ambiance of the local beauty shop would be fun.

I wonder if I should warn her...

Sylvia Toft cut hair to the beat of her own drum. She said it was her art, her creative outlet. And for some reason the whole family let her do it – but truth told, most of the ladies wound up in the city or the next town over for a "fix" shortly after. Most days, Sylvia's was more about the conversation than the hair.

"Just give me a trim," the tourist said innocently.

Sylvia looked at her with concern. "Sweetie, you need way more than a trim. I don't usually trim tourists on Saturdays. You know what they say, don't you?"

"No... I don't."

Sylvia propped one hand on her hip and looked back toward the Tofts. "What's that other thing they say, 'What you don't know won't hurt you' or something? Maybe we should give you a little color while we're at it. How do you feel about fuchsia?"

An hour later Sylvia sat the confused tourist next to Margarette, her hair bound up in a white towel. Everyone in Coraloo knew you didn't just walk into Sylvia's and ask for a trim – Saturday or otherwise. Nobody left the place with "just a trim". *This poor soul has no idea what she's in for*, Margarette thought, remembering the free makeovers that Sylvia regularly insisted on giving her customers.

Margarette laughed out loud, then quickly covered her mouth as she recalled a Christmas party she had attended with Roy at the Prices'. She had made a surely unforgettable impression wearing lime green eyeshadow and a grape-colored lipstick that vaguely complemented her dress. She had learned her lesson – only visit Sylvia's when you have time afterward to tone down "the Works".

Sylvia turned and removed the towel, allowing the tourist's purple tresses to fall over her shoulders.

The tourist's eyes widened. "Ummm... I... I think I should go. My husband's wait –"

Sylvia's voice rang out over the gentle hum of the hairdryer. "Let me just get you dried. Then I'll get you all styled up. Does your husband have any single friends?"

"Not that I know of..."

"Well, I've got this single... let's call her a friend." She nodded toward Margarette. "And this friend –"

"I'm engaged, Sylvia!" Exasperated, Margarette flung the magazine up in front of her face again. Behind it she rolled her eyes and stuck out her tongue at the gaggle of Toft women. She should have known she wouldn't be able to simply come in, get her hair done, and fall asleep under the warmth of the dryer. Why hadn't she just snuck out of town and visited one of the salons in the city?

She and Roy had been dating for nearly eight months, and while they hadn't attempted to keep it a secret, they certainly hadn't gone around shouting about it. Margarette's mother had called it a rebellious fling, a dalliance with the enemy. Her mother's words had stung: *"You can't be serious, Meggy."* Everyone had assumed it would be over before it started. But it was more than a fling.

Margarette had been hoping for at least an ounce of excitement in reaction to her news. She was thirty-seven and beginning to wonder if she would ever find her forever. She knew her family would be a bit upset, disappointed to say the least, but she had hoped they would find it somewhere in their Toftish-ness to be happy for her. But the daggers had flown the minute she stepped foot through the salon door.

"How could you?" a cousin wailed.

Aunt Coraline pretended to faint onto the salon floor and then immediately sat back up, pointing and muttering something that sounded as though she were casting demons out of Margarette's engagement ring.

"He's a Blackwell!" another cried.

"Is he holding you against your will?"

"But what about us? What are we supposed to do?"

"Who's going to make the communion wine now?"

The last one irritated her. Making the communion wine was her art, her craft. She had perfected the process, adding notes and diary-like entries to her notebook on the subject about crushing, boiling, and straining. As far as she knew there was nothing in the church bylaws that prevented a Blackwell from making the communion wine. But she had never considered they might take it from her once she was married.

Her mother set her book down. "Margarette, you should have talked to me first. What a horrible thing to do, making us all eat together as if that wasn't awkward enough. And then you go and tell us..." She flipped her hands up in the air, pointed at her ring finger, and sighed. "And at his age! Really, Margarette? Isn't he a bit old for you?"

Margarette. Her given name. Only those outside the family called her Margarette. To her family she was always Meggy. She hated it.

"I'm almost forty." She continued her flipping and clipping, pretending the spoken jabs weren't bothering her.

"You're thirty-seven, *Margarette*. How old is he? Fifty?"

Maybe if she disappointed her mother more often she would continue to call Margarette by the name she preferred.

"Forty-eight."

Aunt Clara chipped in, filing her nails. "There are too many years between you. It's bad luck."

Nowhere in Toft history had marrying a man of a different age ever been considered bad luck. Had it been so, by now half the women in the room would have broken out in spotty facial warts.

Sylvia stepped in, applying another layer of foundation to the exhausted tourist. "What about Billy Jr? His daddy left him the business what, ten years ago? That boy's been after you since you were born."

"Didn't he ask you to the dance?" one of the other aunts asked. "You know, that Wallace boy's a catch."

"Andrew Wallace is nineteen." Margarette was flipping through the magazine so fast that all she took in was a blur of brides with flawless smiling faces layered in their meringue-like finery. She could feel the heat rising to her cheeks.

Her mother rested her hand on top of hers. "Does age even matter? Isn't that what you said?"

Margarette cast a glance her way. A glance that said, *I am a grown woman and can marry whomever I want.*

"It will all work out." Anna Sue gave her hand a squeeze.

It will all work out. Her mother's words rang true, even though she knew by "work out" she meant someone else would come along, *working* Roy completely *out* of their lives. *Yes, it would work out,* she told herself firmly, *because she loved Roy and he loved her.*

Margarette tossed the magazine aside, no closer to finding a dress she liked. She checked her watch. "Sylvia, it's been thirty minutes. Should we rinse?"

She had papers to grade, lessons to plan, and a float to decorate for the festival. And if Roy's Saturday was turning out anything like hers he would be looking forward to meeting at their usual spot for dinner as much as she was. She did not wait for Sylvia to respond; instead she simply gathered her belongings and moved to one of the reclining armchairs. Without pausing her conversation, Sylvia followed and turned the water to warm.

Margarette rested in the green lounger, head back and feet propped, allowing Sylvia to rinse the impromptu highlights from her hair. Her cousin's long, orange nails dug deep into her scalp, releasing the tension of the week. Sylvia doused her with a rosemary mint shampoo and continued to massage and dig, wooing Margarette into near sleep.

But as Margarette was nearing the point where her shoulders felt light and her heart happy, Sylvia piped up again. "You should really give more thought to Billy Jr. I saw him in that Twittlebottom woman's shop the other day. He was asking about you."

Sylvia and Margarette were close in age and had grown up together. However, their taste in fashion and men were worlds apart.

Margarette sat straight up in the chair and flung back her drooping wet curls, spraying the other Toft ladies with water. "No, I haven't thought about Billy. But you're welcome to him!"

William Butcher Jr? Is she joking? They'd have me marry the mortician rather than the town constable!

She could hear her mother now: "He's a catch, Meggy. It'd be a great match. I adore his mother. He has an apprentice. And he's not a Blackwell."

Not a Blackwell.

She'd had enough for one day. With water still dripping down her back, Margarette Toft hopped out of her chair, hooked her purse over her arm, marched over to hand Sylvia her payment, and stormed toward the door.

I can dry my own hair. Maybe I'll visit the salon in the city. Maybe I'll move to the city. That'll show them. They'll have to drink store-bought grape juice again until they find someone else to make the communion wine. Well, good luck with that because I'll be taking the recipe with me!

She needed to see Roy. Just a glimpse of his smile would set her day right. Like Margarette, Roy was an oddity in his family. He had opted against partaking in the family business, choosing to reside at the base of the hill as the town constable instead of living in a campervan outside of the flea market and setting up shop as a craftsman inside. Not only that, but nearly all of his cousins had red hair, while his locks had come out black.

Margarette twisted her short curly hair up into a wet messy knot at the back of her neck and secured it with a hair tie from her purse.

On her way out the door she heard one of the aunts say, "Poor thing; it's because she's marked."

Margarette turned with a scowl, pointing at her face. "I. Am. Not. Marked. It's gone! See!"

She'd gone all the way through her teenage years succumbing to their superstitions, believing something was wrong with her because she was "marked" – for what she never knew – by a faint birthmark in a dime-sized bumpy blob on the right side of the bridge of her nose. Someone once told her it was because her mother had overindulged in blackberries while she was pregnant with Margarette. It really could have been anything. You didn't even have to have a birthmark for someone to say you were marked. Not that it was hard to be marked. See a frog with one leg? Marked. Get sick from eating strawberries? Marked. Get stung by a bee? *Marked. Marked. Marked.* Margarette's birthmark had faded sometime during high school and only reared its form when she spent too much time out in the sun.

Marked? They have the nerve to say I'm marrying a Blackwell because I'm "marked"?

Outside, the sun remained hidden behind a gray sky as the cool, post-rain breeze sent chills through her wet head. Margarette darted toward the cafe, dodging patrons carrying boxes of festival T-shirts and decorative bunting. From the corner of her eye she saw two men running past in long robes, one carrying a stuffed replica of the Heaken beaver.

Beaver worshippers.

She laughed at the thought. Margarette had no idea what the two men were up to, but she could say with ninety-nine percent certainty the gentlemen were not running off to sacrifice a stuffed beaver. The whole thing was ridiculous, but she loved it… every moment – the ambiance, the excitement, and of course the history.

With the rain at bay the town was stirring once again. For the first time in her memory the sign outside the bed and breakfast proudly proclaimed: "No Vacancies". The whole month would be dedicated to a legendary beaver with antlers, which, as the story goes, not only had the ability to heal arthritic feet but had also won the town's founder his bride. What sort of history teacher wouldn't love it?

A banner, dripping with remnants of the morning rain, hung boldly over the stage, which stood in the same place it had been erected every year since she could remember, directly in the square's center: "The Heaken Beaver Festival". It was something the Blackwells and Tofts didn't regularly argue about – the festival had its place in both families. The Blackwells saw the critter of legend as a symbol of favor, while the Tofts saw it as a way to make money from the Blackwells.

Margarette saw it as the perfect distraction.

CHAPTER 4

Dozens of star-shaped pendant lights hung from the ceiling, casting a soft glow over the cafe's diners. The original brick walls of the former apothecary had been purposefully left exposed and timeworn, complementing the original hardwood flooring. Floor-to-ceiling shelving, once housing remedies and relief, was now home to a collection of ornate vintage glass jars that glistened in the starlight.

Margarette and Roy unofficially claimed The Star on Doka Street as their place – named after the native princess, and mother of the town's founder, Ipunistat, whose name reflected the mark of a star she bore on her nose. Margarette had suggested they try it on invitation of one of her students – one of Coraloo Elementary's most recent additions instructed by his parents to invite everyone to their grand opening. They'd been coming at least once a week ever since. Other than the two, the cafe mostly entertained tourists and more obscure locals who had either long forgotten or married out of their family names. The food was delicious and the atmosphere serene. The Star had nuzzled its way into town by wooing the town elders with appetizers and entrees tastier than anything those who bragged about venturing into the city had ever tasted. It had wooed Margarette and Roy simply by being a place where neither of their families would dine. She had told him it somehow made her feel safe. He knew what she meant. She made him feel the same way.

Roy leaned forward in his seat, his elbows on the hammered, copper-topped table, his hands gripped into a single fist, and his eyes on Margarette, who was studying the menu as though she'd never seen it before.

"Blackwells are known for their ability to make quick decisions," he said.

Margarette peered suspiciously, playfully, over the top of her menu. "Is that a fact, Roy Blackwell?"

"No." Roy raised an eyebrow. "I made it up."

"I know."

He laughed. At times he wondered whether she knew more about his family than he did, and often joked that she was only marrying him for his family name.

A flurry of men dressed in kilts and carrying swords ran past the cafe window.

He often put her to the test. It was a game they played. The kilted men presented the perfect opportunity. "How about them?" he asked, pointing at the clansmen. "Fact or fake?"

She set her menu down and craned her neck to see the men. "Kilts are fact… the tartan is a bit off, though. Swords are fact –"

He opened his mouth to speak.

Margarette raised a finger to stop him. "But the ones they're carrying would have been used for ceremony, not combat. Don't get me wrong, those are some good-looking swords… basket hilt, tassel. But they should probably be carrying claymores with a leather grip – a bit more practical… How did I do?"

He crossed his arms and shook his head.

Her confident disposition changed, as if considering what she might have gotten wrong.

His lips turned into a grin. "You know your swords."

She smiled. "I know my history."

"Margarette Toft, I think you're going to fit right in."

He'd returned to her cottage after walking Aunt Sorcha back to the market the night of the engagement dinner for the same reason – because he wanted her to know. Even though the dinner had gone better than they'd anticipated, he knew it had still unsettled Margarette. He'd offered to clear the table, do the dishes, fix a creak in the floor – anything to be by her side. It was then she had confessed to Roy how, in some crazy, pie-in-the-sky way, she had imagined that his aunt would jump up from the dining table mid-meal and declare a truce between the two families. Then they could all have eaten together and laughed, exchanging stories about the old days and forever dismissing any discord between the Blackwells and the Tofts.

She drummed her fingers on the table. "I can't decide… Want to pick for me?"

He had kind of hoped she would ask. It was another game they played. Roy had found his favorite and saw no reason to steer away from it – pot roast and potatoes. Truth told, he'd come to the point where he practically craved it.

Margarette never ordered the same meal twice. Her goal was to order every item on the menu at least once. Like the cafe's name, the menu was themed on legendary stories of the town's founding, serving entrees like rum-battered fish and curried chicken.

Margarette handed him the cardstock menu embossed on both sides with a smattering of tiny stars.

He looked back over the menu, having read the options more times than he could count. The menu changed with the seasons, accounting for locally grown crops brought in from the surrounding farmland.

"I think it's 'next time'…" he said, tapping his finger on the Ciorbă de perişoare.

Her eyes narrowed. "Maybe we should just have an appetizer."

"You asked me to pick." While she had an affinity for trying new foods, she had repeatedly overlooked the soup, saying she would try it "next time".

"Fine… I'll try the sour soup!" She reached across the table, taking the menu back. "Why not? You know, Roy, I'll probably like the soup…"

"You like everything."

"I know." She turned toward the window.

He wondered what had captured her attention. He watched her, clearly preoccupied with something. "What's on your mind?"

He worried it could be him. Was she questioning their engagement? Last night had been a bit overwhelming, but hopefully it wasn't the precursor of events to come.

She turned back to him. "I've been all over the world, but I can't stay away from Coraloo. I love this town. I love it all. The festivals, the people, the shops, the... Well, I love every bit of it."

"*Every* bit of it?"

Margarette grinned. She sat up, placing her elbows on the table and her chin in her hands. "Okay, some things more than others." She leaned back again, pulling her cardigan tighter around her shoulders and accidentally knocking over the salt. "Oh, shoot!" She quickly picked up a handful, tossing it over her shoulder and into the hair of an elderly tourist.

Roy cringed.

"I hit someone, didn't I? Did they notice?"

Roy shook his head and smiled.

"Sorry, bad habit."

The waitress approached their table, a denim apron tied in a string bow around her waist. She glanced down at the ring Roy had given Margarette.

"Oh my gosh, I heard about this! I guess I should have put it all together. You're the two everyone's talking about. I mean, how many town constables are there? And Miss Toft, I had no idea you were so scandalous! I mean, it makes sense with your sweaters and all. He's older... You dress older."

Roy was older. He often forgot about their difference in age, until perfect evenings out with his fiancée were interrupted by the impertinent chatter of a young twenty-something.

"So, you two are really going through with it, huh? The whole town's talking about it. You're like local celebrities. Even *the others* know. You're like Romeo and Juliet or something. Before long they'll be reenacting your wedding during history week. We'll have an evening where they only serve pot roast and potatoes, and everyone'll dress up like the constable and wear outdated clothes like –"

Margarette smiled up at the waitress. "Angela..."

"Oh, sorry, Miss Toft." She readied herself, poised with pen in hand. "What will you have?"

"Grilled pimento cheese, and can you add a fried green tomato to that?" Roy cleared his throat. She cast a glance his way, scowled, and then returned her focus to the waitress. "And a cup of the Ciorbă de perişoare on the side." She ordered effortlessly, with confidence, as if she ordered the same meal every time they came. The meal would arrive, she'd offer Roy a bite, and then he'd wonder why he hadn't ordered the same thing. While the roast was always extraordinary it was never as tasty as whatever was on her plate.

The waitress turned to Roy. "I know, Mr Blackwell. You'll take the usual." The waitress took their menus and stuck them under her arm.

The usual? No.

Roy didn't want to order the usual. He didn't want to *be* the usual. He didn't want his young, energetic bride-to-be thinking she was marrying a pot roast. He wanted to be Romanian soup and grilled cheese!

"Actually, I'll have what she's having."

"You will?" Margarette and the waitress said in unison.

"Are you sure, Mr Blackwell? I mean, you always order the pot roast. They started plating it the minute you stepped in the door. What if you don't like the soup? Or what if you're allergic to tomatoes and don't even know it?"

"I'm not allergic to tomatoes."

What he really wanted to say was, "Do you think I'm so predictable that I've eaten pot roast at every mealtime for every single day of my life and tried nothing else, including tomatoes?"

He caught a subtle wink from Margarette. She was impressed.

"Angela, just bring Mr Blackwell his meal, please."

"Sorry, Miss Toft. Can I get you two some more water? Soda? The lemonade is fresh." Margarette smiled up at the girl, her look stern but calm. Roy called it her teacher face.

"Water's fine. Thank you."

"Yes, Miss Toft."

The girl scurried back to who-knows-where, hopefully to amend his order quickly and get their food on the go. It felt like hours since he had eaten lunch up at the market.

"She's as talkative now as she was when she was in my class. She had a question for everything back then. 'But what about this, Miss Toft? But what about that, Miss Toft?' I had to give her detention just for talking once! I usually hate to see my students go, but… Well, she's a sweet girl."

Roy laughed, knowing someone else who had the gift of plentiful speech. But he didn't mind, nor did he ever want to see her go. Margarette had brought excitement to his life, and today, Romanian soup.

When the soup and sandwich arrived Roy stared at it, while Margarette dove in. He should have ordered the pot roast. But if he was going to marry Margarette he was going to have to try a few new things every now and then… like this sandwich.

As he lifted the sandwich globs of chunky pimento cheese fell out the sides. He took a bite. A burst of flavors shot through his mouth, then dropped into his stomach like a ton of lead. He took another bite. It was tasty, but his stomach would pay for it later.

He swallowed, wiped his mouth with his napkin, and pulled out a folded-up brochure from his pocket. "I've been thinking about us and our future," Roy began. "I was wondering if I should maybe do something different."

"You've been saying that for months." Margarette took another bite and closed her eyes. "This. Is. Incredible! The flavors and… I don't know. It's the best thing I've ever eaten. This may become my pot roast."

It took him a minute to process that Margarette was suggesting she might order it again and again. But she wouldn't, he was sure of it.

"Take a look."

She took the brochure. "You want to be a pirate?"

He took back the brochure emblazoned with a sunken ship off the coast of the Florida Keys. "Not quite. These men dive for pirate treasure. You get a percentage of whatever they find. I was thinking of investing. You know, taking some risks…"

"Risks, huh? Is this like a retirement thing?"

Retirement.

The word stung, another reminder of the age difference.

He laughed it off. "I've got the bike repairs on the side and my cottage is paid for, so this would be kind of like a bonus. What do you think?"

She popped the last bite of sandwich into her mouth and chewed, keeping her gaze fixed on him until she swallowed. "I think you're amazing, and I love you just the way you are. But I've always had a thing for pirates."

It was the third idea he'd run by her in the past month, but nothing really seemed to grab her attention. She had asked him once what he would do if he could have any job in the world. His answer: a detective. But that was no longer an option, as middle age had put him over the academy's maximum age requirement. So he would have to find something else. Something bold and exciting. Something that would make Margarette Toft the proudest woman in all Coraloo.

Roy took a sip of his soup and coughed.

"Are you all right?"

"The soup… it's…"

She dipped her spoon into the bowl and took a sip, and then another. "It's… well… it's different." She took another taste. She frowned. "Okay, so it's not my favorite item on the menu, but that sandwich is quite possibly the most delectable thing I've eaten in my entire life!"

"You don't like the soup?"

"It's interesting."

"So… you *do* like it? Would you like some more to go? I bet we can get Angela back over here."

She gazed at him, her eyes narrowed, her brows furrowed. And then she took another spoonful. "Fine. I don't like the soup."

"Maybe you should have ordered the pot roast."

She grinned, wadded up her napkin, and tossed it at him. "Maybe you should stick to letting me order the weird stuff and you should stick to what you know."

"But I did like the sandwich."

"Better than the pot roast?"

He crossed his arms across his chest and leaned back in his chair. "Okay. *Not* better than the pot roast!"

She grinned. "Now we can talk about the wedding."

"Are we serving pot roast at the wedding?" he teased.

"I'm not sure. I think my parents want to cover the reception, but then there's that rehearsal thing your family does. Maybe we should set the date first."

"I think that's a great idea, Miss Toft."

"I won't be Miss Toft much longer."

"So, a short engagement? I'm up for it if you are." Roy meant it.

"I agree. A short engagement makes sense. We'll check with the church and see what's available. I'm assuming we'll be getting married at the church."

"Church, field, waterfall..." He meant that too. "As long as we're getting married –"

"No family restriction on location, then?"

"Not that I know of."

Seeing as the Blackwells had once been nomadic – never staying in one place for too long – Roy was certain they didn't hold claim to one specific marital location in Coraloo. In fact, he'd attended his cousin Stephen's wedding in an old tobacco barn.

Margarette pulled a small notebook from her purse and wrote something down. "Roy, I think we should keep it small. Simple. Is that okay with you?"

He wanted to shout, "Okay? Nothing would make me happier!" Just a short hop to the next town over, an 'I do' in front of the justice of the peace, and he'd be good to go. But she'd told him about the notebook, how she had been planning this day since she was a little girl. And he knew his family would be as disappointed as hers if they eloped. So *simple* was the next best thing.

"I'll meet with the florist after we've set the date... Actually, there's not much we can do until we set the date, and we can't set the date until we've met with Pastor Donaldson. Are you sure there's nothing else... something I might not know about? I can't find any pictures of

Blackwell weddings. Are cameras not allowed? Maybe I should talk to your cousin's wife. Do you think Clover would mind?" Margarette took a deep breath. "No, I don't want to bother her. She homeschools all those children! I admire that woman, I really do."

Clover was a mother of five and lived in the nicest campervan Margarette had ever seen. In fact, Margarette was pretty certain Clover and Stephen could have bought a mini-mansion in the next town over for the price they had paid to purchase the rolling home and have it completely renovated.

Roy sat back in his chair, braced for whatever was about to come.

She smiled and wrote something else down in her notebook, biting the inside of her cheek. She took another deep breath. He could see it building inside of her. Stress.

Roy reached across the table and placed his hand on hers. "What do you need me to do?"

"I'll let you know if something comes to mind. But for starters, don't forget about tomorrow night. We'll have to miss the reenactment this year. Too bad because the candlelight walk is one of my favorite parts of the festival."

It was one of his, too.

Roy had run into Charlie Price on his way home from the dinner last night. Now that the families were informed, he'd shared the news of his engagement with Charlie. Not long after, Charlie's wife Velveteen had phoned Margarette, insistent, going on about it "being too late" but saying "they'd make it work". Roy knew the Prices well. Charlie Price managed the family market and Velveteen had taken over his grandmother's bakery, turning it into a successful macaron boutique. He didn't care for the colorful desserts – far too sweet – but the tourists seemed to love them. The Prices were the first outsiders he'd ever really seen his family take to. So the Blackwells had agreed to host, to the great frustration of the Toft family, what Velveteen called the "*fête de fiançailles*". That woman had a way of making everything sound fancy. In short, Velveteen Price was throwing them an engagement party.

Tomorrow afternoon, following the morning service, they would head up the hill to the Coraloo Flea Market – the place where Margarette had said *yes* – to face their families. All of them. Together. In one place.

Ever since their first date he had carried the ring in the left breast pocket of his uniform, just in case. In the beginning they had intentionally kept to neutral ground, avoiding any confrontations with overzealous family members and seeing each other for only a few moments a week. She'd visit him at the station. He'd walk her home from school. They had no intention of keeping their new relationship a secret, as it was near impossible to keep anything quiet in Coraloo.

They'd gone to the Prices' first annual Coraloo Christmas party together with Margarette as his plus-one. She had held gently to his arm the entire night, smelling nice, like warm vanilla. The next day she willingly sat through Charlie Price's funeral, as if having your funeral before you died was the most natural thing in the world. She'd taken notes the whole time, fascinated and honored to be experiencing one of the most notable Blackwell traditions.

A month later she nursed him through a cold, providing homemade soups and hot tea, and stopping by his cottage on her way to and from school for three days. He had made sure to tell her it wasn't mononucleosis or streptococcal pharyngitis. Margarette had laughed and asked if he had ever considered applying to medical school. Roy had said no, claiming he preferred the comfort of his bike shed to an operating room. The truth was, he had never finished university. On one trip she brought him a copy of *Spokes*. She said she'd seen an outdated issue of the cycling magazine lying on his coffee table.

Margarette noticed things like that. She noticed him.

Roy wanted to see her every day for the rest of his life. He hadn't planned to propose when he did. It just happened. He had taken her on a private, behind-the-scenes tour of the Coraloo Flea Market on the day of the market's grand reopening, showing her the ins and outs and introducing her to family members who had voted only a few days prior to allow the Tofts to enter the market. The Blackwells had once had a firm "No Tofts Allowed" policy. There had even been a sign on the outside wall, not that it had kept Margarette away. She'd been to the market dozens of times over the years, but never as a guest. No one had said a word about her lineage. In fact, they seemed to like her.

The market was a flurry of people, scurrying in and out of the shops as if the stores were about to run out of whatever handmade ware was being sold that day. Charlie Price had asked Roy if he would mind being there in full uniform, for a bit of extra security.

Roy had asked Margarette if she'd like to tag along. The familiar scent of vanilla wafted around him. He couldn't take his eyes off her. They stopped under the grandeur of the center chandelier, light flowing through her golden curls. Tourists moved around them, none the wiser as to what was happening.

She stopped and inhaled slowly, breathing in the familiar fragrances of the market that had become so familiar to Roy he forgot to notice them: leather, lavender, fresh mint, charred wood.

"I absolutely think I could live in this place forever," Margarette said.

It was then he knew. He knew for sure. He didn't get down on one knee, but he took her hand and kissed it.

She blushed.

For the first time since his dad's passing Roy felt well, healthy, strong, and whole. He pulled the ring from his pocket and held it up to her.

The market moved on around them. Pickers haggled over the vendors' wares. Macarons baked in the corner shop. Tourists flowed in and out of the storefronts, as pleased with the whole market experience as they were with their hand-crafted purchases. They didn't know what he knew.

"Margarette Toft, can I be yours?"

She stared at him, as if studying the fine lines by his eyes, then replied, "Only if I can be yours."

He placed the ring on her finger.

Still the market carried on, patrons going about their business.
Then, he kissed her.

"Do we have to leave, Roy? Or can we stay here for a while?
Right here?"

He wasn't sure how long they'd stood under that chandelier,
but it hadn't been long enough. Had a tourist not tossed a
handful of change at them, while another applauded, shouting,
"Good show! Good show!" he would have dwelled in that
moment forever.

With their meal finished, the pair stepped out into the bustling circle of Coraloo. The rain had come and gone once again. The citizens were ready, dressed in their finest garb for the historical costume stroll. Maharajas and maharinis, natives, red-bearded children, even a pirate or two walked up and down the streets, the trees aglow with the strung lighting, and the smell of deer meat nachos wafting out of The Beaver's Beard. A hum of music echoed around the glowing town. The stores all stayed open a little later this month as *the others* found their way in and out, searching for Heaken Beaver specials. The children ran through the circle barefooted, pretending to attack one another with their foam antler headdresses.

He took her arm, pulling her close. How two people who had lived in the same town for so long had never met until they did was beyond him. She'd been in every play, ridden in every parade, and had even been named the Heaken Beaver Queen – twice.

All of a sudden he could feel eyes watching them and whispers insinuating curiosity and concern. Even *the others*, the outsiders, somehow seemed to know. It was true what the waitress had said: the whole town knew. When he and Margarette had first started seeing each other it felt like they lived outside the confines of Coraloo, as if nobody but the two of them knew about their romance – as if nobody paid it any attention. But they were paying attention now. Everyone was paying attention.

A Toft and a Blackwell. Even he would have considered the idea inconceivable until he met her. Most Tofts had a way about them.

Money was a priority and church a responsibility. But now there was the ring and everything had changed, as though whatever they had been playing at had become a reality. They had made it official and all eyes were watching to see whether this Blackwell and that Toft would actually go through with it.

CHAPTER 5

1955

There once was a woman named Isabella Donadieu who lived in her own world, distant from the townsfolk. She was the daughter of a traveling troubadour who had made his way to Coraloo for the Heaken Beaver Festival but tragically died mid-performance when a disgruntled audience member, who was not happy with the troubadour's interpretation of "La vie en Rose", hit him with a pair of reproduction beaver antlers. Isabella was promptly given to the priest to be raised as the first orphan in Coraloo. Everyone kept an eye out for her, watching her grow from a distance. They were sympathetic but always saw her as an outsider – an *other*.

It was the priest who had first seen Isabella's talent when he accidentally lit the bottom of his garment on fire and was in urgent need of a hem repair. Seeing him struggle with a needle and thread, Isabella calmly took the robes from him and repaired them until they looked better than new. As she was now old enough to live on her own, the priest purchased a small space looking out over the circle of town where she could practice her trade on the first floor and take up residence on the second.

So Isabella became the local seamstress. The chaos of her childhood now a thing of the past, she set to work creating garments for the rhythms of local life – making dresses and tailoring suits for weddings, birthdays, baptisms, and funerals (the latter for both the dead and, in the case of the Blackwells, the living).

Life ticked along quietly until a certain young starlet by the name of Sister Forrester rolled into Coraloo with her entourage in May of 1946.

The story goes that it was Marcus Poteet who, standing at a fork in the road, detoured an unsuspecting film crew into Coraloo in hopes the producer would see Coraloo as a better place to film *Whispers the Lake* instead of the original destination in the next town over. What Marcus had forgotten to factor in was that the closest thing Coraloo had to a lake, unless they considered the river, was the duck pond his wife Mavis had dug in their front garden, the sight of which sent the crew packing two days later.

Nevertheless, during her two-day respite in Coraloo, Sister Forrester stumbled – literally, after tripping over a dog wearing a turban; it was festival time, after all – into the storefront of Isabella Donadieu.

"I'm looking for something unique," Sister said. "Something extraordinarily different from the rest of those wannabes. Nothing off the shoulder – Dina Blossom went off the shoulder while she was with husbands one and four. And it mustn't be too long. The paparazzi had a field day when Honor Norman tripped down the aisle. Trains should be on tracks, not on dresses. It should be simple, elegant. Can you do that, Miss…?"

"Isabella," she had said. "My name is Isabella Donadieu. And yes, I believe I can."

Sister Forrester's visit created quite a stir in Coraloo. The mayor even named the road into town after her for a few days, until someone let him know he did not have the authority to change road names. Her presence was the talk of the town as she went on to play the leading lady in four hit films, which the Coraloo Theater ran on repeat for months after they had left other theaters. Sister Forrester was a star, but when she stepped out onto the red carpet in her Isabella Donadieu gown, it was the dress that became the talk of the world. It not only made Isabella a celebrity in Coraloo but also caught the eyes of a German princess, a rock and roll star, and an heiress.

The townspeople would later say the only reason Dermot Toft married Isabella was for her newfound fame and wealth. After securing forty-five feathers and the final sequin to a native headdress, Isabella gave birth to her only child, a girl, amid the tulle and fame and

51

frivolities of the festival: Innis Imogen-Laken Toft. "Innis" after a great-grandmother on her mother's side and "Imogen-Laken" because "Innis Imogen-Laken-Ambrosia-Penrose Toft" was much too long.

The painfully shy Innis disliked school so much her mother never made her go. In place of a standard education she grew up at her mother's side, studying anatomy while her mother sketched, and practicing mathematics while her mother measured. She watched as her mother beaded bodices and veils, hand-tacked lace with tiny hidden stitches, and washed her hands incessantly so as not to mar the fabric.

Young Innis welcomed the deliveryman with gloved hands, as per her mother's instructions, and helped to unload crates of silks, satins and organdies, boxes of beads, and spools of gilded threads. She learned three different languages from the voices on the other end of telephone calls, and geography from orders placed with suppliers in exotic places Innis longed to see.

It was the only life Innis had ever known, learning and watching her mother create dresses for women she would only meet twice – once for the consultation and once for the fitting. Innis was wise enough to know the clientele who came and left her mother's studio were different – not from her world. She absorbed their stories of banquets and balls, movie premiers, and mansions on hills. But it wasn't the fame or even the person who wore the dress that held Innis so rapt; it was the adventure of it all – the idea of a life outside Coraloo.

When Innis's father ran off with a belly dancer from the next town over, Isabella and Innis were almost forgotten by the Tofts, and even more so as the smutty dramas of Dina Blossom replaced the swoony romantic films of Sister Forrester. Fashion followed what was happening on screen, and her mother's craft – her mother's chosen art form – merely became a beautifully creative means of securing their financial survival.

Innis sat diligently at her mother's side holding a black amethyst ashtray filled to the brim with turquoise-tipped dress pins as her mother carefully cut the satin *peau de soie* or the double-bonded silk cady, watching as her scissors methodically crunched down on the material. As young Innis grew, Isabella passed on her skill.

"Measure twice, cut once" was her mother's mantra.

One day Isabella Toft paused from her work, pulling a red velveteen ribbon from her basket of extra trimmings. She smiled down at her only child and proceeded to hang her pair of antique German sewing shears around her daughter's neck.

"Have them sharpened on Saturdays and protect them from the morticians."

Her mother had always carried the scissors – a heavy adornment, both practical and pronounced.

Innis knew all about the scissors. They'd come from the fortune teller – a festival *other* – who solicited the shop, scissors hung around her neck, and asked for her skirt to be hemmed. As payment for services she had gifted the scissors to Isabella, declaring them special, unique.

"A pair of scissors is like the mind. Keep them sharp and they will serve you well," the fortune teller had said. Before she left the shop, she warned, "Keep them safe and beware the borrowing hand of a mortician." Then she was gone, never to be seen again.

A good Christian would never have entertained the ramblings of a crystal-gazing old woman, but one who had been hurt by a philandering husband found it easy to look beyond her faith.

Innis Toft carried their heavy burden around her neck, longing to see the world outside of Coraloo but bound by the constraints of occupation and obligation.

CHAPTER 6

Margarette rocked back on the heels of her shoes, her arm held securely in the crook of Roy's elbow, pausing outside the Coraloo Flea Market. Despite the family vote the sign beside the door still read: NO DOGS OR TOFTS – GRANNY BITES!

Granny Blackwell had only been gone for a few months. Word of the Blackwell matriarch's sudden death had traveled swiftly down the hill, halting all Blackwell blathering in Sylvia's Hair Emporium or whatever she was calling it at the time.

Margarette had been at the salon when the news was broadcast. Sylvia had returned from giving Velveteen Price a full makeover, eager to share what she had gleaned from Coraloo's newest residents, and especially how the Blackwells had "gotten to them first". In response, Sylvia had declared she would make it her mission to turn "Velvy" into a Toft, starting with "the Works".

"It works every time! Velvy will be sitting here with us before you know it. She belongs with us, you know. High society. She's not one of them." Not one of them – not a Blackwell.

Margarette's mother appeared in the doorway that separated the salon from the living quarters at the back of the cottage. "She's gone."

Margarette jumped up from her chair, noticing her mother's distress. "What happened?" she cried. "Who's gone?"

"Granny Blackwell. I just came from the post office. Everyone's talking about it. I heard she was unwell... I thought she would live forever."

Margarette thought of Roy. They hadn't been seeing each other very long; not long enough to know whether he would want her

54

company or her distance at a time like this.

Wrist deep in shampoo, Sylvia spoke next. "Well, what are we going to do?"

Silence passed over the women, amplifying the sound of running water as Sylvia rinsed her client clean.

"Did anyone say if they checked her feathers?" Sylvia asked, her mind instantly jumping to the familiar Toft superstition.

Margarette seriously doubted the Blackwells had checked Granny Blackwell's pillow feathers.

She started to reply, "I don't think –"

But Aunt Clara Toft interrupted. "I don't want to be the first to say it, but swirl or no swirl we all know where that woman was headed."

Collective "um-hums" followed.

The ladies fell silent again, as if contemplating their own eternities, then returned their uninterested gazes to the magazines in hand.

But Aunt Clara wasn't finished. "Who wants to go with me? We'll do it tonight. I won't be able to sleep until I know which way those feathers are swirled."

It was an old superstition, and one even Margarette's mother had let go after she had brought it to the attention of Pastor Donaldson and he had politely, without even a chuckle, informed her that a person's salvation could not be determined by the swirl of the feathers inside one's pillow.

This type of conversation would usually have passed over Margarette as salon chatter, but she couldn't take it anymore. "For goodness' sake! A woman has died! Can't we show her some respect? You're talking about sneaking into a dead woman's campervan and ripping open her pillow to look at feathers – a dead woman who just happens to be the grandmother of –"

She caught herself before she could say the word. She didn't know why she stopped short. Maybe because she was about to

reveal to a salon full of Tofts that she was dating a Blackwell.
Or perhaps because she was about to finish with the phrase "my
boyfriend". That sounded so official, so final – a declaration of
the reality she had been facing for the past month and a half. It
was the truth… and worse still, not only was she dating him but
she cared about him, especially in this moment when a member
of his family had left this world for the next.

In the silence of the stares she cleared her throat and
continued, "… many grandchildren."

After that it was some time before anyone had dared make another jab regarding Granny Blackwell. Margarette never knew whether it was because the Toft women had begrudgingly decided the Blackwell matriarch was owed some sort of respect as a worthy opponent – a fallen enemy – or whether Aunt Clara had found the pillow and discovered that either Granny Blackwell would forever haunt her from Hades or she would be standing at the gates of heaven insisting Aunt Clara be refused entry.

Margarette gripped Roy's arm. "I'm nervous. This isn't going to go well."

"Nope." He kissed her on the top of her head.

"Do you think anyone would notice if we didn't show up?"

"I'll be surprised if anyone notices when we do show up."

As strange as it sounded, cancelled plans were Margarette's favorite kind of plans. She secretly hoped none of them would show up. Then she wouldn't have to face it – the bantering, the gazes, the taunts. Her stomach turned.

"What do you think it'll be?" he asked. "Arm-wrestling? Jousting? Or just casual back-and-forth all-out mockery?"

She forced a laugh. "My money's on hammer throwing."

She had known this was a terrible idea the moment Velveteen Price mentioned it. But Velveteen's call had not only been insistent but persistent.

"You absolutely must have an engagement party! We have to celebrate! We'll have it down at the market. I'll cook and gather a few of the ladies to help me decorate. You'll see! It'll be fabulous."

"You want to hold the party when?" Margarette asked, her voice wavering.

"Sunday afternoon," Velveteen squealed. "We should have started planning this months ago. Roy really should have told Charlie he was going to propose."

Margarette had briefly met the newcomers at the back-to-school orientation and then again at their Christmas party. However, after having her own encounter with Sylvia's "the Works" before the soiree, she was certain Velveteen had not recognized her as their son Gideon's sixth-grade history teacher when she showed up at their front door.

"I really appreciate the offer, but surely one day isn't enough time to plan and prepare. I could never ask you –"

"Waiting any longer would be inappropriate and unacceptable. But it's no matter. I can work with what we've got. It's my pleasure, really. And event planning is something I'm starting to dabble in, so you'll sort of be a test case."

A test case.

"Thank you, but I really don't think it's a good idea to mix the families so soon. We've only been engaged a day, and we just told our parents a few hours ago. We'll do well to get them all to come to the wedding. I'm sure you're familiar with the family history."

Velveteen laughed so hard into the phone Margarette had to hold the receiver away from her ear.

"Let's just say I am well aware," she replied. "But we can talk about that another day. Just don't throw anything at me."

Margarette could only imagine what Velveteen meant by that.

Velveteen sighed. "This is about you and Roy, not them. It's your wedding. Don't worry, I'll get them to the party, and that'll pave the way for everything else. Just show up at the market. I'll take care of the rest."

57

"And what if they say no?" But as she said it, Margarette knew the Tofts would never say no. It would be like backing down from a duel.

"They won't because I'm a neutral party. It would be rude to refuse an invitation from me. And besides, I'm having a baby."

"What does that have to do with anything?"

"Nobody ever refuses a pregnant woman."

The truth was, nobody ever refused Velveteen Price, mostly because they didn't know how. She had a pleasantness about her, a charm that wooed and welcomed all who crossed her path. She may have been nearly a foot shorter than Margarette and about two feet wider at present, but based on Margarette's encounters she was always the most prominent person in any room. Velveteen was right – nobody would refuse her.

A cool breeze ushered the couple past the arched threshold and into the market. They were greeted by the glisten of bold chandeliers and the applause of Blackwells – all of them. Men, women, aunts, uncles, and a whole roomful of children, one of whom was wearing a wedding dress that was far too big for her, pooling at her feet and nearly swallowing her whole.

Velveteen rushed over to greet Margarette and Roy, arms flailing. She looked like a hot pink gumball, dressed in an empire-waisted party dress adorned with a rhinestone brooch right where her baby bump started. She carried a pair of matching high heels in her arms but wore sandals on her feet. "Where. Are. They?"

Margarette didn't have to ask about either the heels or the family. She could already see for herself. Velveteen's feet were so swollen they were spilling out the sides of the sandals and the Tofts were yet to arrive. Despite having harbored a secret desire that the whole thing be unexpectedly cancelled by a freak snowstorm in May, Margarette felt disappointed, and truthfully, a bit surprised. The Tofts never missed a moment to show off their finery, nor could she believe they would allow the Blackwells to enjoy this moment without them. *Something was up.*

When she'd asked Aunt Clara if she would attend the engagement party her aunt had smiled knowingly, then asked if Margarette was planning on bringing a date.

Clover Blackwell, who looked about thirty even though Margarette had heard the homeschooling mother-of-five was the same age as Roy, stepped over to greet them.

Clover leaned in to hug Margarette and kissed her on the cheek. "You look lovely, Margarette! Did you buy your dress at the market?"

She hadn't, but she'd visited Uncle Albert Blackwell's Haberdashery on more than one occasion. Margarette and Uncle Albert had hit it off right away, and he'd promised to pass a message on through Roy should he take in inventory he thought might appeal to Margarette's vintage eye. Last fall Albert had made the business decision to expand his range beyond the walls lined with neat little cubbies containing antique buttons and other sewing notions and branch out into vintage menswear, hats, bowties, and cufflinks. Then he'd discovered it would be even more profitable if he could acquire and repair ladies' attire as well.

"I'm truly happy for you both," Clover said. "Velveteen's put together quite a spread. Can I get you anything to eat? A drink, maybe?"

Roy leaned in toward Clover. "I'll take the strongest thing you've got."

Margarette tapped him playfully on the shoulder. She knew he wasn't kidding, but she also knew it wasn't that kind of party. Margarette allowed her future family member to take her by the arm and lead her into the cluster of Blackwells. Margarette was so familiar with the market she could probably have stood blindfolded and named from memory each of the shops and which Blackwell owned them. Of course, she would never reveal this piece of knowledge to any of her relatives; however, she had seen a few Tofts covertly shopping the market's artisan boutiques and aisles of vendors, and knew Sylvia visited Velveteen's macaron shop at least once a week.

The whole feud was ridiculous. She was quite certain most of them couldn't remember why the two families hated one another.

Maybe they should spend a day in my history class.

She strolled into the crowd of celebrating Blackwells as they smiled through bites of finger foods, their hands clutching decorative paper plates. The Blackwells were far more accepting of her than the Tofts were of Roy, but her family would come around. They simply had to get to know him the way she knew him. They had to see that he wasn't a man to be labeled by his name. He was dapper, a gentleman, and an official of the town. She almost swooned just thinking about him.

"Your mother was a Smith, isn't that right?" one of Blackwell men asked.

Margarette's spirits lifted. This man knew her mother. "Yes, she was."

"We were in school together, you know?"

"No, I didn't." She hadn't seen a Blackwell at school since she was in middle school, and had assumed they were now all homeschooled like Clover's children.

"She was quite a looker. Still is, from what I hear." He winked.

As a child, Margarette had loved looking at pictures of her mother as a young woman. It was how she had imagined she would look when she grew up – tall and slender with silky dark hair. Instead, Margarette had taken on her father's attributes, leaving her shorter, dirty blonde, with hair unable to decide whether it wanted to curl or not, and a figure more fleshy than fit.

She raised her eyes and looked through the sea of Blackwells in the hope of finding Roy. He made her feel safe, not that the rest of the Blackwells had ever expressed any intention to harm her. She lifted her shoulders. These people were going to become her family. *Margarette Blackwell.* She loved the way it sounded and had practiced writing it the way a schoolgirl does with her crush, rows of "Margarette Blackwells" in big curvy letters.

"I didn't quite catch your name, sir."

The man extended his hand, but before he could speak the voice of Sylvia Toft boomed around the room.

"Meggy? Meggy? Are you here, Meggy? I can't see you!"

Margarette apologized to the man for the interruption and made her way over to her cousin. "Sylvia! I'm so glad you came."

Sylvia appeared in a rush and took Margarette by the hands. "You look stunning! Not my style, but you know how it goes. I could have done something with your make-up if you'd asked. I can run down the hill and get my case if you want or, you know what?" She shoved her hand into the lime-green handbag that coordinated perfectly with her heels. "I've got a tube of Ruby Dayz right here! Let's go to the ladies' room and get you all fixed up."

Margarette felt herself pulled along once again, but was stopped short by Velveteen, clipboard in hand and looking quite distraught.

She greeted Sylvia with a hug and turned to Margarette in a hushed whisper. "I didn't invite anyone called Meggy. I have exactly every name you gave me, but I don't have a *Meggy*. I've personalized all the party favors and I'll feel absolutely awful if I've missed someone."

"It's okay. Everyone in my family calls me Meggy."

"What? But the cake! Do you prefer Meggy? Is that what I should call you? I can have Charlie run the cake down to that new bakery and order a –"

Margarette took her hand. "I much prefer Margarette."

Sylvia leaned in. "Velvy, the whole family calls her Meggy. You can too if you want."

"Speaking of the whole family..." Margarette turned to face her cousin, arms crossed, changing the subject. "Mother said she and the rest would be here. Where are they?"

"Oh." Sylvia looked back toward the entrance and then up to Margarette. "They're here."

"How did I miss them?" Velveteen wailed.

Margarette eyed Sylvia carefully. It was just as she had suspected. Something *was* up. "Sylvia Toft, where is the family?"

Sylvia turned on her lime-green heels and pointed at the door. "They're outside."

"Outside?"

"Yes... outside."

"What are they doing outside?"

"They have a surprise for you."

"What kind of surprise?"

"A surprise… party."

"Two parties?" Velveteen squealed. "But I planned this party! Are you telling me they planned another one?"

"Sort of…"

Margarette's eyebrows knitted together. She scoured the crowd of perfectly content partygoers; perfectly harmless, happy to do whatever they were asked, trying to make peace partygoers. She spotted Roy with Velveteen's husband Charlie. He caught her eye. She motioned him over.

"Are you okay? You don't look well." He raised a hand to her forehead. "You're not warm."

Margarette thrust her finger toward the door, where Sylvia stood with a larger-than-life smile and her arms extended as if she were displaying a game show prize.

"They're here."

Margarette marched toward the door, arms crossed, teeth clenched, and a good deal of choice words threatening to spill out in a very unladylike fashion. Her mother had said she would come. She would be there. She would come to the engagement party. Margarette soon-to-be-whether-they-liked-it-or-not Blackwell's engagement party. Whatever they were up to, she wanted none of it. They could take their most likely very expensive party and roll back down the hill for all she cared.

"Close your eyes," Sylvia instructed.

"No."

"Oh, pleeeeeeeeeease. We worked so hard, and we're missing the reenactment for this. The reenactment's kind of a big deal, you know."

"You knew about this? You let them do it? If you let them do this, so help me I will go to the city to get my hair done for the rest of my life!" The minute Margarette said it she regretted it.

Sylvia's hands dropped. "We just wanted to make it special for you and…" she nodded toward Roy, "… him."

Margarette pulled Sylvia into a hug, dodging her hair and nearly gagging at the sickly aroma of hairspray and strip mall body mist. She sighed.

Roy put his arm around Margarette and whispered in her ear, "At least they're not in the same room."

With Roy by her side they stepped into the archway to be greeted by a grand shout of surprise. The sea of Tofts parted, revealing rows of picnic tables lined up and decorated in black and grey, as though they were celebrating a funeral rather than an engagement. At the center of it all was a wooden cart filled with Margarette's favorite sweets. Among the assorted tarts – key lime, gingersnap, salted Mayan chocolate – and her Aunt Carol Ann's truffles – who wasn't a Toft but hoped to marry one – stood an ice sculpture in the shape of a gigantic heart. Etched into its center was the letter T.

"Sorry we're late, Meggy." Her mother emerged from the crowd to embrace her, slightly out of breath. "It near killed us carrying all this up the hill, but we did it. I'm not sure what we would have done if the rain hadn't stopped."

Margarette was temporarily speechless. All she could do was point back toward the party behind her.

"I know, Meggy, and Velveteen Price is such a dear to do this. I suggested the event take place on more neutral ground – possibly the Prices' – but she said there were too many of us."

"If she hadn't invited the Blackwells there'd be enough room," a voice shouted from the back.

"I also suggested your uncle's new restaurant," her mother continued, "but as you can imagine Velveteen dismissed that idea – something about a pub not being fit for the event. She insisted we use the market. So here we are!"

Margarette looked out at all the Tofts. These were smart, educated people – doctors, realtors, educators, and entrepreneurs. The Tofts had kept Coraloo running for years, but when the Blackwells had rolled back into town – literally rolled up in their campervans and parked outside the market – the Tofts had gone crazy, as though the Blackwells had unleashed some psychotic plague upon the House of Toft. According to Roy, the Blackwells hadn't reacted with much more civility when they realized the Tofts had practically taken over Coraloo.

"What are we supposed to do, Mother? Attend both parties?"

Her mother looked disapprovingly at Roy.

Roy shrugged. "I say we attend them both."

For the rest of the evening Roy and Margarette stood on the threshold of the Coraloo Flea Market, chatting first to a group of Blackwells on the inside of the market and then turning toward the Tofts as guests on the outside sought to congratulate them. It was all going rather smoothly until one of the Blackwells approached the couple, insisting they come inside as it was about to start raining again.

A Toft stepped up behind them. "Oh, you'd like that, wouldn't you!"

The Blackwell replied, "I'd like you to pack up your party and get off our land."

And the Toft replied, "It's our land, you son of a Heaken beaver lovin' shoemaker!"

There was a sudden rush on the door where Margarette and Roy stood helpless, as if the exchange had prompted a call to arms. Fists were raised and ancient battle cries shouted. Who needed actors for a reenactment? The natives of Coraloo knew their lines by heart.

"Burn it down!"

"Toss them down the hill!"

Margarette was sure she saw a few non-family members rushing up the hill to see what had caused such an uproar. Even her worst day at school had been better than this – and that had been pretty bad. It was the day Culloden Toft dared Ronald Hackett to eat an eraser, causing him to choke and immediately prompting the headmaster, who happened to be conducting an evaluation, to perform the Heimlich maneuver, which sent the dislodged saliva-coated object into Margarette's eye and resulted in her having to wear an eyepatch for a week. Even being banned from the art museum because of a bare-bottomed boy had been better than this. She reminded herself to thank her sixth-graders for being so mature; it was no coincidence that *Romeo and Juliet* was a mandatory part of the curriculum. Had Velveteen not let out a pained wail Margarette was certain she would have been in danger of trampling.

Roy raised two fingers to his lips and whistled, silencing the out-of-breath partygoers. He threatened to arrest the lot of them, Blackwells included, if they didn't immediately return to their own parties.

It was then Velveteen's water broke. The Blackwells asked if they could help deliver the baby. The Tofts declared the baby marked.

Margarette rolled her eyes.

Following Velveteen's departure and Clover insisting she could handle the party, Roy and Margarette watched, seated on the cool floor in the doorway of the Coraloo Flea Market, as the two families observed a temporary truce, switching focus from hurling obscenities to stuffing their faces with crudités and key lime pie.

He glanced over at her, his back pressed up against the stone wall. "I think you should add this to your notebook. People will want to read about this one day."

She grinned, then yawned.

He scooted closer. "I'm sorry."

She inhaled deeply. "I'm not. I think it's merely given us a glimpse of things to come. So now we know." She looked down at her shoes, fighting back tears. She wasn't one for crying in public. "So now we know…"

Why she had thought their engagement would suddenly fix a problem older than the town itself, she had no idea, but she had hoped. "Do you think they'd even care if we left?"

"I'm not sure, but I have an idea." He stood up, a serious look on his face. "Margarette Toft, soon-to-be Blackwell, you're under arrest."

She raised her eyebrows, then smiled softly. He pulled her to her feet and escorted her away from the market as the two engagement parties continued without them.

That evening they sat in the municipal building recounting their favorite parts of the fateful night, turning the horrific into the hysterical. It was a quiet, nice, and oddly romantic way to mark their engagement.

Roy leaned into her. "I imagine our grandchildren will have quite a few tales to tell about this night."

She rested her head on his shoulder, inwardly laughing about the inevitable fate of the ice sculpture. "I imagine there will be a few…"

CHAPTER 7

The rain thudded against the shingled rooftop, echoing across the rafters of the vaulted ceiling. It was not common practice for Roy Blackwell to visit the only church building in Coraloo. He'd never thought much about attending, having never been invited, and it seemed rude to simply show up.

Complete with spire and bell tower, the stone structure was nearly as old as the town. However, despite its regal presence at the tip of the town circle, it was rumored to have had a rather gruesome history. It was the place of worship for three different denominations: Protestants in the morning, Catholics in the evening, and the non-denominationals who worshipped on Tuesday nights. The rest of the week the church was relinquished to young mothers' groups, a homeschool cooperative, the Coraloo community theater, and a ham radio club.

For years there had been talk that the morning worshippers were planning to build their own church, but this had been rumor for as long as Roy could remember. The two services – the morning led by Pastor Donaldson and the evening led by Father Milligan – could not have been more different, but the church remained exactly the same. Most of the time Roy attended the Blackwell church gatherings at the top of the hill. As with most things, including their worship, the Blackwells were perfectly content keeping themselves to themselves.

A mustiness hung over the dusky church interior, as if the rain had found its way inside the cracks and crevices. The dark hues of the stained-glass windows lining the walls portrayed images of the town's founding, followed by scriptures attempting to justify the odd scenes taking place within them. Like the image of two kilted men in sword-to-sword combat accompanied by the verse: "Love thy enemy."

Two rows of rich mahogany pews ran down the center of the place of worship, resting on the church's original wood plank flooring.

Even on this dreary day there was a sense of calm – the same calm Roy felt whenever he was resetting a chain or adjusting the brakes of a broken bicycle. He'd been inside the historic structure on a few occasions – to settle a debate over the communion wine and, once, to tell the non-denominationals to turn their amplifiers down, as per the town elders' request.

A brisk, cool breeze rushed unexpectedly through the church. The heavy wooden doors slammed shut. He turned to see Margarette walking down the aisle, dripping from head to toe, her navy rain boots squeaking as she walked.

He quickly stood and stepped out from behind the pew.

"I'm so sorry," she said. "Max... Well, Max had the whole class in a tizzy. I had to call his parents again."

"What was it this time? Earthquake? Doomsday?"

"Flood. The minute the rain picked up he started shouting, 'The whole town's going under!'"

"It runs in the family." Roy knew the Fox-McGogginses well. They fell somewhere in the line of Tofts but had turned the Tofts' known adherence to superstition into an irrational doomsday fear of the Earth exploding, or conspiracy of some sort. The story changed each time he saw Earl Fox-McGoggins down at The Beaver's Beard.

"We've got a forty-year supply of food right under the house,"
Earl explained.

"Not sure you should be telling people that, Earl. If something does happen –"

"Oh, something's definitely going to happen. I heard it on my radio."

Roy laughed. He was all for being prepared, but the Fox-McGogginses were a bit extreme. He'd been keeping an eye on them for years, certain they not only had a stash of food and water but an illegal arsenal as well. "Well, it's a good thing I

know where you live. I'll be heading over to your house when the
time comes."

Earl squinted and stared hard at Roy, then stood up and said,
"I've got to go", before running from the tavern.

Roy figured Earl Fox-McGoggins was heading home to hide
his forty-year supply of tinned food someplace else.

"I know," Margarette continued. "His mother showed up to take him home carrying buckets. Four of them. To collect rainwater while they walk. Said she didn't want to waste any of it. Sounds like Max gets all his information from his father. I mean, who makes their son pack a week's supply of food in his backpack 'just in case'? Do you think someone should check their house for asbestos? Lead paint, maybe? Can that make you crazy?"

Roy had a sudden urge to have his home thoroughly inspected for asbestos. He immediately started testing himself to make sure he could remember his full name, his parents' names, his street address and phone number, and made a note to check the book for less common symptoms of asbestos poisoning when he got home.

He shook the thoughts away. Once he got started the irrational fear would consume him until he could find enough information to convince him otherwise. In recent years Roy had been afflicted with everything from hay fever to halitosis, angioedema to alopecia. In his mind the symptoms seemed real enough, especially the alopecia. The evidence was in the mirror. But when he challenged the doctor on his sudden hair loss, he was reminded that some hair loss was normal "at his age".

He forced himself to refocus his thoughts, then leaned over and kissed Margarette. She was his perfect distraction.

"Have you seen the pastor?" she asked, removing her trench coat and laying it over her arm.

"Which one?"

The morning worshippers had been unable to keep a consistent pastor for twenty years, so they had settled on a rotation.

"Pastor Donaldson."

They had yet to set a date, but both instinctively knew having the wedding sooner rather than later would be better for their sanity. After the whole engagement party fiasco, it had to happen soon, before one family tried to ambush the other. Roy had already started imagining the Blackwells calling for the shotguns and the Tofts hiring trained assassins. The town would become a scene from some post-apocalyptic 1950s movie. He and Margarette would have to take up residence in the church, but hopefully Earl Fox-McGoggins and his family would be happy to share the necessary supplies.

Margarette and Roy walked to the front of the church hand in hand.

He leaned in closer. "Let's just do it now."

"It's bad luck."

"Really?" As far as Roy was concerned, the Tofts seemed to add to their list of superstitions on a daily basis.

She pulled in closer. "Just kidding."

"Not before the wedding!" Pastor Danger Donaldson laughed, emerging from the vestry and extending his hand. "Sorry for the delay; I'm feeling a bit lightheaded today. How are you doing, Roy? Keeping the town safe?"

Roy forced a chuckle. "Same as always."

"So I hear there's going to be a Blackwell–Toft wedding. Father Milligan said he's had half your family in for confession over the whole ordeal and they're not even Catholic."

Margarette winced. "I heard about that."

"A little extra prayer never hurt anyone," Roy added, elbowing the pastor.

He didn't look well, his eyes narrowed and glazed.

Margarette had told Roy that Pastor Donaldson's last sermon was uncoincidentally about confession, and how it wasn't necessary for Protestants – or anyone, according to his interpretation of the Scriptures – to visit the confessional when people could speak directly to the source. Nor could they confess to cleanse someone else of their sins, especially if that "sin" involved marrying a Blackwell.

"And that's why we're here," Margarette said. "We'd like to book the church, and we'd love to have you marry us."

"Will I need to hire security?" The pastor laughed heartily, bending at the waist, then stopped himself short. "Sorry, another bad joke. Wow, I'm all out of sorts today. I'd be happy to marry you. It seems as though I've got my foot on both sides of the tracks."

It was true. Pastor Danger Donaldson was pastor to the Tofts and a friend to the Blackwells, although Roy wasn't sure whether the Tofts were aware of the family connection. During his first trip to Coraloo Pastor Donaldson just happened to be in the market when Clover Blackwell went into labor. Thankfully, as the son of a midwife who had spoken openly about the details of her career to her children, Pastor Donaldson was able to deliver Danger Blackwell in the middle of the market in front of an audience who, assuming the birth was an elaborate and very realistic Blackwell performance, tipped generously.

The pastor pulled out his cell phone and opened his calendar. "So, when are we thinking? July? August? I'm not on rotation, but I'd be more than happy to pop... pop... pop... back into town!" He paused, exhaled, and rubbed the back of his neck. "Pardon me. I'm not sure –"

Roy eyed the pastor suspiciously. If he wasn't so familiar with the man, he'd have assumed Pastor Donaldson had been drinking on the job.

"Sooner," Margarette said.

"Oh, all right. June, then."

"Sooner," she repeated.

Pastor Donaldson looked up from his handheld device. "How about the 31st of this month?"

Roy looked at Margarette. She nodded. "Perfect."

"Are you sure?" the pastor asked, typing something into his phone. "The town will be nuts by then. Culture week, right? It ends the festival, you know. Are you sure you want to be the grand fennel? Flannel...? Finale! That's it! Finale!"

Roy was almost certain of it now – Pastor Donaldson was sloshed.

"I'm sure you heard about our party last night, didn't you?" Margarette asked, unaware of the clues Roy was picking up from the pastor, who seemed oblivious to his own intoxication.

"Who hasn't? If I didn't live here for a good part of the year, I'd swear someone was making this stuff up."

Roy stepped in, attempting to move the conversation along for their sake and the pastor's. He knew it seemed like absolute madness to get married during the festival. As far as he knew there had never been a May wedding in Coraloo. The Blackwell market would be swarming with tourists, and the weekly events of the festival would be in full swing. Pastor Donaldson was right. Culture week was the craziest week of all with its art walk, shoe making demonstrations, public readings, and final talent show. But that was the point.

"Let's just say we're hoping the festival will keep the families as distracted as possible."

"It's not easy planning a wedding these days. Matrimony's a biiiiig production," the pastor said, stretching his arms wide.

Margarette glanced to Roy. "Um, we're going to keep it simple."

They had already discussed it. There would be no fuss, just a simple ceremony with cake and punch to follow in the flower garden at the side of the church, assuming the rain would stop. And if it didn't Margarette had suggested they take the cake and run, finding a nice little hole where the two of them could eat the whole thing. Aside from a few other minor details, how hard could planning a wedding be?

Pastor Donaldson glanced again at his phone. "All right, I have you both down for the 31st. I'd like to meet with you before the ceremony, call it a bit of pre-marital counseling, if that's all right." He paused, puffed his cheeks out, and exhaled. "Just something I like to do to make sure we're all on the same page, to check that nothing is majorly out of line. Like one of you wants children and the other doesn't… or one of you has a secret life the other knows nothing about. Do either of you have a secret life?" He winked.

Roy laughed, extending his hand to the pastor. "I think we've pretty much talked it all through. I'll give you a call when you're feeling better. Thanks, Pastor."

"Danger. Just call me Danger!"

Roy would definitely have to call him later. Pastor Donaldson had no trouble taking a seat with the Blackwells at The Beaver's Beard, but the barman never asked him what he wanted to drink because everyone knew the pastor preferred water to wine.

The pastor stumbled away, leaving Roy and Margarette baffled by his performance at the altar. A stained-glass window with the image of a cross overlooked them – the one thing all three church groups could agree on.

Outside, the rain was picking up. Lightning flashed through the stained-glass windows, momentarily casting an array of colors across the place of worship. Thunder cracked, the sound reverberating inside the building.

It would truly take a miracle for the wedding to go smoothly and Roy knew it, but he didn't care. Twenty-five days from now they would be standing in this very spot as man and wife.

Margarette lifted her jacket from the pew. "It's getting kind of ugly out there."

He wondered for a moment whether she was referring to the rain or the families. Either way, he wanted her to know he was ready for the storm. "It's safe here."

She turned to face him, reaching for his hand. "I know."

"Do you want to stay inside for a bit longer?"

"I'd like that very much. Do you think Pastor Donaldson will mind?"

He scratched the back of his head. "I think the pastor's back there taking a long nap."

"I could smell it all over him!" Margarette giggled. "It was like he didn't even know... maybe we should keep this between the two of us."

"Just the two of us." He breathed in the church air once again. Everything would be all right so long as he had her. There was nothing a Toft or Blackwell could do to keep him from her. They had survived the engagement party. Surely they could make it to the 31st of May without another major incident?

CHAPTER 8

Margarette sat on a stool, legs crossed, chin resting in her hand at the back of a class of twenty-three sixth-grade students, and yawned, as one after another, the students stood up and presented their projects on Coraloo's history. She had stayed up half the night filling in her calendar for May. Initially she had color-coded it based on festival events, wedding planning, teaching responsibilities, taking Velveteen lunch to thank her for the party, and spending time with Roy.

Somehow, between all the hoopla of the festival and school-related activities, Margarette had added two new colors to the calendar and managed to squeeze in every single one of their events. It hadn't been easy. She'd hoped the festival might sufficiently preoccupy the families so that all thought of wedding rituals would be left to her and Roy, but no sooner had she and Roy shared their wedding date with their parents than representatives from the Blackwells and the Tofts had begun calling. Now that the date was set, both families had rushed to lock in their "we have to" events: showers, blessings, receptions, rehearsal dinners, fittings. She'd made dozens of calls back and forth with the designated family representatives, trying to accommodate them all.

Margarette figured that as someone who had married into the Blackwell family, Clover Blackwell was the best liaison on Roy's side. Clover sweetly apologized every time she answered the phone, clearly trying not to burden Margarette as she listed all the Blackwell events. Representing the Tofts was her mother, who started each dialogue with a sigh but quickly broke off into a list of "but we musts", to which Margarette replied, "I'll take care of it."

On top of the known festival proclivities – thoughts of Norvel Poteet and his cartwheels entered her mind – May was the busiest month of the school year, and she was getting married in exactly twenty-four days. Twenty-four busy, event-filled days. Maybe they were making a mistake in marrying so soon. After all, they'd only been engaged for a few days. Margarette's thoughts were far from the student presentation playing out in front of her.

We could move the wedding to June… No, it starts to get hot in June. The cake would melt at the reception, which means we'd have to wait until late September. School starts back in August and fall break isn't until October. October might work. But if we wait until October we might as well wait until December. I've always wanted a Christmas wedding. But what if something happens between now and then? What if I start to change my mind? What if I hurt him? I could never hurt him!

She'd had this conversation with herself several times before.

This is what I want. I want to marry Roy Blackwell. He makes me happy. He makes me smile. I want to see him every day. I want to be his wife. If we keep the current date we'll be happily married by May and there's nothing the families can say or do about it. But what if…?

"No!" she shouted to the class of very confused sixth-grade students.

"Are you all right, Miss Toft?" a young girl dressed as a pirate asked. "Do you want me to keep going?"

Margarette snapped to attention. "Yes, so sorry. Where was I?"

"I finished my presentation and asked if I could go back to my desk, but you said, no. I don't know what else to say."

"The presentation? You've finished?"

The girl stared at her, confused, as if she'd just told the young girl to eat chalk.

Somewhere on a pirate ship in the South Seas Margarette had dozed off. She had no idea what the girl had said, what grade to give her, or whether the girl needed to say anything more on her topic of choice. She glanced down at the grading rubric in front of her. She'd only written the girl's name. "Great… It was great! Class, let's give her a hand."

The class clapped half-heartedly.

Margarette needed sleep. *Maybe I'll grab a nap before dinner tonight.* She yawned again. "So, who wants to go next?"

A hand shot up. Margarette forced a smile. Perhaps this next one would be unusual enough to keep her awake.

"All right, Max. Why don't you go ahead?"

She wrote his name at the top of the rubric: Max Fox-McGoggins.

Week one of the festival was usually her favorite – history week. For the town this meant reenactments, nightly costume walks around the town circle, and presentations from the Coraloo Historical Society. For Margarette it meant marking reports about the town's history and assigning tasks for the decorating of the float.

It was what she did every year, but she could hardly think about it right now. In fact, she had completely forgotten to leave room for float construction on her calendar. Perhaps one of the other sixth-grade teachers might take on the task.

No, I can't. I won't. They expect me to do it. I can do this. I'll just have to rearrange a few things.

Throughout her sixteen years of teaching she could not recall a year that had made her feel quite so restless. Despite her detailed efforts to create an atmosphere that was both creative and comfortable, even Margarette's classroom was stifling her ability to think clearly. She had been intentional, making her classroom a fun place to learn and giving the room her signature vintage feel, with movie-like posters lining the walls displaying historical events like a cinema premier. A small lamp sat on the corner of her desk at the front of the room, creating an ambiance that seemed to calm the students even on festival days. A plush remnant of ivory carpeting lay beneath the chalkboard, adding an extra bit of coziness. For the most part Margarette's students were well behaved. She gave significant credit to the lamp.

A boy, cardboard sword in hand and wearing a kitchen strainer strapped to his head with a brown leather belt, stepped in front of the chalkboard.

Margarette sat up straight, her tea dress comfortably covering her knees. "You may begin."

"Today I'm Jonathan Toft, the true founder of Coraloo. But what most people don't know is the real reason I lost the land to that scoundrel Mungo Blackwell."

Margarette looked up from the tablet of paper in front of her, praying this wouldn't lead to a slew of phone calls from parents of confused children.

"Mungo Blackwell was a reptoid."

Most definitely phone calls.

"A reptoid?" Margarette tried her best to keep up with the ever-changing slang the students were using these days. She sure hoped "reptoid" wasn't something horribly offensive. Luckily there wasn't a Blackwell in the room if it was. Not that it made a difference. She'd have to call the McGogginses.

"They're the bad kind of aliens," Max Fox-McGoggins said as if she should have known. "You know, body snatchers. Reptile aliens that live inside humans."

"So you're saying that Mungo Blackwell, the founder of our town, was an alien?"

"They're everywhere, Miss Toft. Haven't you seen them? My father says there may be one in this very room."

The classroom sprang to life in a wash of whispers and agitated murmurs.

"Jonathan Toft was brainwashed by aliens!" Max shouted, raising his sword.

Margarette's head fell into her open palm. She was too tired for this. "Class… quiet down."

The room hushed, not so much at her command, but rather to hear what Max would say next. Exhausted or not, she had to know, "And the strainer, Max?"

"My helmet, Miss Toft. It protects us from the aliens – keeps them from getting into our heads."

A hand shot up on the front row.

"Yes, Gideon," Margarette said.

"That's not what happened at all. Can I go next? I've read the history. I know the truth!"

Gideon Price stood up with a fake red beard attached to his face. He marched up to the front of the room and stood directly in front of Max.

Margarette would never normally allow a student to take command of the room in this way, but Gideon had been on a mission to convince his mother that he should be homeschooled, and thus had silently protested by refusing to participate in class until his mother agreed. Therefore, stopping a boy who usually said nothing somehow seemed illogical.

"Ladies and gentlemen," Gideon started. "Lend me your ear as I tell you the tale of Mungo Blackwell. He was a man of –"

Before he could finish, Max shoved him out of the way.

"He was a man of lies! The Blackwells are aliens!" He pointed at Gideon. "They've turned you, haven't they? Everyone knows you're one of them! Where did they probe you? When did they get to you? Do you speak their language? Have you visited the mothership? Take me to your leader!"

Someone in the midsection of the room screamed. Margarette felt like crawling under her desk. She knew exactly what school procedure was to deal with Max, but she didn't have the energy to argue with his mother over the freedom of speech. And the truth was, the Blackwell children *had* turned the Prices' shy, unsocialized son – not into an alien but into a fearless thespian, which Charlie and Velveteen happily embraced.

There was another scream from somewhere in the room. "Gideon Price is an alien!"

Margarette hopped off her perch, her red heels hitting the original hardwood floor with a click in a bid to stop the witch-hunt before it started.

"Sit down, both of you." She walked to the front of the room, waiting for the boys to take their seats. "Neither the Blackwells nor Gideon Price are aliens. And I am quite sure Jonathan Toft was not abducted. History tells us Mungo Blackwell spared the life of Jonathan Toft, giving him the land below the hill and the very land this school and many of your homes are built upon."

"Max, Gideon, I'll give you both a second chance to present tomorrow. But find the truth. What I want is truth. This week has been about the true history of our town. And that's what I expect to get from these presentations. Truth."

There was a knock on the classroom door.

"Excuse me." Keeping an eye on Max and Gideon, Margarette made her way through the rows of desks and opened the door to find Roy standing in front of her with a bundle of blue hydrangeas.

He peeked into the room. "I thought I'd surprise you. I picked them from the garden this morning. But I didn't want to disturb you. I just saw them and knew you'd like them." He kissed her on the forehead. "See you at the cafe?"

She nodded, completely forgetting that the twenty-three students behind her dressed in historical Coraloo garb were craning their necks to get a look at whoever was at the door.

"Thank you."

He tipped his hat and left.

Margarette stood still for a moment with her back to the curious eyes and whispers of her class. She turned to face them and smiled.

A murmur rose up from the middle of the room. "It's not a good match. My mother says she'll turn out just like the scissor lady."

The scissor lady. Innis Wilkinson.

For a moment Margarette imagined herself pushing the cleaning cart up the hill to the market.

Then a response came from somewhere else: "He gave her hydrangeas. It's totally bad luck. And blue! Everyone's saying the wedding will never happen."

Margarette locked in on the two Toft girls – twin daughters of her cousin – and furrowed her brow. She shook her head in a way that said, "Don't cross me. I know where you live."

The girls sat up straight and turned their attention back to the front of the room. She would deal with the cheeky relatives later.

Margarette lifted a stack of pencils out of the glass jar on her desk and replaced them with the flowers. *The girls are right. Why would he bring blue hydrangeas? Doesn't he know what that means? He's sorry for something... What could he be apologizing for?*

Her thoughts plummeted to the worst. She hadn't been married before, but she had been engaged. And she had called it off. Thomas had briefly come up in conversations between them, but had she fully explained? They had talked about so many parts of their lives, past and present. *Maybe I didn't tell Roy about Thomas... but someone else did! He thinks I'm an engagement breaker! That's why he brought the hydrangeas! He's going to call off the wedding!*

Margarette stopped herself, realizing the class was watching her pace the room.

One of the Toft girls spoke up. "It's the hydrangeas, isn't it?"

Margarette could feel the heat pressing into her cheeks. "Superstitions are circumstantial, based on coincidence... Like being in the wrong place at the wrong time." She took in her own words, reminding herself Roy was just being Roy. Perfectly Roy. How was he to know about blue hydrangeas? Blackwells weren't superstitious. No, Blackwells were people of tradition, traditions a bright person like herself had researched. She knew about the Blackwell blessing of the bride and hadn't been a bit surprised when Clover asked to schedule it. She'd bring Thomas up at dinner just in case.

A hand at the back of the room shot up, frantically waving back and forth.

"Yes, Max."

"Like if you pick up a coin and the wrong side is up, and suddenly the flood comes?"

She saw where this was going. "Exactly, Max. It's coincidence. And there is no flood. It's May. It rains a lot every May. And we're not in a flood plain. How long have you lived here?"

"My whole life."

"I thought so. And have you ever seen a flood in Coraloo?"

"No, but my dad says –"

Margarette wanted to get at least five more presentations in before class was over and would rather not give the rest of the time to Max, who was clearly about to do his best to convince the class they needed to save themselves.

"Who's next?"

A few more hands shot up. She stifled another yawn, glanced up at the clock above the chalkboard, and selected a student she had no doubt would be prepared. The student stood, dragging an oversized poster board behind her.

Maybe that's what Margarette needed, a ginormous poster board to hang outside her house. She could display her entire month of May calendar for everyone to see, and if they needed something from her, they'd have to write whatever it was on the calendar. Then there would be no more late-night phone calls. So much to do, so little time. In twenty-four days it would all be worth it, but first she had to make it through those twenty-four days and find a ginormous poster board – a poster board that would be accessible not only to the Blackwells and Tofts, but to the McGogginses, the Hennigans, the Smiths, and everyone else in Coraloo.

Actually, on second thought, she'd better keep the calendar to herself.

CHAPTER 9

1965

Innis Toft stood on a chair, gazing into the mirror at her sharp jawline and long, curly blonde hair, wishing it were stick straight like the other girls'. She flipped it over her shoulder, adjusted her headband, and tried to wink. She pulled her skirt up a bit at the waist so it fell just above the knee. She sighed, wondering if a boy would ever find a girl wearing scissors attractive.

She hurried downstairs and past her mother, who would most assuredly demand she pull her skirt back down. Inside the front door, a poster featuring a gorgeous starlet bride had long faded, along with the fame of Isabella's Bridal. Shops with mass-marketed patterns were on every corner in the city and a new one had recently popped up in the next town over. With sales slow, Innis picked up some work of her own, mostly hemming. Along with her homework it kept her busy – too busy to play at her own designs and definitely too busy for boys... except on Saturdays.

"Do you know what day it is?" her mother called to her from the back.

"I know! I'm on my way, Mother!"

Innis planned to stay out for a while today, but only for an hour. That's all the time she would have. She would walk a little slower past the soda shop or maybe stop in for a minute and pretend she was looking for a friend. Maybe she would stay. Maybe she would meet a boy.

Innis crossed the street and the footbridge as she did every Saturday, eyeing the funeral home on the other side, looking for signs of the mortician, Billy Butcher. *Protect them from the morticians.* Once she was safely out of range she crossed back over and continued her journey toward Wilkinson's Hardware, pausing in front of the ice cream parlor. She looked back. Safe. No one had followed.

A resounding whistle blew out from the shoe factory on the hill. Lunchtime. She was hungry, but she would wait outside the parlor regardless. She craned her neck to see inside, wishing they would see her for once and invite her to come in, to share a soda and a smile.

The row of swivel stools was fully occupied. She leaned against the glass, spying a girl, possibly her age or maybe a little older, wearing glasses and a ponytail – a straight ponytail. The girl laughed. Had she heard something funny? Innis laughed too, hoping it was loud enough for those on the inside to hear as she pretended to talk and wave to an imaginary person on the other side of the street.

She waited. Surely someone would leave soon. Surely someone would see her. Maybe that someone would notice her and say something like, "I haven't seen you around before."

She'd lie and say, "I'm new."

And this someone would say, "Let me introduce you to my friends."

And she'd agree, finally stepping inside for the first time.

The door opened and out walked two boys around her age. Her heart fluttered; she smiled at them coolly. Maybe they weren't as dull as she assumed. They sure didn't look dull.

"Hi there," she braved.

"Nice scissors," one of the boys said with a laugh. "Can I see them?"

No one had ever asked to see the scissors. If she let him would he call her, take her to a film, buy her a soda?

The scissors seemed to grow heavier, pulling at her neck. She wanted to take them off, throw them in the river. But she knew she couldn't. This boy could grow up to be a mortician for all she knew. *Then what?* She never knew what. She only knew she had to keep them safe. Only two people outside the boutique were allowed to handle the scissors: Walter Wilkinson and his son Wilkin.

82

She shook her head, at a loss for words, standing there staring into the boy's beautiful eyes. Why couldn't she think of something clever to say? This was her chance. He was the first boy from the soda shop who had said more than two words to her... He'd said six. She longed for a boy to kiss her, or to push her playfully into the pool like she'd seen in a film last summer.

She started to speak, but the other boy spoke first.

"Shot down by the scissor girl! Too bad. She's choice!"

The boy shrugged. "Maybe next time, Scissors."

Scissors? Had she been nicknamed... by a boy?

Innis's heart soared. She would come by next week to see if he was still there. *Scissors.* A nickname. Surely only a boy who was interested in a girl would give her a nickname. And even if he wasn't interested, she didn't mind, because at least now she felt known – known by a boy.

She watched as they walked away, laughing. One boy kept his hands in his pockets, while the other talked with his hands. She wondered what they were laughing at. An inside joke? A memory? Her? No, they couldn't be laughing at her, because he'd given her a nickname.

She picked up her pace, watching people as they passed by, recalling them by their nuances – a nervous twitch, the clicking of heels on pavement, or a slight hum. Her eyes shifted from side to side, always looking, always watching, always protecting the scissors.

She quickly ducked inside Wilkinson's Hardware, the door clanging shut behind her, and exhaled. *Safe.* She had been to this shop every Saturday since the day her mother had entrusted her with the scissors, with the exception of any Saturdays that fell during the holidays. Then she would be forced to wait a week, as would her mother, who refused to cut a single thread while the scissors were not suitably sharp. Wilkinson's Hardware was dark, dull, common, normal. Here she was known by her given name, not a nickname.

"Hello, Innis." A teenaged Wilkin Wilkinson emerged from behind the counter, his hair in a classic crew cut, unlike the boys at the soda shop who wore theirs a little longer.

Innis forced a smile and tugged her skirt down. "Hi, Wilkin. Will it take any longer today?"

"No. About an hour, same as usual. You're welcome to wait. Mom made cookies if you want to stick around. I could show you how we sharpen the scissors… or we could do something else."

He always asked her to wait, his mom always made cookies, and Innis always said, "No, thanks."

She carefully removed the scissors from around her neck, feeling an instant release from the weight she carried with her every day.

"It's a nice day," Wilkin started.

It was always a nice day according to Wilkin, even when it was raining or Innis had just trudged through a foot of snow.

She forced a smile.

Dull.

"Are you going to the festival?" he asked.

"I… I'm not sure."

The door to the shop clanged shut. Innis glanced back to see the boys she had encountered earlier walking into the store. She pulled her skirt back up an inch.

"Well, maybe I'll see you there," Wilkin replied.

Her eyes were on the boys, but a shout had sent them swiveling back toward the door, their attention fixed on someone else outside the shop.

She wanted to wave to them, shouting, "Hey, it's me… Scissors." But she didn't.

"So will I see you there?"

"Where?"

"The festival." He cleared his throat and lowered his head. "I'll walk with you… if you want. Just in case something happens to the scissors."

"Maybe." She wasn't really listening, and in any case she'd never been to the festival. It wasn't safe. "I'll be back in an hour. Be careful with the scissors."

She left as she always did to go back to her mom's shop, where she would wait alone as she always did.

But before she was out of earshot he said, "I'll wait for you", as he always did.

84

Outside the fitting room, Margarette flopped down into the armchair, partially upholstered in a charcoal gray velvet and intentionally left open at the back revealing a heavy wooden framework. La Robe de Mariée seemed the perfect place to find a dress. It was advertised in every bridal magazine from the city to Coraloo. Margarette had clipped the address weeks ago, adding it to her list.

However, wearing her eleventh dress – strapless, layered, exposed boning stabbing her under the arms and in the ribs – she was beginning to have serious doubts. It was their fifth and final stop of the day, having saved "the best" for last. Right now Margarette wished she wasn't the kind of person who saved the best for last.

Why do I save the best for last if I know it's going to be the best? Why not shop the best first, find what I want, and get it done with?

But she was a historian, and research was in her blood. Even if she found "the dress", she would still have wanted to weigh up her other options before making a final decision. But now she was out of options all together.

She just wanted to marry Roy. Her Roy. The Roy she'd met while filing a complaint against Father Milligan. She smiled at the memory… It had been an absolutely lovely gesture for the priest to voluntarily pull her weeds for the third time that week. The problem was she and Father Milligan had totally different ideas as to what constituted a weed. Before Margarette had written the first word on her complaint form Roy had suggested a stakeout.

"Excuse me, Constable."

Roy Blackwell looked up, making direct eye contact.

Margarette looked away, uncomfortable. She had a habit of

gazing down or off to one side, unintentionally attaching her focus to something random like the buttons on the constable's shirt. It was a hard habit to break. She blamed her grandfather, who had told her looking boys in the eye before she was sixteen would make her cross-eyed.

But this was no boy. This was a man.

"Mrs Toft, isn't it?"

"Miss Toft," she corrected, forcing herself to look at him and realizing she had never really seen him before. He was handsome, debonair in that classic movie kind of way.

"Can I help you?"

She realized she had spaced out, lost somewhere between the vintage spectacles and the crinkles on his forehead. "Um, yes. I need to file a complaint. Against Father Milligan."

"You want to file a complaint against Father Milligan?"

"Yes. That's what I said."

"The priest?"

"Is there another Father Milligan?"

Roy laughed. "What's he done this time?"

Father Milligan had a reputation for being "helpful".

She smiled, looked away, and then reminded herself to look back. "He's ruining my flowerbeds. It's innocent enough, but no matter how many times I tell him my weeds don't need pulling he keeps showing up. At my house. Before sunrise. And attacking my dahlias. I swore if he showed up again, I would file a complaint.

"And he showed up again?"

"This morning. So here I am, filing a complaint."

Margarette suddenly found making eye contact with this man wasn't that hard. She shifted on her feet, stepped closer, and tried to hide her smile. Why did she want to smile?

He leaned back in his chair. He smelled nice, like soap and nutmeg... or was it cedar? Why did she notice how he smelled?

"I'm afraid I'm going to need some evidence."

"Evidence? He's nearly picked all my evidence!"

"Miss Toft –"

"Please, call me Margarette."

Call me Margarette? Had she just said that? He was the constable! What did she care what he called her? He could call her Meggy if he wanted. Actually, not that. He could call her anything but that.

Roy rubbed the back of his neck. "Margarette Toft, I'd be honored if you would accompany me on a stakeout."

"A stakeout? To catch Father Milligan?" She laughed.

"We'll catch him in the act. Then I'll help you replant your dahlias."

She inhaled, at a loss for words. Why was she getting all swoony over Roy Blackwell? He'd been the constable since she was in secondary school and had to be at least ten years older.

"I think that would be lovely." Seriously? Lovely? What was wrong with her? Was she actually considering this? The man was a Blackwell for goodness' sake. A Blackwell! It was pointless even giving an inch to the situation when it absolutely could not be. Blackwells and Tofts just didn't marry. Marry? Had she really thought the word marry? Stop it, Margarette! Stop it!

"Well then, Miss Toft, shall we go catch ourselves a priest?"

She was about to say yes when she had a sudden thought.

"What will you do with him if you catch him?"

She glanced at the empty but extremely tidy holding cells. Interesting. A man of order. Stop it, Margarette, her inner voice – which currently sounded a lot like her mother's – told her. He's a Blackwell. A Blackwell. She'd studied them for years and knew more about his family than her own.

"Cuff him, fingerprint him, then lock him up until he can properly identify and classify his destruction by genus and species."

He's smart.

She laughed. Why had she laughed? It wasn't that funny.

He smiled.

They must have crossed paths dozens of time, maybe even hundreds. But in that moment, there was something she had never seen in the constable before.

The next morning they went on their first date: a stakeout to catch a priest picking dahlias.

She had toted her notebook of wedding clippings around to each shop, pointing out bits and pieces of dresses she liked to the boutique attendant. This had proved to be of little help, as each attendant insisted she try on what all the other brides were buying.

Margarette had run into these "other brides" at every shop they visited – notebook-less twenty-somethings who knew exactly what they wanted. She glanced over at herself in the mirror. Her hair was a frizzy mess from the dress that had come off over the head two shops ago. Her eyes were heavy, her make-up faded, and her lipstick had embarrassingly wiped off somewhere in the lining of a dress back at shop number one.

She stared at the rejected dresses hanging in front of her, then glanced down at her mostly exposed chest, certain that if something fell down there it would be lost forever. She sucked in her stomach and tried to breathe. *Nope. Nope. Nope.* Sure, she could make this one work, if she wanted to suffocate to death. Margarette tried to be objective. Her mother had said it was "the dress". However, Anna Sue Toft had also said the last ten were "the dress".

"It's the one, Meggy!"

"You look gorgeous, Meggy!"

"Stunning!"

"Oh, this is it!"

A few tears and sniffles into the handkerchief. "My baby girl is getting married."

"This one is so you, Meggy!"

Although snug, the current bridal gown did have a kind of vintage feel. Toss a red crinoline underneath and she'd look like something straight out of the American Wild West. She could just see herself standing at the front of the church swishing the skirt back and forth, dancing the cancan number from *Orpheus in the Underworld*.

Maybe the Toft and the Blackwell ladies will want to join in. Yes, that's it! Roy's Aunt Sorcha and my Aunt Clara will be side by side, kicking up their heels in all their Blackwell–Toft glory. It's not the wedding that will unite the families, it's the cancan!

She tried to laugh at the ridiculously hopeful thought, but the dress was too tight, and not the kind of vintage she was looking for.

Her mother snapped her out of the pleasantry of her musing. "I see a smile. I was right… It's the one!"

Margarette shifted to the right and then to the left, exhaling loudly. "No, it's not the dress. But can you do the cancan?"

"Oh, good grief, Meggy." Anna Sue turned back to reevaluate the rack of dresses, momentarily pulling out number seven and then pushing it back in between six and eight.

Number seven was Margarette's favorite of the eleven dresses; however, it wasn't quite right – somehow forced to look antique with its factory-manufactured lace appliques. But it wasn't hideous, and it had been a decent fit… sort of. Maybe she should settle for it. But what if she bought it, had it altered – making it non-returnable – and then found the dress she really wanted? She'd regret it for the rest of her life and have to tell her children stories about the wedding dress that wasn't. They'd ask to borrow the only-looks-like-an-antique dress, but they wouldn't be able to because the manufactured lace appliques had turned orange, failing the test of time.

She had twenty days to find a dress. *Twenty days*. She had already ordered the flowers, addressed the invitations, hired a photographer, finalized the wedding attendants, hesitantly scheduled for Sylvia to do her hair – only her hair – and confirmed the date again with Pastor Donaldson, who apologized profusely for his behavior, claiming he did not know what had come over him, and contrary to rumor he had not been "hitting the communion wine". Roy had offered to help with the preparations, but astoundingly it was all going to plan… except for the dress. And he couldn't help with that.

89

Her mother stood on the platform in front of the mirrors, turning from side to side as she examined her backside, sucking in her cheeks and lifting her chest. "Meggy, why don't you stand up and give the dress one more look. It really complements your figure," she said, aiming her words at their reflections.

Complements your figure. In other words, "You could do with losing a pound or two."

Still held tight by dress number eleven, Margarette wriggled in the chair, hoping to dislodge herself as a human wedge. She used her hands to push off the sides of the seat the way she'd seen pregnant women do, managing to raise herself up a little. She flopped back down.

"I can't. I think the dress ate my feet. It's trying to take out my lungs, too."

"Don't be so dramatic, Meggy."

She extended one hand to her mother and one to the boutique attendant – who obviously worked on commission, because with every dress Margarette tried on she gasped alongside Margarette's mother and said, "Yes. Oh, yes, mademoiselle! This is the one. I'll ring it up for you!" – and allowed them to pull her to her feet.

Margarette hiked the pounds of dress up above her ankles. Oh, how she longed to break out into the cancan at this very moment. The song would be stuck in her head all day. She stepped up onto the platform, shuffling to face the three-way mirror. She shifted the bodice of her dress and pulled it up so it completely hid her bosoms, at which point the attendant came up behind her and shimmied it back down.

"You've got to give him a little something for the imagination, mademoiselle."

"Definitely not the dress. I think I'll change."

Margarette gathered the dress up again so she could see her feet, climbed down from the platform, and pulled back the gray velvet curtain that ushered her into the extra-large fitting room. Her mother trotted along behind her, unzipping and helping her step out of the dress. At that moment Margarette was truly grateful her mother had come along, despite their differences.

After she changed back into her black pencil skirt and blouse, she strolled out into the sea of whites, off-whites, candlelight whites, and bridal whites. *Good grief!* She'd never realized there were so many shades of white. Was this really necessary? Did she even need a wedding dress? Maybe they could just elope? Roy wouldn't complain. The Tofts would call it a bad omen. The marriage would certainly be marked. Roy would be marked. And she would be marked… again.

"Sweetheart, you could always wear my dress. We could let it out a bit at the sides. It could be your 'something old.'"

Something old, something new, something borrowed, something grew. She had almost forgotten about that part. For years she had wondered why "grew" seemed oddly out of place, not to mention grammatically awkward, until she learned that brides living outside of Coraloo needed "something blue". Then it all made sense. Some Toft along the way had decided to make the rhyme their own – strange, but their own. She pulled the notepad from her purse and made a note to locate each of the four items, including the "something grew".

"Thanks, Mother, but I'm not sure a size eight would ever fit into a size two."

"Have a sip, mademoiselle." The attendant handed her a crystal glass with the name of the boutique etched into it. She awkwardly caressed Margarette's stomach with French-manicured nails. "It'll help with your tummy puff. Maybe if the dresses fit a little better, you'd find one you like."

My "tummy puff" isn't the problem! Okay, it might be a bit of the problem… Margarette glanced down at the beverage, inhaling a faint aroma of hay. She held the glass away from her nose, swirling her finger around what appeared to be a bloated blueberry trapped in a nest of sprouts. *Smile and don't be rude.*

We probably should have passed on a second round of dessert. But it was spiced chocolate cake… She glanced at the watch on her wrist, which had belonged to her grandmother. Like the lemon-shaped earrings and every other piece of jewelry Margarette wore, they were a reminder of a time when ladies wore white gloves on special occasions and store clerks would never have dared to point out another woman's... tummy puff.

Margarette had no idea when they would get to come back to the city, with all the activities the Blackwells and the Tofts had lined up for her. She glanced once again at the rack of options. This was it, her last opportunity to actually see a dress in person and try it on. She needed to decide, but she couldn't. Her dress was out there somewhere. She just had to find it.

"Well, Mother, you can't say I didn't try. There's a quaint little secondhand boutique around the corner... You never know..."

"For goodness' sake, Meggy – you might as well see if you can't dig one up at that market of theirs."

That's not a bad idea. Maybe Roy's Uncle Albert can find what I'm looking for. Margarette couldn't believe she hadn't thought of it already.

"Sweetheart, if you're going to marry a Blackwell you might as well look good while you do so. We'll find you something nice. You still have a few days."

"You know, I could always wear a toga... or just go naked," she joked, nettling at her mother.

"Margarette Toft, you can't be serious." Her mother tilted her head, drawing the corner of her lips into a tired smile. "I'm really trying here, and you won't let me help with anything else. I want to be a part of this."

Margarette laughed. "I know, Mother." She linked her arm through her mother's. "How about we grab a cup of tea and a sweet treat? Let's do a bit of shopping while we're in the city... And pop into the secondhand store. I'll only be a minute. In and out."

Now that she had planted the seed in in her own mind, Margarette was excited about talking to Uncle Albert. A vintage dress from the flea market. It was the perfect idea!

Anna Sue pulled another dress from the rack and held it up in front of the mirror. "Maybe I should get married."

"I'm not sure how Dad would feel about that."

"Oh!" She smacked Margarette playfully on the arm. "You know what I mean."

Margarette didn't know what she meant.

"Seriously, Meggy? I meant a vow renewal, complete with exotic honeymoon. It's a thing people do when they get my age. Your father and I could use a little freshening up, if you know what I mean. You do know what I mean, don't you?"

This time Margarette knew exactly what she meant, but she didn't want to think about her parents "freshening up" their marriage, so she quickly changed the subject before her mother could give her "the talk" they'd already had when she was twelve.

"How does that tea sound? I don't need to stop by the secondhand shop after all. Maybe I'll find a dress online." She wouldn't. "I'll just start scrolling and whatever I land on that'll be my dress, as long as it doesn't look like anything on that rack, or the rack over there, or that other one, and especially not the black thing in the window. I bet that one would spice up your marriage."

"Very funny. Your dad prefers red."

"Mother!"

"I'm joking, sort of." She sighed. "This is the chicest shop in the city. If you're going to find a dress it'll be here."

Maybe her mother was right. She hadn't tried them *all* on. She walked over to the rack directly in front of her and frowned. These were quiet possibly the trendiest dresses anywhere, so much so she had mistaken the one on display for lingerie, and the last one the attendant swore was exactly what she needed but squeezed her in such a way Margarette was afraid she would pop out, exposing herself halfway down the aisle. The children would scream. The aunts would faint. Roy would arrest her for indecent exposure and refuse to marry a floozy. The only man who would ever marry her after that would be William Butcher Jr. They'd fire her from Coraloo Elementary and she'd have to push a cleaning cart up the hill for the rest of her life like Innis Wilkinson.

She took a breath to escape from her runaway thoughts. "They're not for me. I'm not this... this *fancy*. Do you really want me walking down the aisle looking like a hat box?" she said, holding up a dress comprising two hoops: one at the bottom and one at the top.

A familiar look crossed her mother's face – the overly pleasant smile, the tilted head, the lips slightly parted because something Margarette did not want to hear was about to come out of her mouth.

"Maybe you're rushing into this."

Margarette snatched up her purse and took off toward the boutique's reclaimed door.

"Meggy, wait! You forgot your alfalfa sprout water! Please wait! I drove, remember?"

Margarette stopped beside the intentionally half-naked mannequin. "I don't want the water, but I do want Roy Blackwell! And yes, I said B-L-A-C-K-W-E-L-L."

"Keep your voice down, sweetheart."

"Do you really think anyone here cares that he's a Blackwell?"

"Well, maybe. You never know. Some of our people did move to the city back in the seventies."

Margarette reached for the door handle.

"Please hear me out," her mother pleaded.

She sighed. "I'm listening."

"It's just that I was talking to Juanita and her son Billy –"

"Unbelievable! You're still trying to set me up with William Butcher Jr, aren't you? Little Billy Butcher? The mortician? You've been talking to Sylvia too much. You do realize the irony, right, Mother? His last name is Butcher and he dissects dead people for a living."

"But they're a good family. Family is so important. And you can't deny he's handsome. And he has an apprentice. An *apprentice*, Meggy!"

Over the years they'd had this conversation more times than Margarette could count on both hands: "Family is important. You marry into the family. The unity between two families is a bond that will spread to your children and your children's children. The impact of a bad family union could devastate an entire society. And a healthy income is always helpful."

"Why don't you take one last look around, just in case? I'll meet you back at the car."

But Margarette didn't feel like taking one more look around. She turned toward the door again, fully intending to head straight to the secondhand boutique before she left the city. Her dress would be there. She'd walk in through the door and it would be right there, waiting for her. *The dress.* She'd slip into the boutique's makeshift dressing room – secondhand stores always had makeshift dressing rooms – and ease into the dress, which would release a soft, faded fragrance of outmoded perfume, slightly musty, old, worn... and to her, delightful. She'd look up into the wall-mounted mirror and gasp, "It's absolutely perfect!"

A warmth so lovely spread over Margarette it pushed away any thoughts of Billy Butcher, his apprentice, and alfalfa sprout water, forcing her to smile among the sea of ivory silks and taffetas.

"Is there something else I can show you, mademoiselle?"

Lost in her musings, Margarette barely heard the shop assistant. Through her dazed thoughts she turned to see *the dress.* The dress from her imaginary secondhand shop encounter. The dress that fit perfectly in the makeshift dressing room. Simple, elegant, and quite possibly authentically vintage. If not, the designer had done a remarkable job pulling it off.

"I was on my way out, but that dress. The dress you're holding..." Margarette stared at the intricacy of the lace. It was unlike anything she had seen in the dozens of bridal magazines she had scoured.

The attendant placed her hand under the full skirt of the dress, holding it out for Margarette to see. "It is a one of a kind, mademoiselle. A Bella Fottasi."

Bella Fottasi. The name wasn't familiar.

"Can I try it on?"

"Of course, mademoiselle. I'll just –"

Margarette suddenly froze. Her mother was waiting in the car.

"Actually, would you mind writing down the information?"

"Of course, mademoiselle."

Bella Fottasi. She had jotted down a lot of designer names, but had never come across this one.

She glanced at the door and then back at the dress. One of kind. It could quite possibly be gone before she could make it back.

"I'll try it on."

Moments later Margarette stood in front of the mirror. The Bella Fottasi fit as if it had been made especially for her. The satin hung long, pooling slightly behind her ankles and delicately falling off her shoulders. Elegant, modest, gorgeous. And she could breathe. Her mother had been right – this *was* the shop. She hated that she'd have to tell her… maybe she wouldn't. She searched under the arm for a price tag. Nothing. She knew it would be expensive – she could feel it in the fabric – but her mother had offered to pay.

The assistant helped her step out of the dress. "This is the one." All the assistant's earlier pushiness was gone, replaced with a genuine sense of approval.

Margarette smiled. She couldn't wait for Roy to see it… at the altar, of course, and not a peek before. She wasn't going to let anything, including a pre-wedding peek at the dress, jeopardize their marriage. Maybe there was a bit of Toft in her after all.

"Yes, this is the one."

"I'll check the price for you."

Looking at the dress hanging alone from a gold hook beside the mirror, Margarette exhaled. It was the perfect fit, so no need to pay extra for alterations. As an afterthought she looked inside the dress for a label, something to acquaint her with the designer. But there was nothing. No name, no logo… not even a size.

The assistant returned with a card in hand. "I am terribly sorry, mademoiselle, but this particular dress is spoken for. It is my error."

Her elation fell to devastation. "There must be some mistake. I don't understand."

"No mistake. It is… a special situation."

Special? Of course it was special! It was the dress. Her dress.

"But please, if you need any further assistance… " Margarette took the business card, intentionally aged to fit the feel of the rustic elegance adopted by the store, and slipped it into her handbag. She glanced back at the dress. *One of kind. A Bella Fottasi. My dress...* She wasn't going to let it go with an error and a business card. If she could unearth the obscure traditions of the Blackwells she could track down the maker of this dress.

CHAPTER 11

Roy sat on a stool at the front of the room with the chalkboard behind him. Rows of sixth-grade students stared back at him, their eyelids heavy in the early morning. Someone toward the rear of the room sneezed – most likely a cold or allergies. He hoped it wasn't contagious. The florist and the priest had presented before him. He was quite certain their lives were far more exciting than his, but Margarette had asked. It was a simple request.

"Five minutes. That's all it will take. I want to try something new this year. I want the students to really know their community. I want them to be engaged, you know?"

"Before you reveal to them that at one point in time our families fought over a dead man's shoes?"

"If that part's even true. Besides, I covered that last week."

He returned to the subject of her class. "What will I say?"

"Tell them about life as the constable of Coraloo. You're kind of a big deal, you know."

He didn't know. "A big deal? Like a celebrity?"

She raised her eyebrows playfully.

He pulled her in close. "Should I be getting paid for this?"

"By paid do you mean you'll let me cook you dinner?"

"How about I cook you dinner? You've been so busy. Surely I can do something to help with the wedding."

"I have it under control. Besides, I should be making you dinner, seeing as you're doing me such a huge favor. But, I won't argue with a celebrity. So you'll do it?"

"I'll do it."

"Great! Just tell the paparazzi you don't have time for pictures."

Roy didn't feel like a celebrity. Constables in other towns could use industry terminology like "crime rate" and "arrests per capita". This year's crime rate consisted of a cat, a dog, and a mouse that had managed to find themselves stuck to the same sticky trap. He wondered if animal control had managed to save the fur.

But when Margarette – Miss Toft – introduced him, the class cheered and hands shot up for questions before he'd even sat down. Margarette motioned for everyone to lower their hands. She gave him a wink, to which half the class responded with "Ewwww" and the other half with "Ahhhhh".

Roy rubbed the palms of his hands against his khaki trousers, sitting up straighter on the stool, suddenly feeling more confident and unfamiliarly proud of his "celebrity" status.

"Well, like Miss Toft said, I'm the constable and it's my job to keep you safe." Since nothing ever happened in Coraloo he figured he'd actually done a decent job of keeping everyone safe.

A hand lifted on the right side of the room. "What's it like to be in a car chase? How fast does your car go?"

Roy forced a laugh, his chest tightening – maybe heartburn, or muscle strain, possibly angina. He'd check the book when he got home. He didn't even own a car – he had no need for one. His bicycle worked just fine.

"I can't say I've ever been in a car chase." Roy laughed. "I chased a runaway dog out of the flower shop, does that count?"

He laughed again. The class didn't. Margarette smiled.

Roy rubbed the back of his neck. "Okay, who else has a question?"

A boy wearing oversized glasses raised his hand. "How many people have you killed?"

Roy threw a quick look over at Margarette. His beautiful Margarette. How had he gotten so lucky?

She looked back, bemused, and shrugged.

"I've never killed anyone."

The boy spoke again. "But you've shot someone, right?"

Roy shook his head. "Nope. Never had to shoot anyone. I don't even carry a gun."

"But let's just say, hypothetically, that you needed to shoot someone. You would do it, right?"

Roy's mouth fell open. He hardly knew how to answer. "Let's hope it never comes to that."

A girl on the front row: "Have you ever been shot?"

Roy considered this for a moment. He had, in fact, been shot at when he first took the position as constable. Norvel Poteet, a decorated war veteran and once avid hunter, had sworn up and down a bear had taken up residence in the Coraloo Municipal Building. When Norvel thought he had the bear in his sight, he took it. Luckily for Roy he'd heard tell of Norvel's hunt and asked his neighbor to hide the shotgun shells. However, when Novel had careened into the station, wildly surveyed the landscape, taken aim, and pulled the trigger yelling "BANG!", the lack of a bullet had done nothing to prevent Roy falling backwards off his chair in shock, clutching his heart and knocking his head hard against the cold stone floor.

Norvel's gun had immediately been confiscated and replaced with a postmaster's bag, as the town was in need of a postman and Norvel was in need of a pastime. Roy did, however, permit Norvel to carry a slingshot, just in case, which Norvel confessed he used to secretly hunt the mail bears – not to be confused with male bears – as mail bears had a peculiar taste for stamps.

"I've never taken a bullet, if that's what you mean."

Another hand. Max Fox-McGoggins's this time. Roy could only imagine what would come out of that boy's mouth. He'd already heard about the aliens and the flood from Margarette.

"Has the increase in tourism had any effect on the crime rate in Coraloo?"

Crime rate. There it was. One of those words they used in the city or the next town over, and a perfectly logical question until Roy paused to answer.

"Because my dad says we need to keep an eye on *the others* this time of year. Those tourists are government agents in disguise, stirring up trouble."

Roy coughed, trying to hide his laugh. He should have known there would be more to it than a vague interest in the crime rate.

Another hand shot up. "My dad said you caught a government agent! Are there really government agents in Coraloo?"

Another voice: "He didn't catch a government agent; he caught Gideon's dad. He's a Chinese spy. Isn't that right, Mr Blackwell?"

Gideon Price stood up. "My dad's not a government agent or a spy! But if he was he wouldn't be dumb enough to get caught."

Roy laughed at the memory. "Gideon's right. Mr Price isn't a spy, which goes to show you should be sure of your evidence before you accuse anyone."

Roy's own grandmother had accused Charlie Price of colluding with the Chinese government because he'd chosen to wear a suit to the flea market one day. The former banker was hardly a spy, but Roy had taken him down to the station to let him cool off in a cell. Truthfully, the sorry debacle had merely been a formality to calm his grandmother and keep the accused Charlie from endangering himself by picking a fight with the wrong Blackwell. By the time the whole escapade had fully unraveled they'd discovered Roy's cousin was embezzling money from the flea market. But old Shug Blackwell was hardly a spy either, just a lonely, lost man in need of redirection.

Roy didn't consider himself lonely by any means, but lately he was feeling a deep tug toward redirection. He'd have been happy helping Margarette with the wedding, even if helping entailed holding a pen and marking to-dos off her list. But she'd insisted she was managing. Nevertheless, Roy was sure the dark circles that had appeared under her eyes were not part of her plan. But they were no matter; she was still the loveliest lady in Coraloo.

"Class," Margarette spoke up, pulling the students' attention away. "Mr Blackwell will take one more question."

Nearly half the class had a hand in the air. Maybe he should give himself a bit more credit.

"When you were little, did you want to be a constable?"

The question hit Roy hard. He hadn't wanted to be a constable or even to spend the rest of his life in Coraloo, for that matter. He had studied law at university, with dreams of one day managing his own firm in the city. His father's unexpected illness had forced a return to Coraloo to help out at home and be with his mother, so he had dropped out of law school and done the next best thing: he'd run for office and won. How he'd won remained a mystery to Roy. It was common knowledge the Tofts had made up a huge proportion of the town's population during the late nineties, as his Blackwell cousins had yet to roll back into town. Some said the Tofts voted for him because he was the first dark-haired man to cross the threshold of the municipal building after the church bells rang on the day of the election – another of their mysterious superstitions. It didn't matter. He'd held the position since he was twenty-five and had continued uncontested ever since.

"When I was a boy... I actually..." He rubbed the back of his neck again and glanced over at Margarette, who was poised on a stool at the back of the room. "Well, I actually wanted to be a professional cyclist. My father and I were planning to ride the Tour de Loo."

The Tour de Loo was a small ride starting in central France – a retaliation from a collaborative of tiny towns in the north of France, disgruntled at being left out of the larger races and therefore missing out on the benefits of the resultant tourist trade. His father had read about the ride in one of his cycling magazines.

The minute Roy said it a field of hands sprouted up in front of him. So much for one more question.

"Do you ride now?"

"Didn't you fix my bicycle last year?"

"What kind of bike do you have?"

"Why didn't you ever do it?"

Why didn't you do it?

He didn't know what to tell them. He had passed on the Tour to study... he hadn't thought he had the time... He'd been due to return to law school in a few months. With a law degree he'd have been able

102

to work in the city, away from Coraloo with its flea market and absurd festivals. He'd told his father they would do it the next year, but his father never rode again. It had started in his legs and progressed quickly. He'd been wheelchair-bound before Roy was even sworn in.

"It just wasn't in my future."

The room was still, quiet.

Margarette was watching. She knew the truth. He'd told her a bit of it. She'd said he needed to forgive himself. He'd said he didn't know how.

"Hey! Do you want to know what's in your future, Constable?" Max shouted. "My dad's building a time machine in the backyard for when the government comes looking for us. He wouldn't mind if you wanted to try it out. Shouldn't hurt much."

Despite the fact that he had never shot anyone, had never been shot, and would not agree to Max Fox-McGoggins's request that he be the first man to travel through time, Roy figured he had quite possibly been their most interesting guest. Although the barber had spoken in depth about the time he'd sliced his hand open and needed thirty-six stitches but had proceeded to trim the hair of the entire boys' basketball team that same afternoon. And the doctor had made it quite clear twenty-twenty vision was not a requirement for brain surgery. Roy hoped Dr Toft was joking. He'd had his appendix removed three years ago, and often wondered whether the good doctor had taken out some of Roy's sanity too. He'd never been quite the same since. Roy found the electrician and the record shop owner fascinating as well. Both had been to university to study one thing but had come out the other end to do something totally different.

He watched Margarette as she gently corrected one of her students at the back of the room.

She deserves more. Somebody more exciting. Somebody with better stories to tell.

Somewhere between the baker and the accountant, Roy decided it was finally time to do something about it. He had been bored and stagnant for far too long. He needed great stories to tell her over dinner at the cafe, and should he be invited back next year he wanted to be able to say more than "It just wasn't in my future." He needed the excitement he had craved – the thrill of the ride, racing down a hill with the wind blowing in his face. He'd wasted too much time listening to the locals pitch him on the most recent home-based business and even more time plowing through brochures of innovative opportunities promising leisure-filled days and financial freedom. He had both of those things, but they were not what he wanted. He wanted his own story. He wanted to tap into his inner Sherlock Holmes.

But who was he kidding? He'd inevitably head back to work. If he hurried he might catch Bert Thompson's call and invite him out to lunch again.

Roy kissed his bride-to-be on the cheek, leaving her to finish the rest of her school day. Then he wandered back to the municipal building, paying little attention to the locals or to *the others* who had seemingly taken over its streets.

Back at the station his latest case sat on the desk unfiled. He picked up the file of events relating to Ms Brimble and her pet menagerie and walked it down to the basement. He unlocked the archives – a rather large coat closet housing a lone filing cabinet holding every case and complaint in the history of Coraloo. The three-drawer cabinet was packed with manila file folders dating back to before Roy had been born. He thumbed through the files, past the BAs and the BOs, until he found the file's new home. He pushed the drawer shut, but it slid back out. He gave it a shove, again, and then again, but something was keeping the drawer from closing.

He removed a stack of files, opening the first and thumbing through it. Just another moonshiner. As far as he knew home brewing wasn't a problem anymore, especially since Coraloo's young people had declared the process an art form and it had been legalized in three states. He'd been holding on to a jug of the contraband, confiscated way before his time, as it was surprisingly effective in removing fingerprinting ink. The next file wasn't much more exciting – trespassing. He continued to thumb through the accounts of unresolved misdemeanors and minor infractions. Crime just wasn't part of life in Coraloo. He should go back to law school or take up a trade.

But he was about to be married. And if everything went as he and Margarette hoped, he'd be a father one day. Maybe he'd hold on a bit longer and take early retirement.

Roy slammed the file back down in frustration and shoved the drawer shut, but the heavy cabinet fought against him and the drawer bounced back, hitting him hard in the arm. He rubbed his instantly aching shoulder and leant over to shut the drawer once again when a name suddenly caught his attention.

WILKINSON, WILKIN.

Wilkin Wilkinson?

Curious, he removed the file and carried it up to his desk. The faded file was old, dated before Roy had returned to Coraloo, back in the days when he had been too busy studying to come home. He glanced up at the framed line of former constables watching him, eyeing him, evaluating his every move.

Roy didn't know much about Wilkin except that he and his wife, who was as aloof and awkward as Wilkin, worked up at the flea market keeping the place tidy. Wilkin had a reputation for bouncing between the town's two establishments – one a tavern and the other also a tavern; however, the proprietors of the latter insisted it be referred to as "the pub" so as not to confuse the tourists. Wilkinson tended to favor the original of the two, so much so he would be eligible for a preferred customer card at The Beaver's Beard if such a thing existed. In fact, it was not too long ago that Roy had been called in to break up a shouting match between Wilkin and a silent portrait of Mungo Blackwell carrying a rather large beaver upside down by one of its oversized antlers.

"Are you calling me a liar?" Wilkin shouted up at the painting. "No beaver calls me a liar!"

Roy watched from the bar, wondering how long he should allow Wilkin to shout at the wall art before approaching him.

"Come down here and fight me like a man!"

The Beaver's Beard quieted, all eyes on Wilkin. Roy was certain a few bets were taking place under the table to see who would win should such a fight take place – Wilkin or the beaver.

Wilkin turned around, the light from the antlered chandeliers reflecting in his eyes. He was wild and angry, insisting someone bring him a ladder so he could show the Heaken beaver what a real beaver looked like. When no one responded Wilkin started stacking chairs to give him the extra height he needed.

That's when Roy stepped in. "What seems to be the trouble?"

"That beaver called me a liar, and I want to fight him!"

Roy scratched the back of his neck. He'd need to be creative with this one or someone, most likely Roy, was going to get hurt. "That's fair. Let's take it outside."

Wilkin appeared to think for a moment before responding. "All right. But who's going to get that beaver down?"

Roy looked around, surveying his attentive audience and praying he could get Wilkin outside. He had no desire to see a 100-and-something-year-old painting have a hole punched through the middle. "I guess I will. Why don't you go outside and wait?"

Wilkin nodded and did as Roy suggested. Roy watched Wilkin leave and waited, counting to ten before heading outside and making up some story about how the beaver was too chicken to come down and fight. However, when Roy stepped outside, he saw Wilkin walking away – calm, hands in his pockets, a gentle limp – toward the Coraloo Flea Market.

But other than that Roy had never known him to cause any trouble. He flipped open the folder and thumbed through the pages – out of order, incomplete, and filled with a stack of bizarre photographs. The first was the image of a woman and Wilkin. She was beautiful… far too beautiful for the wide-eyed Wilkin, carrying a jar of what Roy assumed had placed most of the other files in the drawer – moonshine.

The young woman in the photograph had blonde curls piled up on top of her head, black-rimmed glasses, and a pair of scissors hanging around her neck. At first Roy could have sworn he was looking at Margarette, but it was the heavy scissors that gave her away. Innis Wilkinson.

"So old Wilkinson was just another moonshiner. Not surprising."

He set the photograph of the couple aside and quickly reached for the second. He brought it close to his eyes and then reached for his glasses. The detail of the photograph slowly came into focus. The picture had been taken in the basement, right outside the archives door. Somebody was holding up a dress. A wedding dress. And in front of it, written on a strip of paper, was the word "EVIDENCE".

His mind reeled with assumptions, his imagination taking him to dark places he dared not tread. He sifted through the file's documents – maps, descriptions, photographs – until he found what he hoped he never would. An accusation. An accusation filed by the Acteurs Agissant Acting Troupe. The charge: murder.

CHAPTER 12

In the tradition of the Coraloo Flea Market, lantern-like lights flanked the doorway of "Sorcha's", welcoming shoppers to examine her wares. Inside, rows of cedar shelving held bolts of hand-dyed ribbons and linens arranged in a delicate pastel-colored rainbow. Her shop smelled woodsy and clean. Roy stood on the wooden box at the center of his Aunt Sorcha's ribbon shop, fighting the urge to scratch the itch on his lower back as his aunt fidgeted with the eight yards of pleated tartan wool covering his bare thighs.

Thoughts of Wilkin Wilkinson occupied Roy's mind as he scanned the sea of passing shoppers beyond the shop's entrance. Were they unknowingly walking alongside a murderer? Did Innis know?

A trio of tourists, shopping bags hanging from the crooks of their arms, entered the store, giggled, and asked if they could take a picture with him.

"Is this part of the show?" one of them asked.

It took him a minute to realize they thought the man having his kilt altered in the middle of a shop was market entertainment. The Blackwell children had become quite famous for their market interpretations of the Blackwell family history and had even made a bit of spending money by setting out an old boot to collect tips.

"No. No show." Roy laughed. "I'm getting married."

"Today? Is it open to the public?"

An awkward question, he thought.

However, the market's new success had brought with it a slew of curious patrons fascinated by the Blackwell clan.

"No…" As if their wedding wasn't going to be spectacle enough, they had limited the guest list to family only – not Coraloo residents who swore they could trace their ancestry back to one feuding family or the other but only knew Margarette as *that* Toft and Roy as *that* Blackwell. And tourists were definitely not on the list.

"Go on, now. Shoo!" Aunt Sorcha commanded, gesturing with her hand for the girls to move further into the shop and away from Roy.

There was another jingle of the doorbell and then another.

Roy looked down on his aunt from where he stood on the fitting platform. "I can come back another time if you want."

"You don't have time."

Aunt Sorcha was right. Sixteen more days. Sixteen days and Margarette Toft would be his wife.

Margarette had the notebook with her every time they ate dinner, met for lunch, or stepped out into the festival for a breath of fresh air. She wouldn't even let him carry it. He certainly considered himself no expert when it came to wedding planning, or in any way knowledgeable of anything to do with wedding goings-on for that matter, but Margarette wasn't acting like herself. She seemed distracted, hurried. The photograph in the Wilkinson file had given him an idea. An old idea. A way for him to help ease some of the wedding burden. He just had to ask.

"Shoulders back, chest out," Aunt Sorcha insisted, playfully poking Roy in the hip with a pin.

"Watch it!" he joked.

Roy's mother had carefully packed away his father's wedding attire just in case. His father would have approved. His mother would have cried. The wearing of the Blackwell plaid kilt was tradition.

All of a sudden, she jabbed him in the leg.

"Ouch! Easy!"

"You ought to have that mole checked out."

"What mole?" he turned awkwardly, trying to see the back of his calf where Aunt Sorcha was working to let the hem out to knee length. He hadn't noticed any alarming moles, and he checked often.

"Nope. Just a piece of fuzz." She had already stuck him at least ten times, but he was quite certain that last one was on purpose. He tried not to think that Aunt Sorcha was subconsciously revealing her true thoughts about his upcoming nuptials through a thousand little pinpricks.

"How's the bride?" Aunt Sorcha pulled at the black sleeves, pinning and tucking the five-button waistcoat.

He waited for her to follow up with something snarky, but she didn't.

"Amazing."

"I can see it all over you, Roy. You're quite taken with her, aren't you?"

"Quite." He laughed. He was far more than quite taken.

Another prick to the shoulder.

"Easy with the pins."

"I've gotta get it just right. Not a Blackwell married who didn't look the part on his wedding day. And since you're wearing your father's wedding attire it's going to take a bit of adjusting."

"Guess I'm a few pounds heavier."

"You're the spittin' image of him, just a few years older. He'd be proud."

Would he? Would his father have been proud of the constable of Coraloo? A constable who sat behind a desk, scrutinized every bodily ailment, and tried to satisfy his love for the ride with the repair of a few flat tires and the occasional seat adjustment.

"And how's the groom gettin' on?"

He exhaled. "Good. Fine. I'm good."

"Are ya? Wedding jitters?"

"No, nothing like that."

"We like her, no matter she's a Toft. She doesn't act like one. Pretty thing. Book club decided to give her a new last name until she properly took yours. We're calling her 'DuMont'. After a character in our book. Margarette DuMont. Has a nice ring to it, don't you think?"

His face warmed and Roy finally relaxed. If that was their worst – renaming his fiancée – he could handle it, and Margarette would get a good laugh when he told her.

"All right, you can step down. Don't let the pins fall out."

"What do I owe you?"

"What kind of question is that? We're family. But maybe you could fix my bike."

"Tried to ride down the hill again?"

"None of your business what I'm doing with that cycle. The chain's come off again."

"You can fix that yourself, you know. I can show you how."

"I know, I know. But I'd much rather you do it."

"All right, then. It's a trade."

"Is there anything else you're wanting to ask me, Roy?"

There was in fact something he wanted to ask her. Something oddly inspired by the Wilkinson photo. Something important. Something special. Something for Margarette. He nodded.

His aunt laughed, clearly knowing what he was struggling to find the words to say. "I figured it was coming. I'm not sure what Granny would say about it, God rest her soul, but the rest of us have already discussed it."

Roy stepped down from the box to thank her but was interrupted.

"Excuse me, ma'am, will you take three for this?" A woman with one pair of sunglasses on top of her head and another on her face, carrying an enormous purse, held up a bolt of the crafted ribbon.

Roy could see the suppressed anger on Aunt Sorcha's face rising to a boil. It was a known rule of the market: don't haggle with the Blackwells. Haggling was saved for the temporary vendors who set up in the center of the market.

Aunt Sorcha raised a finger. "Get out!"

"I beg your pardon!"

"You heard me. Get! Out!"

"But I'm a customer. And the customer is always right."

"I don't know what world you woke up in, missy," Aunt Sorcha tossed a bolt of her handmade ribbon from one hand into the other, "but around here –"

Out of the corner of his eye amid the flying ribbon, Roy spotted Wilkin Wilkinson. He was hobbling along with his usual limp, carrying something large.

"Think before you throw another one, Aunt Sorcha!" Roy called out. "I'll be right back."

Slung over his shoulder in a zipped white bag, Wilkin's package looked suspiciously like a body. Roy's common sense kicked in. *Ridiculous.* But the charge had been murder. Could it be? Did he have a murderer on his hands? If Wilkin had taken someone's life before, wasn't he capable of doing it again? Surely not. And definitely not so out in the open. He'd have to be crazy to do something like that. But looking more closely at Wilkin's two long braids and fedora, Roy had to admit that from where he was standing Wilkin Wilkinson might not be far off the mark when it came to crazy.

Roy took off after him in the kilt, weaving his way through the slew of shoppers with his aunt yelling behind him, "Don't you go messing up my measurements! We'll have to do it all over again, and I ain't got time for any of that!"

Roy knew full well he'd have to deal with a customer complaint later that day. The woman would storm through the door of the Coraloo Municipal Building and claim she'd been publicly humiliated by Aunt Sorcha or that a store clerk had assaulted her with a bolt of ribbon.

"A bolt of ribbon, you say?" he would ask. "Are you sure it wasn't food?" Most of the complaints he received involved flying food.

The woman would reply with something sarcastic like, "Of course it wasn't food! I think I would know if I'd been hit by an airborne macaron!"

Then he'd say, "All right, just fill out the form."

And she'd reply, "Form? I have to fill out a form? Can't you just make the old woman apologize? She threw me out of her shop. I've never been so embarrassed in my life! I have the right to shop wherever I like."

The woman might or might not fill out the form but would almost certainly find humor in the antics of his family members at some point, hoping the next time she returned with friends she would manage to bait one of the family members into "performing" for her again. Most of the time the complainants never even picked up the pen.

Having the market open six days a week, as opposed to two, had brought a real change of pace for the town and for Roy. More tourists equaled more whiners. Sure, it was more work, but not the kind he wanted. Not like this cold case, which was looking warmer and warmer by the minute.

Roy didn't know what he would say when he finally caught up with Wilkin. He couldn't just come right out and say, "So, I found this file. Apparently, you were accused of murder. Is it true? And is that a body you've got there?"

He snuck through the crowd of unsuspecting passers-by and amused patrons watching the Blackwell children reenact the death of Mungo Blackwell. For a moment he lost sight of Wilkin. Roy turned, searching the market, only to find a man and woman seated in the corner of the market, pointing and laughing at him like two disrespectful children.

"Nice legs, Constable!" the man shouted. "Can I borrow your skirt?"

The woman shoved her collaborator playfully. "It's not a skirt, it's a kiln… a kip… a kilt."

They were locals. Roy had seen them in town before, but not like this: drunk, and in broad daylight. The taverns were probably competing for customers again and running some sort of special. He hadn't received word of it, and he'd issued no license for alcohol to be sold at the festival. The Blackwells had opted not to serve alcohol within the market, so the couple hadn't come undone on these premises. Roy was considering arresting the two for public intoxication when he caught sight of Wilkin again.

He picked up his pace until Wilkin was clearly in view, tailing him until he was nearly at the arched front entrance. A couple of tourists snapped photographs of the kilt-clad Roy, pointing and clapping as if he were a part of the market's entertainment. Wilkin looked back and Roy ducked, but not before they locked eyes.

There was a moment, a pause, as if Wilkin were trying to read Roy's intentions. Then Wilkin ran, leaving his limp behind but still carrying the mysterious white bag.

"Wilkin! Stop!" Roy cried.

But the man kept moving, picking up speed, racing as though he had never had a limp at all.

Roy doubled his pace, straight pins attacking him at the knees, wrists, and shoulder, until he leapt out of the market and landed in a puddle outside. He groaned, shook the mud off his boots, and, remembering his quest, looked to his left and then his right.

There was no sign of Wilkin. It was as if he had vanished.

After returning to the market to leave his wedding attire with Aunt Sorcha for alterations, he spent the rest of the morning searching for Wilkin. It was then, after asking around, that he realized there was no known residence for the Wilkinsons in Coraloo.

Back at his desk, Roy flipped through the pages of Wilkin's file once again. Surely there couldn't be a murderer running loose in Coraloo? But with so many tourists, how would anyone know if someone had gone missing? And why was there no further information in the file? No notes relating to an investigation, a trial, an acquittal, or anything else. It was as if someone made the charge and the acting constable had done his end of the paperwork, but then instead of investigating he'd buried the file in the archives. How would anyone in their right mind not investigate an accusation of murder? It didn't make sense. He could think of nothing but Wilkin for the rest of the day. Especially the charge – murder.

The door to the station opened and slammed shut. Roy looked up to see Earl Fox-McGoggins looming.

"So, what are you going to do about it?" Earl thumped his hand down on the Wilkinson file.

Roy glanced down at the file in front of him. "Do about it?"

He gently pulled the file out from under Earl's hand and closed it. At first, he thought Earl might be referring to the Wilkinson file, but given the metal colander on his head, he realized Earl was most likely referring to something else.

"How can I help you, Earl?" Roy wanted to ask whether he would be dealing with an alien invasion or a troll under the bridge today, but he held his tongue. Earl was a nice enough guy. Odd, but harmless.

"We have a thief in Coraloo. What are you going to do about it?"

"A thief?"

"That's right. Someone stole the recipe!"

Roy stared at Coraloo's resident conspiracy theorist. "Recipe?" He was afraid to ask anything further. There was no telling what the Fox-McGogginses were cooking.

"You know. *The recipe.*"

Roy shook his head, having no inkling as to what recipe the man was talking about. Unless... but surely Margarette would have told him. "Are you talking about the communion wine?"

The man threw his arms in the air, nearly knocking the colander off his head. "Why in the world would the Coraloo Historical Society have locked up the communion wine recipe?"

Roy could have given him a few reasons. That particular recipe had nearly launched two sweet old ladies on the communion committee into a full twelve-round boxing match. But if it wasn't the communion wine recipe, then there was only one other recipe that would cause such distress. And it would explain a lot, including the behavior of the drunken couple at the market. About ten years ago one of the teens had found the recipe in the library, stuck between the pages of *Great Expectations*. No one would ever have known about it had the boy not tried to pass out samples of the beverage as part of his presentation for the Coraloo High Science Fair.

Roy followed Earl to the scene of the crime, which happened to be on the other side of the municipal building. "When was the last time you saw the recipe?"

"Are you joking?" The Fox-McGogginses lived above the Coraloo Historical Society and had unofficially named themselves its curators when no one else stepped up for the job. "How am I supposed to know? This place has been awash with tourists since the festival started. I can't hardly tell the lookers from the watchers!"

"The watchers?" Roy glanced up at the man's makeshift helmet and gave up any hope of receiving a sensible answer. "Never mind."

"It was here. Right there on display... but I can't recall the last time I saw it."

"So it could have been gone for some time."

"I do my job!"

"I know you do, Earl."

"We have a thief in town! That's what's happened. What are you going to do about it? Should we lock down the town?"

"I'm not sure that will help us right now."

Earl narrowed his eyes. "You know as well as I do, Roy, something strange happens during the festival. Something unexplained. People tend to be a little crazier, more reckless. Maybe it's the full moon."

Roy had to agree. It had been a slow festival so far. "Maybe." But Roy knew full well that this year's madness had nothing to do with the moon and everything to do with a mysterious moonshiner.

"So whodunnit?" Earl asked.

"No idea. But how about we keep this to ourselves?"

"Good idea. We don't want to let the perp know we're on to 'im."

That wasn't why, but Roy agreed. People just didn't steal in Coraloo and what he didn't want was mass hysteria.

The last time mass hysteria broke out the town did end up in a week-long lockdown. It happened after a blackbird became trapped in the church bell tower, when one of the Tofts openly and boldly announced, mid-service, "A bird in the tower brings death by the hour!" Half the town was convinced they were about to be stricken with the plague. The Tofts had sworn at the town meeting that the last time a blackbird had been trapped in the tower and finally got out it had flown into the house of a third or fourth cousin, and that third or fourth cousin had contracted the avian bird flu and died before he was even diagnosed. Immediately after the meeting there was a run on the hardware store for nails, and townspeople started boarding up their windows, afraid to open the door for fear of the "bubonic bird" getting inside.

Unsure how else to quell the madness that was gripping the town, Roy did what any good constable would have done: investigated. The truth, he discovered, was that the third or fourth cousin was actually a fifth cousin who had sadly died, aged ninety-seven, three days before the bird of legend had trapped itself in the tower. By this point Roy and half the town had developed sore throats and muscle aches. But, as further research revealed, the bird flu was most often spread by ducks, and 99.9 percent of the time was passed on after coming into close contact with a person carrying the illness. Seeing as no one in town had – or had ever had, for that matter – the avian flu, Roy finally persuaded everyone, and eventually himself, they could safely unlock their doors.

"Thanks for keeping this between us, Earl. I'll let you know as soon as I find anything."

Roy stepped out of the museum. Across the way, a group of townspeople had gathered in the circle beneath a collection of umbrellas at the central stage to find out whether they had been voted citizen of the day. Shoppers and others milled about. Artists and merchants stood beneath the blue and white tents, never-minding the day's drizzle, each one of them a suspect.

Roy decided to head back to the office, file the report, make a list of suspects, including the couple from the market, and have a chat with Pastor Donaldson.

Margarette would be waiting for him at the cafe a bit later. The rain suddenly ceased and the sun poked through the clouds. Roy breathed in the day... a new kind of day. A busy day. A full day. The sort of day he hadn't experienced in a very long time.

CHAPTER 13

May 3, 1976

Innis had faith that love would come, like a promise as yet unfulfilled, but she had never expected it to walk through the front door of her shop. She knew every young man in town and wanted nothing to do with any of them. They were all dull, boring. She wanted an adventure. Someone mysterious. Someone who would whisk her – and the scissors – away from Coraloo. When her mother passed away Innis stayed put. Now a tailor, her days were spent shortening skirts and arguing with old men about the correct length of their pant legs. The satins and silks were no longer delivered from distant lands and the clientele was far from famous.

It was a Saturday when it happened.

The bell on the door clanged. "Good afternoon, Innis."

Innis sighed. "Hey, Wilkin." She walked over to the cash register and pulled out a five-dollar bill. It's what she had paid to have the scissors sharpened for as long as she could remember. "I'm more than happy to retrieve them myself. I can walk, you know."

"I don't mind. Gets me out of the shop."

The truth was, she very much appreciated the delivery. That way she only had to pass the mortician once a week as opposed to twice. She was acutely aware that the mortician had noticed her Saturday trips and made a point of handing out advertisements from his doorway at the very time she passed on her way to and from Wilkin's Hardware. This was awkward, as Innis felt the only truly safe way to deal with the situation was to walk on the other side of the street. He would wave hello and she would look the other way.

How bizarre, she would think to herself. *Dead people don't read advertisements.*

Wilkin shifted back and forth on his feet. "I brought you something, Innis."

"Oh?"

"Dad's selling it in the store. He bought it from a traveling merchant."

Her ears perked up at the word "traveling".

"A merchant?" It wasn't unusual for newcomers to peddle their wares during festival week.

"He's in the beauty business."

He?

"Says he's helping his wife."

Wife. Not what she wanted to hear.

"A salesman for his wife's beauty business is selling to a hardware store?"

"Said he's branching out and we should, too."

"Do you have the scissors?" she asked, suddenly panicked and no longer distracted by the *married* salesman.

"Of course!" He handed her the scissors. "I can put a new ribbon on them if you like."

"Thank you. This one will do." She had considered changing the ribbon on several occasions, but it was the one her mother had chosen, and it would do just fine.

"As I was saying, I brought you something."

She eyed him curiously. No one had ever brought her anything except unsatisfactory clothing and unsolicited advice.

He handed her a glass bottle, elegantly etched and ornate, with a heart-shaped top and a tiny gold bow hugging its neck. The label read "Jus de Beauté".

"It's beautiful." She removed the lid, gave her wrist a spritz, and inhaled the fragrance of citrus and roses. Realizing Wilkin was watching her, she looked up and caught his eye, and for a moment she saw something. Something she had never seen in him before – an understanding. It explained why he offered to deliver the scissors every Saturday and why he had just presented her with a gift. Her heart skipped, but her head reminded her she didn't want that kind of understanding. Not from him. Not from the scissor sharpener.

Dull.

She looked away, not wanting to give him false hope of a future relationship. Theirs was strictly business.

He looked to the ground, blushing. "Are you going to the festival tomorrow?"

How was she to answer?

"I mean, you know, in case something happens to the scissors... I would be there. Things can happen during the festival, you know. There's no telling who will show up in town. I hear the council's bringing in professional actors this year, mixing things up a bit. Trying to liven people's spirits around here, with the shoe factory closing and all. A lot of people are going to be out of work."

For the first time in all the years he had offered she considered enjoying the festival events. He would protect her... and the scissors.

But then the door clanged again, and all understanding was gone as a new face caught her eye. She pushed her glasses further up the bridge of her nose with her forefinger so they properly framed her eyes, and quickly yanked down the scarf that had held her hair away from her face, allowing the curls to fall delicately onto her shoulders. A young man – adorned in a long, bejeweled purple coat with military-style buttons and a high collar – pushed past Wilkin to approach the wide-eyed Innis. His eyes were dark, as if they had been lined with black eye pencil, enhancing the thickness of his eyelashes against his thin, pale face. He wore a top hat, banded with a matching purple bow, pulled down over his forehead. Behind him stood five others, dressed as ornately and bizarrely as their leader, holding large bags in their hands.

The young man took her hand, kissed it, and, in an accent unfamiliar to Innis – Swedish, or maybe German – introduced himself. "I am Jean-Michel, and we are a troupe of traveling thespians in need of a talented tailor. We were told you were an expert in such matters, but I see you are much more than that. For I, throughout all my travels... in all my many, *many* leading roles, have never been at a loss for words... for never before have I seen such beauty."

Completely taken with the silkiness of the young man's tone, Innis did not notice the clanging of the bell, or that Wilkin Wilkinson had left the bottle of perfume on the counter. Nor did she notice the bags of wearable thespian paraphernalia the actors had proceeded to drop at her feet.

She was certain she had never seen a man so handsome in her entire life. His presence overwhelmed her with childhood memories she had long ago forgotten – the actresses with their exotic stories and the fabrics from far off places. A desire to travel the world she longed to see soared through her once again – a desire to leave Coraloo and stand at the side of Jean-Michel hemming his glittery pants for the rest of her life.

He gently released her hand and gazed into her eyes, slipping his free hand into his pocket – along with her pincushion. She started to speak, to question the abduction of her pincushion. But then he spoke again, this time with a hint of an accent she had not noticed before. The words spilled from his tongue.

"I would find myself humbled by the use of your talent to reattach this wee button to my coat."

Never had anyone asked her to sew on a button in such a way. "Of course... Let me just write up a ticket for you."

"Our illustrious troupe is to perform before your humble townsfolk tomorrow afternoon. There will be no cost for you to attend, fair woman, as I would be honored if you would be my guest."

Had Innis been in the right frame of mind, and not wooed by the glittery presence of Jean-Michel, she would have remembered that all the public productions were free of charge.

He spun around in a circle, lifted an arm, and bowed in front of the smitten seamstress.

Then Jean-Michel backed out of the shop, leaving his ticket behind, and leaving Innis too in awe of him to wonder anymore about the whereabouts of her pincushion.

CHAPTER 14

The melodic strum of a traveling troubadour echoed below her, followed by the faint cheers of patrons participating in the festivities. The rich aroma of freshly fried mini-doughnuts rose up the hill from a vintage campervan, which had been forced to spend the week in town after blowing out two tires at the town's entrance. Word spread a team of contortionists had stumbled into Coraloo late in the night looking for a place to stay and offering up their talents in exchange for lodging. It was all part of the norm, the enigma, the unexplained that worked with the nuances of Coraloo to create the most memorable month of the year.

However, Margarette had chosen to give it a miss today. For the Blackwells. For Roy.

She stood at the entrance of the Coraloo Flea Market, excited, nervous, and hardly able to believe what was to happen. The last time she'd entered the building she had been arrested. On purpose. By her fiancé. The jail was the quietest place in Coraloo, and Roy was there. Stealing a few moments alone with him was all she craved these days – moments free of her sixth-grade students, floats, wedding flowers, and unnecessary family portraits her mother insisted they take while Margarette was still a Toft. Even a simple wedding came with certain expectations. Expectations she had set for herself a long time ago. Expectations that included the perfect bridal gown.

Margarette stepped into the remnants of a busy market day, the artisan boutique shops lining the walls of the market aglow with their tiny wall lanterns. The three crystal chandeliers hung boldly, sparkling their welcome above the aisles of vendors covering their awning-shielded tables of antiques and collectables as they packed up for the day. This was about to become her life. A life with a family of gypsy-like artisans – the Blackwells. It was their heritage, their livelihood, their history.

She inhaled the warm fragrance of handcrafted leather goods, dried herbs, and baked goodies. It was like Roy's smell... an aroma that made her feel safe and loved.

Margarette moved casually and comfortably through the straggling customers toward the back of the market, with hand-hewn wooden tables and benches dressed up in blush-dyed table coverings and jars of fresh florals. She adored Aunt Sorcha's hand-dyed linens and owned more than her fair share of the matching ribbons. At the head of the tables sat a large wooden armchair, draped with grapevines and local wildflowers like a fairy throne. Looking at the simple attire of the Blackwell ladies milling about – Clover Blackwell barefoot in a gauzy long-sleeved dress and the other ladies, bold in personality but demure in presentation – made her question for a moment the blue pinstriped dress and red heels she'd chosen for the occasion.

Her tummy fluttered with anticipation. She prayed they wouldn't ask her about the wedding dress or lack thereof. Uncle Albert said he'd keep an eye out, reassuring her that her quest would remain a secret between the two of them. She was trying, she really was, but nothing seemed quite as right or as lovely as the Bella Fottasi. The attendant had said it was one of kind, but she had to know for sure. Margarette spent her planning hour at school scouring online sites each day, hoping to find the dress, but its origin remained a mystery. There wasn't a single mention of the designer to be found. Even if Bella Fottasi happened to be some elite designer who made clients sign a contract of anonymity, surely someone would have slipped up at some point. But the designer and her wares were nowhere to be found.

Coming to terms with the fact that the Bella Fottasi was not meant to be, she had called La Robe de Mariée to order dress number seven.

"And what is the date of your wedding, mademoiselle?"
"May 31st."

"We will be cutting it fine. The distributor is in Egypt... hand made. Allow time for alterations... You said, size 8... Correct?"

"Correct."

"We will need a deposit and then you can pay the rest when the dress arrives."

Margarette gave her the card number, reminding herself she could work with dress number seven. Seven was beautiful, and more her style than the others. It wasn't the Bella Fottasi, but she had no other choice. As the attendant said, she was already cutting it fine.

"We need to schedule your fitting... How does April 10th sound?"

Margarette tried to process the date. "I'm sorry. Did you say April 10th?"

"Yes, mademoiselle."

"But the wedding is May 31st..."

"Yes, that is what you told me."

"I'm sorry. I'm a little confused... I thought you said April 10th."

"Yes, mademoiselle."

"But the wedding is May 31st... May 31st."

"Yes, that's what..."

There was a pause. An awkward, uncomfortable pause. A pause that told Margarette exactly what she feared. The attendant had assumed she was getting married next year... which would make sense, seeing as that was what any normal bride-to-be would do. "I am so sorry, mademoiselle. We cannot have your dress this soon. All our distributors require at least six months to a year. You are welcome to revisit our sample rack. We have some lovely gowns there."

Sample rack? She had visited the sample rack... Eleven had come from the sample rack. She didn't want eleven! She wanted number seven... from the boutique rack. But not really... No, what she wanted was the elusive Bella Fottasi. And since La

Robe de Mariée was the first, and only, place she had heard the designer's name it surely wouldn't hurt to ask.

"Ma'am, there was a Bella Fottasi –"

"We do not sell a designer by that name."

"You do… I saw it. One of your attendants was carrying it, and I tried it on. Can you check to see whether it sold?"

"Mademoiselle, I assure you we sell no dresses by that name. I have never even heard of your Bella Fottasi."

Had she imagined it? Had she been in such a frenzied state that she'd made it all up? She didn't know what else to say, or what to ask. Surely the attendant would know. There had been no tag, no label. Maybe it was something else. Maybe the attendant had been wrong. But then she remembered the business card.

She hung up and flipped through her wedding notebook, retrieving the business card. On one side, in elegantly scrolling gold letters, was the name Bella Fottasi, and on the other a phone number. She typed in the number and waited to the fairylike tune of gentle violins, the fluttering of a flute, and what sounded like birds chirping in the background. Then it stopped, and a small beep sounded.

"Hello? Hello?" Maybe she was supposed to leave a message. "My name is Margarette Toft. I saw one of your gowns at La Robe de Mariée in the city. It was… exquisite… perfect. I'm not even sure if it was in my price range… Maybe I shouldn't have said that, I'm sorry… That was probably rude. But I would love to talk to someone to find out if you have another… I was told it was one of a kind… My wedding is in a few weeks and I don't even have my dress. It was a swift decision… we need to be married as quickly as possible. Family reasons… But you don't need to know all that about my family. Sorry again. My number is –"

The phone clicked. Someone had hung up at the other end. Someone had been listening and they'd hung up. She dialed the

125

*number again. Maybe she'd rambled too long and the message
had been cut short. She would only leave her number this time.
But instead of the birds and the violins there was nothing. She
hung up, confused. Maybe she would try again later... Or maybe
she would stop eating dessert and wear her mother's dress.*

A hand-lettered invitation had cordially invited her to the day's event –
the Blackwell blessing of the bride. Roy said it was a tradition – a day for
the ladies of the Blackwell family to "feed her and fix her up".

Clover stood off to one side, flanked by her two teenaged daughters,
Fiona and Finella. She waved Margarette over, then returned to
directing the flurry of Blackwell women who were scurrying about.

"Ladies! She's here!"

In a matter of seconds Margarette was surrounded, her red heels
removed while someone behind her gently pulled a comb through
her curly locks. Clover carefully extracted her from the huddle with a
giggle. "It's all about you today. They mean well. It's tradition, and you
know how they are about tradition. I promised Roy and Stephen I'd do
my best not to let them overwhelm you."

Margarette laughed. She knew all about their traditions... even the
Blackwell custom of holding your funeral before you die. It was a bit
morbid in her opinion, but after Roy had explained a bit it oddly made
sense. Roy had organized his funeral the year before they met. He told
her he'd talked about his father and the cycling trip they should have
taken together. He occasionally brought up the trip, but she never
probed.

"Ladies! Ladies!" Clover called her clan to order, clapping her hands
in such a way the ladies halted and turned their attention to her. "Let
us bless the bride!"

Margarette was hurriedly ushered in her bare feet to the floral
throne and a crown of laurel placed on her head by one of Clover's
youngest, Fie. Two teenaged girls and a few other littler Blackwell girls
from other families – Margarette had no idea which they belonged to –
positioned themselves in front of her.

"Ladies and… ladies." Fie opened her arms wide and bowed to Margarette. "I present to you the marriage of Beatrice Blackwell."

Margarette had seen the Blackwell children perform the Blackwell tales for the market's patrons on more than one occasion. The tales were legendary even among the Tofts, told in such a way as to keep the children in bed at night – like some grim fairy tale meant to frighten its hearer from venturing into the forest. She had heard the tale reenacted in front of her more than once as a child, but it didn't exactly end with a happy ever after. Her father's version had been even more gruesome than the historical tale. She realized the brainwashing her parents had been propagating all along. The moral of their story: if you fell in love with a Blackwell, he would kill your father. This obviously wasn't part of the spectacle taking place in front of her.

She watched in awe as one of the girls, dressed as the groom – because boys were prohibited from the bridal blessing – escorted another dressed in layers of white fabric and what looked like a bird nest on her head.

One of the girls leaned in to Margarette. "This first part actually happened before the wedding, but we didn't want to do a costume change."

Margarette held her giggle. She couldn't wait to learn every one of their names.

"Oh, Beatrice!" the one dressed as the kilted groom began. "Will you be mine?"

"Forever and ever!" the other gushed.

The bride and groom walked between the other girls, holding out sprigs of mint like a canopy for the couple to pass through until suddenly the bride fell hard to the ground. Margarette gasped, to the delight of the girls.

The groom stooped down and lifted his bride. "I will lift you whenever you fall. I will carry you wherever we roam."

At the muffled sound of sniffles, Margarette turned her attention to a seated grouping of older women, all dabbing their eyes with cotton handkerchiefs. She couldn't wait to know all of them, too.

The retelling ended, performed exactly as she had read in her research, with a sudden shower of potpourri pouring down on her as the other girls tossed it into the air by the fistful. The ladies seated at the long tables stood, then clapped and cheered, as did Margarette.

Early in their courtship Roy had offered to loan her a book of family history if she was interested. Margarette thanked him but declined, admitting she had already read the book of Blackwell history five times. Not only was it part of the sixth-grade curriculum at Coraloo Elementary, but she had written her senior thesis on it at university, to which the professor responded with, "Extraordinary! Fascinating! How did you come up with such a tale?" However, he had almost flunked her until she produced documented evidence from the town archives, to which he'd replied, "And you *know* these people?" She'd had no idea at the time how well she would not only come to know them but to love them.

The wee Blackwell leaned in. "It's okay. We all cry at the end, but don't worry. Roy will carry you, too. Want them to do it again?"

Margarette wondered, in fact, if Roy would request he carry her down the aisle in homage to "The Tale of Beatrice Blackwell".

Before the tale could be retold, two older ladies each set a large galvanized bin on the floor in front of Margarette. They stepped away and then returned with pails of steaming water, which they proceeded to gently pour into the bins, then motioned for her to place her feet inside. She wriggled her toes in the warmth of the water. One by one the Blackwell ladies rose from their seats and added something to the water, accompanied by a word of wisdom. A sprig of lavender for rest. A bit of mulled cider for longevity. And so it went until every lady had placed her item in the bin.

Then Clover approached and placed a cluster of clovers in the steaming water. "For friendship."

Friendship.

The two oldest Blackwells crouched down and proceeded to wash Margarette's feet with warm cloths that smelled of lavender and rosemary. After the washing she could feel the women digging into her heels and pressing through her arches. If it hadn't been for all the other ladies staring at her she would have fully enjoyed the best foot massage she had ever received. Just when she thought they were done, one of the ladies dripped warm, fragrant oils across her feet and proceeded to rub them into her skin.

Margarette fought to keep her eyes open. It had been a long week. Alongside wedding planning she had, against her better judgment, taken her class on a field trip to the post office. Hadn't she learned her lesson about mixing festivals and field trips? She had sworn she would never, ever, do it again, but Norvel Poteet had asked. In fact he had practically begged, and Margarette couldn't deny him.

Norvel had led the students on a guided tour of the Coraloo postal service, explaining all the ins and outs. He was excited, prepared, and clearly proud of his position. She'd had to issue three detentions for inappropriate language – at least, she considered it inappropriate language. It was hard to tell these days; it seemed as though the students were repurposing words and making up new ones each week. At one point she had found herself saying, "I don't care if your grandmother uses it every day. You're not using it in my class!" And to the one who had argued the word wasn't really a bad one because he'd watched a movie about it, she had assigned a thousand-word essay on the word "the". Norvel was satisfied and none the wiser to the sneaky misbehavior of sixth-graders, and her students were officially educated in the goings-on of the Coraloo postal service. But she was exhausted.

Margarette was jolted from her musings when she felt a set of small fingers fidgeting with her hair. The owner leaned in, and in a tiny voice said, "Blackwell ladies usually keep their hair long, but we'll see what we can do."

Do?

Margarette was so entranced by the tingling in her toes she didn't care what they did to her hair.

The voice came again: "Would you ever consider dyeing it red?"

She turned sharply toward the girl, convinced for a moment she had been replaced by her cousin Sylvia.

"You do have lovely hair. I always wanted to be a blonde, but Mum says red is beautiful. She says her red hair made her look like a gypsy and that's why the Blackwells took to her so quickly. But Uncle Roy loves you and you don't have red hair." The voice faded to a whisper. "And you're a Toft."

The girl's innocent comment flung her back to the reality of their unapproved union, overshadowing the restorative intention of the gentle tugs and pulls at her hair. She would always be a Toft. Neither family approved; however, one was willing to take her in, while the other wanted nothing more than to push Roy out and replace him with The Butcher. Margarette laughed inwardly at the thought. She truly loved her family. They would come to terms with her marriage eventually, just as they had come to terms with her leaving Coraloo for university and phoning from Thailand suggesting she might not come back. No wonder her mother thought Roy might come and go. *"Toft girls marry well."* It was what she had been told since she was a little girl. "Toft girls marry wealth" is what they really meant. Roy Blackwell might not be wealthy in the eyes of the Tofts, but he had more heart than all of them put together.

"They're almost finished," the young girl cooed.

Margarette breathed in the fragrance of dried flowers.

Then another voice piped up – Clover's. "Please don't hate me."

Margarette sat up straight, a bobby pin jabbing her behind the ear. "What?"

One of the elderly Blackwell women helped Margarette to her feet and escorted her up and down between the tables as the ladies whispered blessings over the soon-to-be newest member of the Blackwell clan, speaking words of hope, peace, and unconditional love over her marriage.

Margarette had no idea what Clover was referring to. Why would she hate Clover over such a beautiful, selfless moment? These ladies were loving her in a way she had never been loved before. Sure, it was a bit awkward walking barefoot on the cold floor with her hair twisted into braids and dried flowers sticking out like hedgehog quills, but hearing the ladies' blessings was one of the loveliest moments she had ever experienced. In fact, she wished she had somehow thought to record their blessings so that she could replay them any time the Toft women offered up another potential suitor.

She looked over at Clover, whose head was buried in her hands. *Something's wrong.*

Margarette mouthed the word "What?" just as Clover looked up from her seat.

Clover mouthed back, "I am so, so, so, sorry!"

A knot formed in Margarette's stomach. She trusted Clover, so whatever came next was clearly going to be disturbing. She knew that the Blackwells did some odd things. But what if there were secrets, arcane rituals of the past of which she was unaware? Her mind raced as she began to conjure up ideas of the absolute worst traditions the Blackwell ladies might impose upon her. Would they bury her alive and have Roy dig her up? Or perhaps they would cover her in bubble wrap and throw fruit at her to test her mettle? She didn't know where that thought had come from. Maybe all the fragrances slathered over her body were inhibiting her ability to think straight. Was she being slowly poisoned? She glanced back at Clover and firmly reminded herself that if Clover had survived whatever was about to happen, then so could she. Maybe.

The eldest Blackwell, Aunt Sorcha – whom Roy was so fond of – led Margarette back to her throne. Margarette suddenly felt like the wife of the town's founder, the Maharini of Kuru. Maybe this was a test of faith or a biblical test of will. She imagined herself sitting before two women, one with a child in her arms. Would she really have to proclaim, "Divide the child!"?

Margarette snapped out of her contemplation, making eye contact with a very confused woman who was clearly trying to attract her attention without breaking the solemn silence or dropping the large white box she held before her, tied with an even larger hand-dyed pink bow.

"Oh! Is that for me?" Margarette glanced over at Clover, who now had her whole body turned away, refusing to watch the proceedings. Whatever was disturbing her, Margarette assumed, was about to come out of that box. *Could it be snakes?* She'd read about a few snake-handling churches in the south. That was it! The Blackwells did want to test her faith. She knew it!

The lady presented Margarette with the box. Margarette leaned down a little and gave it a subtle shake. Silence. Not a hiss. *No snakes.* Clover occasionally glanced back and then looked away, stuffing her face full of cake in some kind of wild comfort-eating gesture. Margarette wanted cake way more than whatever was in this box.

The lady nodded for Margarette to open the gift, the silence heavy with expectation. Margarette could have sworn the ladies were inching onto the edge of their seats. She felt as if a creepy clown were inside, waiting to jump out and pie her in the face. But the Blackwells weren't crazy; they were eclectic.

Margarette slowly untied the bow. It was beautiful and soft, and she absently thought it might look nice tied together as a tree trimming. She rolled it up and set it aside to use at a later date. Then she breathed in slowly, carefully lifting the lid and setting it to one side as well.

Her heart raced as she made out the outline of a bodice through thin layers of paper. It was a dress! The Blackwells were renowned for their intricate craftsmanship and attention to detail. Would this be as lovely as the Bella Fottasi? She laid her hand on the tissue paper and smiled up at the women. She wanted to remember this moment. The moment she first laid eyes on her dress. The dress the Blackwells had made for her. She mouthed "thank you" to the ladies, who returned delighted smiles and clasped hands.

Clover was now on her feet, pacing back and forth, and stuffing her face with pastries. She refused to look at Margarette.

A gasp escaped Margarette's lips as she carefully lifted back the folds of tissue paper to reveal layers of badly yellowed fabric pieced together in a style out of fashion by nearly three decades. Margarette held back tears as she pulled it from the box, stood to her feet, and held it up to what she would normally have described as her fairly healthy frame. This dress looked as though it would fit a twelve-year-old girl, not a thirty-seven-year-old woman who started a new diet every Monday and ended it with cake on Tuesday.

Aunt Sorcha stepped toward Margarette and proudly proclaimed, "Every Blackwell bride has worn this dress, including Roy's sister, mother, and grandmother."

The ladies cheered, toasting their glasses of Blackwell mulled cider to the new bride, followed by, "Won't she look lovely?" and "It can be altered" and "Do you remember when such and such wore the gown?"

An unpleasant aroma wafted around Margarette – the odor of generations of perfume emanating from the dress, mingled with something else that Margarette couldn't quite place. She glanced up to see Roy standing in the distance, waiting. He'd said he would walk her home.

A sickening feeling settled in the pit of her stomach as the reality set in: they actually expected her to *wear* this dress – this yellowed, outdated abomination of pearls, lace, and taffeta. It had been reworked so many times a few straight pins remained in the bodice. Surely this was a joke. But Clover's apology and evasive face-stuffing tactics had said it all. This was real. She wanted to scream, "But what about Bella Fottasi? That's my dress, not this!" *Oh please*, she thought. *Not this.*

She looked back up at Roy, his face a smiling beacon of hope. He would help her. He always helped her – like when he'd saved her flowerbeds from Father Milligan and when he'd participated in her Citizens of Coraloo Day at school. Roy could simply explain to the Blackwell ladies that Margarette wanted to choose her own wedding dress – a dress like the Bella Fottasi. Comforted by the thought, she took a deep breath to compose herself, quelling her rising panic, and with a forced smile mustered up her most gracious words of thanks for the Blackwell women. They were, after all, offering their most precious family heirloom to a Toft. They were welcoming her into their family.

At the conclusion of the event, Margarette was left with a stack of cards on flower-pressed stationery filled with the Blackwell blessings spoken over her, a new hairdo, clean feet, a full stomach, the most horrific dress she had ever seen in her whole life, and a profuse apology from Clover, who swore it looked better on.

Roy put his arm around Margarette. "How was it? Did they treat you well?"

She inhaled his smell. "It was nice."

"This one was important to them. I give you my word that I'll protect you from any of their wilder shenanigans, but you know our ways…"

In truth, Margarette liked their ways. She just didn't like the dress. How could anyone – Blackwell or otherwise – like the dress? Surely he would understand; she just needed to find a way to tell him. "Do you remember when I went to the city a few weeks ago?"

"When you went shopping with your mom? Sure. My family didn't talk about freshening *their* marriages, did they? Because once you get them started down that road…"

Roy could always make her smile.

"No… but when I was there I saw a dress. It was perfect. It looked… Well, it looked like it belonged here in the market, if that makes any sense."

"Not really."

"It was already spoken for, but I'd never seen anything like it. It was as if…" She tried to bring it back to something he would understand. "It was as if it had a story. A history."

They stepped out of the market and stopped at the top of the hill. Coraloo waited for them below, lit up by glistening gas lamps, casting a warm glow over the striped tents and crisscrossed bunting.

Then he kissed her. "You don't know how much it means for me to hear you say that."

Relief flooded through her. He understood what she was trying to say.

"All the women in our family have worn that dress. It represents our history, and it's how I always imagined my bride. I was a bit nervous you'd find something before the blessing."

She pulled away from him. "What?"

"The dress… it has a history. Like the dress you saw in the city. That's what you were about to tell me, right? That you like the dress."

She wanted to shout, "Heck, no!" but instead she gripped the box, secretly wishing a strong wind would jerk it out of her hands and shove it down someone's chimney, where it would be ignited into an eternal flame, sending the dismal dress down to the depths of Hades. But she couldn't say that to Roy.

"It's one of a kind."

134

CHAPTER 15

M argarette needed a neutral opinion – someone to help her honestly analyze the situation; an unbiased third party. So she phoned the first non-Blackwell/Toft she could think of. Velveteen Price.

Velveteen ushered Margarette inside the Price cottage. Margarette was very familiar with the cottage, as not only had she attended the Prices' Christmas party, but the cottage had once belonged to her grandmother. She knew all too well what the place had looked like before the Prices moved in. Velveteen had transformed the cottage from a bad attempt at mid-century modern to a rustic-chic mini palace. The wallpaper had been stripped and the carpet pulled; however, Velveteen had left the gaudy stained-glass bee hanging in the kitchen. Margarette had no doubt that at one time the light fixture had been a very expensive purchase on her grandmother's part, but it now looked perfectly comfortable glowing in the Prices' farmhouse-style kitchen. The illuminated bug had scared her as a child, but now it served as a sweet reminder of her childhood.

"Margarette, I'm so glad you called. Please, have a seat… a cup of tea, a sweet? I just pulled a tart out of the oven, my very own recipe. You do like tarts, don't you?"

Margarette did. She still had four of them in her freezer left over from the engagement party.

"Tea would be lovely. And I never pass on a tart." She knew she shouldn't… *But if I keep eating, then surely I'll be too big for that monstrosity of a dress.* She chuckled. *Yes, that's the solution. I start a sweet treat diet now, and by the wedding day no amount of alteration will make that dress work…* She stopped this train of thought, surprised at how

135

callous she was becoming, and set the large white box and her wedding notebook on the couch, gently moving aside the baby paraphernalia.

Velveteen placed Margarette's slice of tart and cup of tea on the coffee table. She looked fabulous. Ridiculously fabulous considering she'd given birth a little over a week ago. Even in her yoga pants and long T-shirt she appeared perfectly put together. She was wearing make-up, and already looked smaller than she had before she announced her pregnancy.

"All right. Show it to me."

Margarette pointed to the box.

"It can't be that bad."

Margarette sat slumped on the sofa, hiding her face with a cushion. She was exhausted after another week of trying to teach a class while her students were way too distracted by the festival to take in her talk about the history of the town's founding father.

"Are you telling me it's so bad you can't even look at it?"

Margarette nodded and sighed softly as Velveteen stepped over and placed the sleeping baby, Agnes Price, in her arms. *Agnes.* It was a name that had thrilled the Blackwells and devastated the Tofts, leaving many of Margarette's relatives feeling there was no further hope for the Price family, having named their daughter after the recently deceased Granny Blackwell.

"Will it, like, burn my eyes out or something?"

Margarette nodded again.

"It can't possibly be as bad as this place was when we moved in. Did I tell you about the wallpaper? Dahlias! Big fat dahlias all over the place!"

"Those were my grandmother's dahlias," Margarette said defensively, trying not to laugh.

The Tofts had been absolutely frantic trying to find someone in the family to buy the house for fear that it might fall into the "wrong" hands. Everyone knew they meant Blackwell hands. In fact, Margarette's mother had tried to insist she buy the place. Margarette had considered it but was afraid she might find something better and be stuck with a fixer-upper. And while dabbling in DIY sounded like fun, she thought she'd be better off leaving the fixer-upper to someone with a bit more talent in that area. Someone exactly like Velveteen Price.

"I'm lifting the lid…" Velveteen joked. "I'm removing the lid…" Then came a shriek. "Dear Lord! What is this? There's no way that Clover Blackwell wore this thing! I know Clover, and I know she does a lot of strange Blackwell things… but this? How many rhinestones are on this thing? Surely the sleeves were added. Puff sleeves didn't come back into fashion until the eighties."

Margarette gave Agnes another snuggle, attempting to settle her after her mother's gasp of horror. Velveteen neatly folded the dress back into the box while Margarette imagined the dress suddenly springing to life, zombie-like, and pinning her to the sofa until she relented and agreed to put it on.

Velveteen went over to the sink and washed her hands, then carefully took the baby from Margarette. She was a natural mother and had turned into a bit of a germaphobe during the final month of her pregnancy. She admitted that she'd become a little irrational due to hormones, spending hours scouring the floorboards, cupboards, even disinfecting book covers, in an attempt to sanitize the house. Her husband Charlie had to step in when he found her perched precariously on a ladder bleaching the ceilings. No one set foot in the Price home without removing their shoes, washing their hands, and adding an extra-thick layer of hand sanitizer before holding sweet little Agnes.

"Margi."

Margarette had no idea why Velveteen called her that. Maybe it was an attempt at "Meggy". She'd let it slide.

"I get it," Velveteen continued. "I totally get it. That thing would have taken a flying leap off the side of a bridge by now if I was in your shoes." She sighed. "All right, no. No, it wouldn't. Not if Charlie really wanted me to wear it. I might have altered it a bit, after I'd had it steamed, dry cleaned, and sanitized. Do you think we can alter it? Maybe we could, you know, fix it. I did a bit of sewing back in design school…

not clothing, mostly curtains. But seriously, anything's better than what you've got going on here."

Margarette fought back tears, her notebook-full of wedding ideas she had been clipping since she was a little girl seeming to taunt her with all its unfulfilled wishes. The hobby had started one December when her parents received an influx of Christmas catalogs. She had sat for hours, flipping through the pages. Her mother said she couldn't keep them – too much clutter – but Margarette would cut out the things she liked before tossing away the rest of the magazine. So Margarette had set to clipping: a living room set, a recipe for oatmeal chocolate chip cookies, a wedding dress. Over the years she had begun to organize her clippings into neat notebooks. Occasionally she would flip through them, removing the taped images she no longer liked and adding new ones. She'd started planning her wedding well before she decided that a wedding would be in her future. In recent years she'd even created a notebook for motherhood, with articles on breastfeeding, tips for sleeping at night, nursery decor, and cute baby outfits. The notebooks were a way for her to organize her thoughts, setting them aside for later.

But there was nothing like the Blackwell dress in any of her clippings. In fact, it was the farthest thing from how she had envisioned herself on her wedding day. She could just imagine herself being carried down the aisle – something else she needed to talk to Roy about – her body shrink-wrapped into the bodice and the rest of the dress trailing behind in a yellowed blob of sequins, rhinestones, and lace.

But it was just one day. One moment. And Velveteen said she would have sucked it up and worn it for Charlie. Could Margarette do that too? For Roy? She wouldn't have to wear it very long. Just for a few pictures… A few pictures that would hang on their wall for the rest of their lives, for their children to see, and their grandchildren and their great grandchildren. Imagine if she and Roy had a girl of their own: would she then have to wear that thing on her own wedding day? Would it ever end?

Holding the baby with one arm, Velveteen wrapped the other around Margarette. "What can I do to make it better? I could spill something on it or put it in the stove and accidentally cook it. The Blackwells would believe it was an accident if I did it."

"It's horrible. I don't think I've ever seen anything so horrible in my entire life." Margarette felt safe to speak her mind in the Price home – neutral territory. She could say whatever she wanted, and Velveteen wouldn't try to explain the situation away with family traditions or backwards superstitions.

"But Roy wants me to wear it. He absolutely wants me to wear it. He says it's their history. You should have seen his face. I don't get it… Maybe I do… Am I being selfish? I don't think I'm being selfish. Maybe I'll show up at the church in something else and hope he doesn't notice."

Velveteen took Margarette's hand. "I have an idea. The Blackwell ladies are meeting here for book club tomorrow. How about I gently explain the situation? Tell them you want to find your own dress? I'm sure they'll understand. Or I could tell them that I know this woman who was forced to wear the family dress but didn't want to wear the family dress –"

"Clover wore the dress."

Velveteen positioned herself on the couch in such a way as to nurse Agnes. "Right… Clover wore the dress. Did they drug her or something? I'm telling you, there is no way Clover Blackwell intentionally wore that dress. Have you talked to her?" She paused, adjusting Agnes's position.

"No, but I probably should."

"Your only other option is to tell Roy the truth."

"I couldn't! He'd be devastated. I'll just have to wear it. That's all there is to it. I will wear that… that… *thing*. And I'll be married and the Blackwells will be happy and my family will be…"

She hadn't told her mother – or any Toft – about the dress. If she was going to wear the dress, she thought it best to keep it a surprise. She really didn't want to give her mother yet another reason for her not to marry Roy.

Velveteen sat up and looked Margarette dead in the eye. "Tell him the truth, Margi. Don't let your marriage start off this way. You have to be honest with him. He's your forever."

Her forever. Roy was going to be her forever. She'd known it from the first time he'd shown her what was on the other side of the hill. It was verbally their second date, but technically their third. As the stakeout had ended in a rather long conversation with Father Milligan, who had given them a lecture on "pruning the vine", they later decided that the encounter had been more of an education than a date.

For their second official date he'd taken her to see the other side of the hill. It had just been the two of them, away from their families, their work, and their everyday life. Margarette had visited parts of the world most of the people in Coraloo could not even locate on a map, but in all her years, she had never once seen what was on the other side of the market – rolling hills of farmland dotted with country homes, their occupants living happily away from the constraints of grading papers, parent–teacher conferences, and aunts ready to ship her off to live with the next available non-Blackwell. And on a knoll so high, yet a distance away, Margarette had thought she could see a manor hidden among the cedar trees with tall turrets and a long driveway that wound through the valley and up to the hill, like a fairy tale.

He had brought a bouquet of wildflowers, tied with hand-dyed ribbon from the market, as well as a picnic lunch – in a basket, complete with all the accouterments – from the market as well. The market was taboo as far as her family was concerned. The Tofts said a person could find everything one needed outside of Coraloo by driving the short distance to the next town over or driving into the city.

Atop the hill on their unintentionally secret second outing – she had told no one about the second date or the two firsts – Margarette had rambled on about books. Books she had read, purchased, and caught a glimpse of in the cells on the first floor of the Coraloo Municipal Building.

"I bet you'd like the bookshop," Roy said. "My cousin Stephen runs the place. He gave up a pretty high-profile career to come back to the market. He said this life was easier. He needed to get away and start over. I could take you there sometime, if you like."

She'd been to the market, but she would very much like for him to take her there. The clouds moved slowly over the hill as life in Coraloo moved even more slowly behind them. In front of them peace overtook conflict, replacing any notion she'd had of feuding families and expectations.

The sweet smell of freshly hung tobacco swept up and around them. Margarette inhaled slowly – the moment, the season, the company; holding on to it as a new memory, she never wanted to let it... him... go. Then she exhaled. The aroma had always been a part of her life, like Roy, but she had never noticed it... never really noticed it... until now. She imagined the two of them somewhere else... anywhere else. Away from the place where the names Toft and Blackwell were synonymous with Montague and Capulet.

"Do you ever want to get away... to escape Coraloo?" she asked. "Like, go on an adventure, see the world in a way you've never seen it before?"

"He looked into my eyes and said, 'I believe I already have.'"

Velveteen sat with her mouth open as Margarette recounted the events of that second date.

"He really said that – 'I believe I already have'? Oh, Margi! You have a gem of a man."

Margarette smiled at the memory of the hilltop date. She hadn't even gotten to the best part. They'd shared the picnic lunch, the handmade cheeses, the pastries, and the infamous Blackwell cider.

As the sun was beginning to set, he looked over at her again and asked, "Miss Toft, would it be all right if I held your hand?"

In that moment she had seen the beauty of the Blackwells and the true gentility of Roy. And in that moment, she knew she was ready to leave behind her life as a Toft. She wanted to be part of what had made this man the way he was. She wanted to be a Blackwell, even if she could barely sew on a button and heated up the majority of her meals on the stove top. And she wanted, more than anything, without a question or second guess, to marry Roy Blackwell.

"He asked to hold your hand? Oh, glorious! That is the most romantic thing I have ever heard. You must wear the dress! If he wants you to wear it, then by all means wear it, wear it, wear it. Just wear the dress. And if it makes you feel better, I'll wear whatever you want me to wear inside out and backwards." Even if Velveteen wore her whatever inside out and backwards, she would still look good.

"What happened to honesty and starting my marriage off with the truth?"

"Oh, there will be plenty of truth coming from that man. If it will get you down the aisle and into the arms of Roy Blackwell, wear that dress."

Margarette flopped back against the pillow, defeated. "You've been hanging around my cousin Sylvia, haven't you?"

"How am I supposed to respond to that?"

"There is no appropriate response to 'Sylvia.'"

Velveteen squeezed Margarette's hand. "I'm kidding about wearing the dress... sort of. A man like that will love you no matter what you're wearing. Just walk right up to him and tell him the truth."

"I'm not very good at these things. What if we... fight?"

"He loves you. He'll want you to be happy. He'll listen."

Velveteen was right. She needed to tell Roy the truth...

Maybe.

CHAPTER 16

Roy wondered whether Bert Thompson would surprise him and decide to meet him at the market for lunch. But it was not Bert, or lunch for that matter, that took Roy to the market. It was Wilkin Wilkinson and the missing recipe. Two cases, both a mystery. He'd spoken earlier that day with the pastor and the couple, all of whom admitted to feeling slightly intoxicated but denied drinking, let alone distilling moonshine. Roy had no other leads, but he wasn't giving up. Things didn't go missing in Coraloo, at least not since he'd been constable.

Roy stepped through the open archway. Other than the tavern, the market was the only place any of the people he questioned had ever seen Wilkin. The man had run from an officer of the law, which was enough in itself for Roy to bring him in for questioning. But if Roy couldn't track Wilkin down, he could certainly have a word with Wilkin's wife Innis.

The Coraloo Flea Market was uncharacteristically crowded. The festival below was drawing quite a crowd, and the morning rain had them seeking shelter within the confines of the market. Some blamed the rise in festival attendance on the Tofts, who were secretly quite fond of the increased revenue the tourism had brought to the businesses below the hill. Others blamed it on the flea market.

Roy shivered in the cool morning air, noticing a slight headache coming on. He'd had a few headaches in recent days. *What if...* But there was no time now for speculation. Roy scanned the sea of damp shoppers. No sign of the couple. At the far end of the rows of vendor stalls – occupied by resellers of collectables and an expansive variety of vintage odds and ends – Roy spotted Charlie Price engaged in what appeared to be a rather comedic conversation with a vendor.

Roy shouldered his way through the crowd until he reached the canopy-draped booth of carefully priced and labeled antique car adornments, once crowning the front of some very pricy automobiles. He picked up one resembling the head of a woman with wings, turning it over in his hand. The label read: "1926 Buick Goddess". He set it down again.

"I'll give it to you for three fifty. Sells for over four hundred."

Roy knew this game, but he didn't play it. "I'm working today."

Charlie turned with a smile. "Aren't we all?" he said, casting a wink at the vendor on the other side of the table. "But I sure would like to get my hands on that 1952 Nash."

The vendor leaned in. "I'll give you a good deal."

"You already told me your good deal, Frank." Charlie and the vendor laughed. "Velveteen has me on lock down. No more buying until Agnes is at least five."

"And you're going along with that?" Roy asked, aware of Charlie's knack for haggling and reselling.

"Course not. But truth is, I don't have much time to buy and sell these days. I miss it."

Arms crossed, the vendor on the other side of the booth chuckled. "Old Charlie's not as much fun as he used to be. At one time I could darn near sell him my whole table."

Charlie returned the laugh. "Not quite the *whole* table, but probably the table itself if I could make something off it."

The vendor held up a wool blanket with a large red stripe banding the front and a white cross at its center. "It's Swiss Army... I'd say around 1941... Tempting, isn't it?"

"I know, I know." Charlie shoved his hands into his pockets. "I'd love to have it for my own collection. Always wanted one of those things. But I promised Velveteen, and I have it on good authority that someone out there is pumping out a pretty decent, high-quality reproduction of those these days."

"Oh yeah?" the vendor asked, narrowing his eyes. "And whose authority is that? I might need to have a few words with my competition."

"The internet," Charlie responded flatly.

The vendor laughed so hard Roy wondered if the man had forgotten to breathe.

"I didn't know I was that funny," Charlie said.

"You're not," Roy replied, enjoying his part in the camaraderie.

"So, what brings you here, Constable? Lunch? Shelter from the Tofts? I hear they're in the market for pitchforks, something about burning you at the stake."

The vendor started laughing again.

"Actually, I'm here about the Wilkinsons."

"The Wilkinsons?" Charlie asked. "Are they in some kind of trouble? Is there something I should know about?"

Roy didn't want to give anyone cause for concern, especially not Charlie Price. "I'm not sure, but I'll let you know if anything comes of it. Do you know where I can find either one of them?"

Charlie shook his head. "Good luck. They keep their own hours. The two of them pop in here and there, sweep the floors, change a few lightbulbs, and then leave to go who-knows-where. The market's spotless, so I can't complain. Funny thing, I don't even have contact information for them – no phone, no mailing address, no nothing. My business mind tells me to let them go; there's no telling what those two are up to. But I just don't have the heart to do it. They've been here since the place first opened."

No phone, no mailing address. Those two were definitely hiding something, and even if it wasn't murder Roy was determined to find out what it was.

"So, no sign of them today?"

"What day is it? Sunday? I can't even keep my week together. Sometimes I wonder if opening the market an extra four days was worth it. Sundays are the shortest but the hardest five hours of my week. Open in time for the morning service-goers to grab a snack, and closed so the evening service-goers don't feel guilty if they don't make it back in time for service. Monday can't come soon enough. A whole day to spend with my girls and Gideon."

Roy was also a fan of Mondays. It seemed like the whole town shut down for the day, just to take a rest from the busyness of the weekend. In fact, the town elders had agreed most of the shops should shut down, as a sort of forced day of rest. A few people had complained until they'd actually taken the day off and realized they felt a whole lot better for it.

Charlie yawned. "Excuse me. I'm looking forward to Agnes sleeping through the night." He yawned again. "The Wilkinsons... I'd say you're more likely to spot Innis than Wilkin. She doesn't say much, sort of a mystery, but if you hang around long enough, you'll see her pushing her cleaning cart around. Now that I think about it, I'm not sure there's anything that cleans in that cart. Have you ever seen anything inside it?"

Roy had never thought about it before. But when he saw her, he'd take a look.

"Oh, and since I've got you here, Vee and I would love to have you and Margarette over for dinner sometime soon. I guess she and Margarette had quite a discussion about the dress."

The Blackwell dress. It was the only practical thing he'd been able to do for the wedding, and he felt kind of proud of himself.

"Thanks for the invitation, but it might have to wait until after the wedding. The families have Margarette running from one side of Coraloo to the other."

It was true; Roy hadn't been able to snatch more than a few minutes with her in days.

"Well, after the wedding it is. See you around, Roy. I have bills to pay, a market to run, and a good few weeks of sleep to catch up on."

Roy took up his stance, positioning himself near the temporary vendors. He crossed his arms and watched the array of shoppers scurrying to and fro, dashing in and out of storefronts and digging through the wares of the temporary vendors. He checked his watch. He'd been here nearly an hour, but there was no sign of Innis. The market closed at five on Sundays, and the parade was due to start shortly. He'd told Margarette to watch for him waving to her and her students as they went past. He studied the shoppers, moving hurriedly about, but there was no sign of Wilkin or Innis.

This was pointless. Those two had been around the market for as long as anyone could remember. He considered shoving Wilkin back into the filing cabinet where some constable before him obviously thought he belonged, but there was something about the way Wilkin had looked at him the other day. And then he'd run. Why had he run? Innocent men don't run... Nor does their limp mysteriously disappear.

In the distance he could hear the theatrical voices of the Blackwell children. "If you want to marry her, you must fight for her! Fight now, or forever hold your peace!"

Then another child: "I have no reason to fight you!"

And then another: "I have no reason to fight you!"

Then: "But I will fight you, Blackwell!"

Someone rang a bell. Roy imagined two of the boys were now slugging it out for the audience. The patrons applauded and cheered, tossing their coins into a pair of old work boots set out by the children. His head pounded and his throat felt a little tight. He hoped he wasn't coming down with something... something incurable, something life-threatening.

Think about something else.

He didn't have time to be sick. He didn't have time to search the book. He needed to find –

"Are you looking for me, Constable Blackwell?"

Roy whipped around to see Innis Wilkinson standing behind her cart. He cast a glance inside. *Empty.* Her curled locks were much longer than in the photograph he'd seen inside Wilkin's file. A few strands fell down the sides of her face while the rest was tied up with a black scarf into some semblance of a bun. Black rimmed glasses perched on the bridge of her nose. She was thin and spoke quietly, sounding older than he had assumed. This made sense, since according to the file Wilkin was in his sixties.

He cleared his throat. "Mrs Wilkinson?"

"Yes, sir. I ran into Mr Price. He said you needed to see me. Have I done something offensive?"

"Offensive?" he laughed. In his mind offensive equaled everything this woman with the odd shears hanging around her neck was not. "Oh, no. I'd just like to ask you a few questions. It's something I'm working on… for the safety of the town."

He hadn't planned what he would ask her and decided he couldn't come straight out and ask, "Is your husband a murderer?" So in that moment, with the confused woman looking up at him, he didn't exactly know where to start.

"You work here with your husband, yes?"

"Has Wilkin done something offensive?"

Roy cleared his throat, noting the dry tightness once again. *Why is this so hard?* "I don't think so. It was just a question."

"He's always by my side. Always has been." This time she giggled, catching Roy off guard.

He rubbed his tongue across his teeth, afraid that some of his breakfast might be visibly stuck between them. He hadn't expected to get much out of her, let alone a laugh.

"Excuse me, sir," she added. "It was a memory."

"A memory?"

"I was engaged."

"That seems typical."

"Oh, not to Wilkin."

This was getting interesting. Innis had been engaged, but not to the man she had married… *Could her former suitor be the man Wilkin had murdered?*

Roy wrangled his thoughts, forcing himself to not make any unjustified assumptions. "I guess I should just get right to it, Mrs Wilkinson –"

"I guess you should," she replied bluntly.

"You see, it's come to my attention –"

The sound of hurried feet and a shout of "Stop!" interrupted his thoughts.

He turned to see a woman rushing toward the door, hugging herself tightly. He looked back to see one of the Blackwell women waving frantically in his direction.

148

"Excuse me, Mrs Wilkinson…"

Roy took off after the first woman, wishing he'd had the chance to finish his conversation with Innis first. He caught up with her just shy of the arched entrance. The market seemed to come to a standstill. All eyes watched him, cameras raised to snap his big moment.

"Ma'am, would you mind putting your arms down by your sides?"

The woman hardly looked the type to shoplift, dressed as she was in her fur coat, and carrying one of the fancy handbags they made at the purse factory in the next town over. However, it was a bit warm out for fur.

"That's her!" Aunt Sorcha shouted, waving her arms in the woman's face. "That's her! You got her, Roy. That's the woman. That's the thievin' witch who stole my ribbon. Arrest her! Take her in! Shove her in the clink and show her what Blackwells do to thieves. If you won't, I'll take her round back and we can fight it out."

"It's all right; I've got this." He turned to face the woman in fur. "Your arms, please."

"This is outrageous! You'll be hearing from my attorney. I have rights! Do you see this?" she shouted to the onlookers. "I have rights!"

"Ma'am, I mean no offense. If you'll just show me what's in your arms we can put an end to this and all go home."

The woman scowled at him and hugged herself tighter. "No."

Roy thought for a moment. Either he was facing a lawsuit or a bona fide shoplifter. He scratched the back of his neck, realizing he'd need to be creative. "Can I buy you a pastry to extend my apologies for any embarrassment we might have caused you?"

Aunt Sorcha stood on tiptoes, eye to eye with Roy. "Roy Blackwell, I will excommunicate you from the family if you don't arrest this thieving witch right now! Comes into my store tellin' me it's not high quality… Says she's seen it cheaper in the city. Says it was made in China! I'll fight her, Roy! Right here and now, as Granny Blackwell's my witness. I'll not let our good name be sullied."

Roy gently drew his aunt to his side. "Again, my apologies. She's senile."

Aunt Sorcha punched him in the rib. "I'll show you senile!"

He would explain it all to her later, though he probably should not have called her senile… He'd have to grovel for the next month or so, but she'd come around.

The woman's expression changed. "There's no need. I'll be on my way."

"Please, ma'am. On behalf of the town of Coraloo, allow me to express my sincerest apology." Roy addressed his aunt. "Excuse me, but I need to find this lady a seat. It's a scorcher out there. Could you possibly grab her a glass of water?"

"A glass of water? Are you up to your ears in it? That Toft woman's softened you, Roy! That's what it is! Call me senile, but I'm not the one who's marrying a Toft!"

Roy rolled his eyes.

At that moment, a young man of possibly thirteen or fourteen inched past the woman, a heavy backpack pulling at his shoulders. The woman cast a glance his way, then back at Roy.

Roy grinned. "Excuse me, son. Would you mind running to fetch this nice woman a cup of water since the crazy old woman here refuses to do so?"

The boy looked frantically from the fur-adorned woman to Roy and back again, confused and out of sorts, sweat beading on this brow. "I, I, um… She made me do it! I'm a minor, you can't arrest me!"

"He's a liar!" the woman shouted. "I've never seen this boy before in my life."

"I'm not taking the fall again, Mam-aw."

Roy helped the lady to her feet. "Do you want to show me what's under that coat now, ma'am?"

The woman scowled at him and slowly opened her coat, revealing her accumulation of pilfered goods.

"All right, then. Let's get you two down to the station."

Aunt Sorcha leaned in to him. "How long'll you be holdin' the goods for evidence? If you dust for fingerprints it won't be good anymore."

"You'll have your ribbon back by the end of the day. And, for the record, I don't think you're senile."

"I knew what you were up to, Roy Blackwell. Where'd you think the children learned to put on shows the way they do?" She elbowed him playfully in the ribs.

Roy led the pair of shoplifters out of the shop, down the hill to the Coraloo Municipal Building, and into one of the newly cleaned cells, swearing that he would lock the old woman up for life if she proceeded to use profanities against her grandson.

With the grandmother in one cell and the young man in the other – the two shouting blame at one another through the brick wall – Roy diligently filled out the paperwork. For once Roy's strict cleaning regime had not been in vain.

On his desk sat a backpack filled with sterling silver: a sugar bowl, a milk jug, and a decanter. Roy said he would give them twenty-four hours in the cells for shoplifting and then let them go. He was proud of himself. Had he not noticed the knowing look between the boy and his grandmother he'd have had no reason to ask the woman to remove her coat, exposing three bolts of ribbon, two books, a string of pearls, and a Barry Manilow CD that Roy later determined had been filched from one of the vendors. The vendor said she didn't need it back. Roy might have had a bit of compassion for the light-fingered woman had she not chastised him for what she considered the uncleanliness of the cell. He'd had to excuse himself at this point before he said something impolite.

"I'm heading out to the parade," he said. "Can I bring you two anything?"

"How about a little justice for an old woman?" she screamed. "You can't keep me locked up in here. I have rights, you know. I'd like to see the person in charge."

Roy grinned as he glanced back at them before exiting the Coraloo Municipal Building. "*I'm* in charge."

Thoughts of the victorious capture momentarily replaced his newfound obsessions with Wilkin and the missing recipe. The rain had finally come to a stop and the town circle was full and bustling.

151

He breathed in the festival aromas of Coraloo: apple cider doughnuts, popcorn, and burgoo – typically a Toft family reunion treat, but also a Heaken Beaver Festival tradition, brewed from whatever meats and vegetables the family members decided to toss in it that day. Roy made a note to stop by the church and see how this year's batch was coming along. Last year he'd had to break up a disagreement between two parishioners – one from the morning service and one from the evening – who had disagreed over whether soy was a legume or a vegetable. One of these days someone was going to have to give in and build another church or two.

Citizens had already started lining the sidewalks in anticipation of the Heaken Beaver Parade. Children wore oversized antlers and vendors roamed the street pushing their carts of balloons and cotton candy. The Tofts were scattered about, adorned in their Sunday best. The men stood with their hands stuffed into the pockets of their suits, while the ladies in their dresses, hats, sunglasses, and high heels, waved at one another across the street. The Tofts would use any occasion to dress up.

Roy jogged across the street just before the Coraloo High School band struck up a tune in the distance. Somewhere behind them Margarette was riding on the float that she and the class had spent the last two weeks putting together – the reason she'd had to skip their dinner. She had left him a voicemail message:

"I'm so sorry, but I have to cancel dinner tonight. I'm literally up to my ears. I'm standing in a very large pile of some sort of brown mesh. And now…" Her tone suddenly changed. "Charles Michael, the tail belongs on the beaver!" Then another change in tone. "Just a few more days. I love you. See you tomorrow, maybe. Okay, bye."

It wasn't like them not to have dinner at the cafe, but the float and some wayward sixth-graders, who for some unexplained reason had been dropped off at the school without parental supervision, had diverted her attention. Roy understood. She'd seemed quite relaxed when he'd picked her up from the blessing, which was exactly what he'd hoped for. He knew the Blackwell ladies would treat her well. And then there was the dress. He was thankful they'd agreed to let her wear it.

152

He'd taken one piece of stress off Margarette's wedding planning plate, and that was all that mattered.

Roy pushed his way through the crowd until he was in front of Shepherd's Hardware. This would be the best spot to see her. He'd promised to wave. She'd said to look out for the giant beaver riding a pirate ship, giving Max Fox-McGoggins full credit for the design. It was the first time in Roy's life he remembered looking forward to the parade. The format was always the same: high school band, tap dancers, and lots of beaver costumes followed by the Heaken Beaver Queen riding behind in a convertible. But it really wasn't the parade he was looking forward to; it was seeing Margarette. A scuffle of raised voices attracted his attention.

"It's my body. I can do what I want with it!" a man shouted.

"My store is not a piercing parlor!" another shouted. "It's a hardware store… that sells groceries!"

"Who's gonna stop me?" the man yelled, weaving back and forth.

Roy took hold of the man's shoulders, pulling him away just in time to prevent him from landing a fist on Mr Shepherd's face.

"That's enough, now. Norvel, what are you doing?"

"He's blasted!" the shop owner declared. "Running through my shop, making a mess of everything. Then he goes and tries to stick a nail through his nose."

"It's *my* body," Norvel blubbered. "I can do what I want."

"Not in *my* shop!"

Roy turned to face the postman, immediately wishing he hadn't, as he took in a full-on exhale of liquor and bad breath. He urged himself not to gag.

"Norvel, I didn't think you were a –"

Before Roy could finish his sentence, Norvel swung again, landing a punch squarely on Roy's jaw – a much harder one than he thought a man Norvel Poteet's age would have been capable of.

"Well, that's enough of that." Roy pulled the handcuffs from his waist belt and secured them around Norvel's wrists.

"It's my body. I –"

"You can sleep it off back at the station."

Roy had never known Norvel to partake of alcohol, but the festival sure was bringing out the worst in everyone. Three arrests in one day. This was new.

Norvel tried to writhe his way to freedom. "False arrest! False arrest! You've got nothing to hold me on! It's my body!"

"You have the right to silence. You do not have to say anything, but it may harm your defense if you do not mention when questioned something which you later rely on in court. Anything you do say may be given in evidence."

Norvel tossed his head back, forcing Roy to do the same. Roy hated dealing with drunks.

However, he didn't hate what he had just seen as a result of the head thrust. It was a sign much like the others that hung in front of the shops in Coraloo. He frequented Shepherd's Hardware at least once a week to refill his pantry and stock the refrigerator. A newcomer suggested Bill Shepherd add "and Market" to the store's name to account for the groceries on the right side of the shop. Bill had laughed, replying, "That will only confuse everyone." The Shepherd family had owned it for as long as he could remember. But sure enough the sign was there, as he had always known it to be, only he had never paid it attention: "Wilkinson's Hardware Company".

"The sign," Roy said to the proprietor. "You didn't see fit to change it?"

Bill shook his head. "I just never got around to it. Had the window done and thought that was enough. Dad took over after the Wilkinsons closed it down... you know the story... After the Wilkinson boy and that Toft girl disappeared."

Toft girl?

"Innis?"

"That's the one."

"Are you sure she was a Toft?"

The man scratched what was left of his gray hair. "As far as I remember. She was an odd one. Quiet. An orphan, I think."

A memory, far off and distant, returned from Roy's childhood. He remembered people talking about how the two had gone missing. And with no one to help him work the store old Wilkinson had been forced to shut it down. Three arrests and a unique twist to the Wilkinson puzzle within a matter of hours. *Innis Wilkinson was a Toft. Not too bad for a day's work.*

Roy straightened his shoulders and headed back toward the Coraloo Municipal Building. He took the long way around the back, having to stop and warn the bumbling drunk to refrain from pulling antlers off children's heads and keeping an eye out for Margarette.

"Norvel, what have you been drinking?"

"I haven't been drinking… just my usual tea. What kind of man do you think I am? I go to the morning service!"

"Sure smells like you've been drinking more than tea."

Roy knew that smell.

"That's my mouthwash, Roy. Come on, you know me. I bought it for my halitosis."

Likely story.

Roy had a feeling that if he could track down Norvel's supplier he would also find the missing recipe.

Norvel dropped to his knees. Roy fought to pull him back to his feet. As he finally managed to get Norvel stable, he saw the backside of the pirate ship passing him by.

He'd missed her.

CHAPTER 17

May 4, 1976

As part of the annual festival's events a stage had been erected in the center of town, complete with a fading red velvet curtain fringed with golden tassels. A company member from the Acteurs Agissant Acting Troupe stepped boldly out onto the stage dressed in sequined black-and-white-striped pajamas. Around his ankle he wore a shackle that clanked when he walked.

"Ladies and gentlemen…"

Innis looked behind her. Only a smattering had shown up for the late evening performance, as most of the town was already asleep. She sat poised in the front row, alone, at the invitation of Jean-Michel. She had dressed for the occasion, having applied her mother's lipstick and a dab of her perfume. She'd worn a white sweater and tied her locks up with a large black bow. The scissors hung in their usual place around her neck. Those in attendance whispered that they had never seen Innis Toft look so lovely or so grown-up.

"Tonight's performance will inspire. It will awe. It will make you weep. It will grip your soul in ways you never imagined. Ladies and gentlemen, I present to you… the Acteurs Agissant Acting Troupe's performance in a dramatic and modern retelling of *Great Expectations*!"

Innis sat with her hands in her lap, mesmerized as one of Charles Dickens's greatest novels played out in front of her. She absorbed every word of it as a marvel. She had read the novel. It wasn't her favorite, and at times she'd found it less than entertaining. She much preferred something wild and untamed like *Tarzan of the Apes*… or like Jean-Michel. However, while she knew all there was to know about Pip, Innis had never seen his story performed with such passion and color. Oh, the colors – royal blues and violets, fuchsias and crimsons. The actors shimmered as they moved. She felt a bit of belonging, a piece of the performance, as if every stitch, hem, and salvaged sequin had its own part to play. *Her* part. The role where she had spent hours repairing the theatrical garb for this very moment. Awestruck by the collaboration of elaborate costuming and heavy theater make-up, Innis had to remind herself to breathe. She imagined herself as Estella – beautiful and unattainable. Pip loved her, and in Innis's version she wholeheartedly loved him back.

She kept her eyes fixed on Jean-Michel. Even during the intermission she did not move or step away to look at the booth of odd paraphernalia and snake oils the troupe had brought with them to sell. Three hours later, as the group drew the show to its romantic conclusion, only a handful of spectators remained, the rest of the crowd so overwhelmed by the performance they had retired to their cottages to calm their nerves and quiet their senses.

"The unqualified truth is, that when I loved Estella with the love of a man, I loved her simply because I found her irresistible." Jean-Michel gripped his hands over his heart, falling to one knee. "Once for all; I knew to my sorrow, often and often, if not always, that I loved her against reason, against promise, against peace, against hope, against happiness, against all discouragement that could be."

He jumped to his feet and walked to the edge of the stage, his heavily black-lined eyes fixed on Innis. Her eyes locked into his gaze for a brief moment, but then she looked away, afraid he would see into her thoughts, afraid he would see her for who she really was – dull, like unsharpened scissors.

"Once for all; I love her none the less because I knew it, and it had no more influence in restraining me, than if I had devoutly believed her to be human perfection."

He winked. Innis blushed.

A dry-ice-induced fog spread across the stage. A few of those who had remained in the audience coughed and rubbed the water from their eyes.

As Jean-Michel took the hand of an overly made-up young woman in his and exited stage left, Innis applauded, her heart pounding and her mind whirling, wholly captivated by the performance.

Earlier in the day the Coraloo Actors' Guild had reenacted moments from the town's history – the naming of the town and an epic battle over land. But this had been something entirely different. Something breathtaking and fabulous like she had never seen before.

The scattering of vaguely amused onlookers drifted back to their cottages, some crossing the footbridge and others finding their way back to the bed and breakfast to rest for the next day's events, but Innis stood firm as she waited for her Pip, her Jean-Michel, to take his final bow.

One by one the actors returned to the stage, bowing as Innis alone showed her approval of their epic rendition. There was only one actor left by the end. He floated to the center of the stage, spun in a circle, and bowed dramatically, bobbing up and down like a glittering fish. Once again he focused on Innis, stepping slowly toward the front of the stage.

He was the most fascinating man she had ever met. And unlike the tag she had stuck upon herself, *he* was anything but dull. She imagined him lifting her onto the stage, taking her hand in his, and carrying her off into the evening mist. He placed his hand over his heart, yanking a rhinestone button from his long blue velvet coat. Then he tossed it out into the crowd-less crowd, whereupon Innis caught it, inwardly vowing she would never let it go. Her first thought, *I can sew that back on.* Her second, *Momma, he's not a mortician.*

CHAPTER 18

Roy stood outside the Coraloo Municipal Building with a box of decorations – the same ones used to adorn the Coraloo Municipal Building for as long as he could remember. Not that he had any intention of winning the festival's storefront decorating competition. He never won; he just wanted to participate. The judging wouldn't take place until the weekend, but Roy figured he might as well get started.

He checked his watch. Margarette was running late.

"Hello, Ms Brimble!" he called, waving to the woman who was now fully clothed and walking her dog. "I see Alfie's doing all right."

Before he knew it, Ms Brimble was standing in front of him with her arms flailing, harping on about how long it had taken animal control to free her Alfie, how that mouse had died anyway, and the cat had needed stitches. Thankfully, Norvel walked by at that exact moment.

"Hey, Norvel! How are you feeling?"

Roy had released Norvel early that morning, insisting he go home, shower, and be ready to reveal the name of his supplier. Norvel had insisted he had no supplier, nor was he a drinker.

"My head's throbbing," he said.

Roy understood – not that his own persistent headache was the result of overindulging on illegal liquor; it was more of a nagging at the back of his neck that he couldn't shake. Aunt Sorcha's peppermint oil had helped a bit, but the pain was still there.

"Thanks for shutting me down..." Norvel glanced over at Ms Brimble. "I imagine police business is kept confidential?"

Roy had called Bill Shepherd over at the hardware shop to ask whether he would be filing charges. When he'd said no, Roy had asked a favor – Bill wouldn't tell anyone about Norvel. But something was off. Sometimes Roy felt as though he knew the people of Coraloo better than he knew himself. And he knew Norvel Poteet. The man was a bit frantic, but Roy had never known him to be a liar.

"Norvel, you know Ms Brimble, don't you?"

"Of course I do." The postman tipped his cap toward her, his slingshot sticking out of his back pocket.

"Have you heard about what happened to her dog Alfie, Norvel?"

Norvel looked down at the dog, then back up at Ms Brimble. "Does he have the mange?"

Roy had once read that humans couldn't get mange; however, scabies was a real possibility.

Ms Brimble gasped, hand over heart and visibly offended. "Of course not! My Alfie is a ped-a-bree."

"Beg your pardon, ma'am," Norvel said, squatting down to pet Alfie. "It's just that I noticed those bare patches on his face. I've a cream that might work for that."

Roy spotted Margarette standing not far off. He hadn't seen her arrive. He smiled over at her, but she immediately looked down at the ground. Was something bothering her? He'd already apologized for missing the parade. She said she understood.

"You'll have to excuse me," Roy said, backing away from the two deep in conversation.

"How'd I do?" he asked Margarette, motioning toward the couple.

"Matchmaking?"

"Distracting, more like." Roy stepped up onto the first rung of the ladder to hang the aged red-and-white bunting over the bulbous strung lighting.

"Roy, I need to talk to you about something."

"Everything okay?"

"No… not really."

He looked down at her. His initial instinct had been right. Something *was* bothering her.

"I'm on my way back down."

"No, stay up there. I think it'll be easier that way."

Easier?

"All right."

"Roy Blackwell." Her tone was stern and matter of fact. He'd heard her use her teacher voice with a few students she'd seen misbehaving in public, but never on him. She took a deep breath and continued. "I hate the dress."

The dress?

It took him a minute to process what she was saying. Then he remembered the Blackwell wedding dress.

"No one in their right mind would wear that thing. Velveteen said I should tell you the truth. Roy, I know it's been in your family a long time, and I know how important tradition is to the Blackwells, and I don't want to do anything to jeopardize my relationship with them, and please don't be mad at me. But it doesn't fit, and I'll have to lose weight. Lose weight, Roy! That means no more chocolate cake at the cafe. And it has a very distinct smell. I may have to keep it in the garden shed until I return it."

"Return it?"

"I didn't want to lie to you because I love you, Roy Blackwell."

He stood up on the ladder, staring down at her. He had never seen her like this before – so agitated, so defiant, and all over a dress. He didn't understand. It was just a dress. Only he could see that it was about more than the dress. They had agreed to keep it simple, just enough to satisfy the families and say, "I do." But even though Margarette tried to brush off the stress and pretend she was managing, the truth was that most of the burden had fallen on her. Both families were pulling her so hard, in opposite directions, he was worried she might split into two.

He inched down the ladder, scratching the back of his head. "Margarette –"

"Roy... I've made a decision. I..."

He looked closely at her, her eyes heavy and tired.

"You don't have to wear the dress," he said gently.

"I don't? But I thought..."

"I don't care what you wear." Relief flooded over him. *So all along it was just the dress bothering her. I was beginning to think it was me...*

"But the tradition... and the Blackwells."

"I guess we'll have to make some new traditions."

Then she cried. And he held her.

Did he really care about the Blackwell traditions? His side of the family had stayed in Coraloo, while the rest had relocated when the shoe factory closed. He was surprised that when the Blackwells returned to Coraloo after their long sojourn they still accepted him as one of their own; he didn't even have to attend a ceremony or partake in some bizarre ritual. In fact, they thanked him for "holding down the fort" while they were away traveling the countryside, hopping from festival to festival with their homemade wares while he'd stayed behind – his father employed in the next town over, his mom an active part of the Coraloo Parent–Teacher Association.

He remembered hearing about the mass exodus as a boy. His sister Clara had dismissed the rest of the Blackwells as a bunch of gypsies, saying she would change her last name before she moved away. Eventually she had. She'd married a missionary and was currently living in a small village in Africa. His mother had kept her mouth shut on the subject. Roy knew all too well what she thought of the Blackwell name and had joked on more than one occasion that his father should have taken her name instead.

"They're strange, but they're family," his dad had always said.

Roy never knew why they didn't associate with the other Blackwells. As far as he knew there were no hard feelings. They had left when he was young, so he'd hardly known them.

But then, when they'd rolled back into town, one might have thought the citizens of Coraloo were preparing for war. There had been shouts of rage at the town hall meeting:

"Send 'em back!"

"It's not their town, anyway!"

"We own this town! Make them stick to the hill!"

Roy had been a high school senior when it happened.

Despite their long absence he'd grown fond of his family since their return, especially his aunt Sorcha, who had scooped him up like a son after his mother passed. He had learned to respect their ways and even found value in some of them, like having his funeral. He knew what he needed to do; he just wasn't ready to do it.

Roy pulled her close. It felt so good to hold her. "I'll talk to the family. I'll tell them you aren't going to wear the dress."

A tear rolled down her cheek. "You would do that?"

"I'd do anything for you."

She paused, distracted, momentarily somewhere else. Then she clinched her fists at her sides and looked him sternly in the eyes. "I'm going to wear the dress."

"But you said –"

"I want to wear it. I've decided to wear the dress."

"Yoo-hoo!" a sweet voice sang out from behind them. "I'm so glad I caught you both."

Roy turned around to see Claudette Twittlebottom – as wide as she was tall, hair flipped out at the ends, a bright pink scarf tied around her neck, and the owner of the new high-end gift shop – eyeing him in a way that he almost considered inappropriate.

Claudette had clearly had no idea what was coming when she put down roots in Coraloo. Like the new cafe, neither the Blackwells nor the Tofts approved of her imported gift cards and luxury dishware, insisting sweet little Claudette would take their business. A representative from each family had shown up at Roy's desk asking to have her evicted for disturbing the peace, to which he'd responded that hanging a large canopy of pink balloons over the door did not constitute disturbing the peace. Roy had to hand it to her – she was a fighter. Claudette was always coming up with new ways to draw in the tourists.

"I don't know why I wasn't invited to your little shindig up on the hill. Anyhoo… I just thought I'd drop by and bring you two some little somethings from the shop," she said, inching her way closer. "Just some sweeties and my Jubilee Jam." She handed Roy a basket of jars with the packaged sweets in the middle. "No charge."

"That's nice of you Ms... erm..." Roy took the gift, stepping back from her.

She smelled like roses and mothballs.

"You can just call me Claudette."

"All right, then. Thanks for the... erm..."

"Sweeties."

"Yes, the sweeties. Thank you, Claudette."

Once Claudette was out of earshot, he turned to Margarette. "Where were we?"

She looked better now, more relaxed.

"I should be going. I need to run by Sylvia's. I'll see you at the cafe. Seven?"

He kissed her on the forehead. "Seven."

Roy stepped inside the municipal building, set Mrs Twittlebottom's basket down behind the desk, and looked at the empty cells, remembering only a week or so ago when he and Margarette had sat there celebrating their engagement, just the two of them, free of any wedding plans and unsolved cases.

At that moment, the phone rang. Roy answered. "Coraloo Police... Slow down, Earl. You've got a lead on the recipe? I'll be right over!" He hung up the phone, leaving the sweeties and the disheveled cells for later.

Three streets over, Margarette sat in an empty salon chair using her clipping scissors to dissect Sylvia's stack of outdated magazines. She didn't even know what she was clipping, and she hadn't checked the back of a single one of them. *Poor nameless faces... Clip, clip, clip.* She felt foggy and confused.

She had done it. She'd been thinking about it all day at school, and when the dismissal bell rang she'd marched right over to the Coraloo Municipal Building without putting another thought to it, expecting to sit down at Roy's desk and tell him exactly how she felt about the dress. But he had been outside... on a ladder. And she'd had to wait while Roy sorted out the affairs of Ms Brimble and Norvel Poteet. Looking up at him she'd begun to wonder why she'd even come. Margarette hated arguments or confrontations of any kind. But despite her aversion to conflict, disrupting the family peace seemed to be what she was best at these days. What had she thought she was walking into? For a moment she'd almost walked away, but when the path became clear she had done it. She'd told him exactly how she felt about the dress.

The way he'd looked at her. The way he'd held her. He'd said he would do anything for her.

She dropped her head back against the edge of the padded chair. She'd said she would wear it. She'd told him she would wear the dress. What happened? That wasn't the plan.

Sylvia paused between hair rollers, having almost covered Margarette's whole head. "I'm almost done here."

"It's all right. I was just coming in for a wash and blow-dry, anyway. Thought it might calm me down a bit."

"What's going on? Is it man trouble?"

Margarette could feel the ladies lifting the vintage dryers off their heads, leaning in from their kitchen tables, and pausing their games of Euchre as if Margarette was about to jump up and shout, *Not anymore! I've finally come to my senses. I've decided to marry The Butcher... I mean... the mortician!*

"I'm tired, that's all."

A collective "um-hum" passed around the room.

"I think I'll head back out. I've got some errands to run before I meet Roy for dinner." She hoped they'd all heard.

"Have you found your dress yet?" one of the aunts asked, wearing a sheepish grin.

Wait... Did they know about the dress? How did they know about the dress? Margarette scowled at Sylvia, who pretended to be lost in intense concentration as she squeezed permanent solution onto a cousin's rollers. Sylvia knew everything.

"Yes," she answered honestly. "As a matter of fact, I do have a dress."

"How was the blessing?" another asked, inciting more giggles.

Another jab. Wouldn't they like to know?

If the old biddies wanted to play this game of "Let's See How Far We Can Push Margarette", then she'd play back.

"Absolutely lovely."

"Did you see old Innis at the market?" Sylvia asked.

"Old Innis?"

"Cousin Innis," Sylvia said, correcting herself.

"Do you mean Innis Wilkinson, the cleaning lady? She's a Toft? How did I not know this?"

"We don't talk about her much."

Margarette was shocked, not so much that the Toft ladies hadn't talked much about a family member, but at the glaring reality that Innis Wilkinson was a distant cousin.

"I heard Innis abandoned the family... ran away," one of them added.

"I heard it was that Wilkinson boy who made her that way... you know, *different*."

"I heard she wears those scissors because she thinks she's protecting them from something."

"I heard she was born during the festival."

"You mean she's marked too?"

All eyes were now on Margarette.

"I'm not marked!" Margarette discreetly put her clipping scissors back in her purse for fear the ladies would begin to make some sort of deeper connection between her and her scissor-wearing cousin. No one had ever mentioned Cousin Innis to her before... Never. Margarette half-thought they were making up the family connection in another attempt to woo her into the arms of anyone other than Roy. She wouldn't put it past them.

"They say she could have been traveling around the world with a celebrity by now. Instead she's working as a janitor with that husband of hers. It just goes to show what happens when you don't marry well."

That's it. I've had it! Margarette thought, fuming at the Toft ladies' thinly veiled insults. If being "marked" meant marrying for love over money, for virtue over family name, then she was more than happy with the label. *Better to be marked than to be a Toft!*

CHAPTER 19

The first floor of the municipal building was busy. The Wilkinson case occupied Roy's thoughts and the missing recipe filled his once-empty prison cells. He'd had two more arrests that morning for public intoxication, both parties swearing they hadn't touched a drop. Roy had taken time to thoroughly investigate all the booths for possible distributors and was keeping a close eye on *the others*, who now included a puppeteer, an origamist, and a family of celebrity impersonators. Earl Fox-McGoggins's call had been a bust. A false lead. Roy should have known better than to follow the man to Mayor Hennigan's, only to have Earl confess that he might have left the museum unlocked, but still had serious suspicions about the mayor. Roy was not a bit pleased he'd canceled his dinner plans with Margarette to pursue Earl's misleading accusation.

Roy checked the clock on the wall. He had a few minutes before it was time to head over to the cake tasting. The Wilkinson file lay open on his desk, and beneath it the case of the stolen recipe. He thumbed through the pages again. He just couldn't imagine old Wilkinson murdering anyone.

Roy picked up the phone and dialed the state detective, hoping his old university roommate was working today.

There was a "hello" at the other end of the line.

"Henry? It's Roy! How goes it…? And the family…? How old is she now…? Before you know it you'll be marrying her off. Yep, getting married in a few weeks… No, she's not crazy. Blind, maybe… I wouldn't say I'm busy…" Roy leaned back in his chair, feet up on the desk. "Same old, same old… Keeping the peace… I'm staying healthy. A few aches and pains, but nothing to worry about. You know how it is… Promotion! You don't say…? Well, congrats… Sure, sure… I'm up for a celebration…"

Roy sighed, listening to Henry ramble on about his recent promotion. He dropped his feet down and sat up in his chair. Even if he found the recipe and solved the Wilkinson case there would be no promotion in Roy's future. This was it. Constable of Coraloo.

"Right, the reason I called… So, I'm calling in that favor. It's an old case, but I was wondering if you wouldn't mind looking into it. Case number is 9453 and the name is Wilkinson… Married to an Innis Wilkinson. If you don't mind digging into it a bit more for me, I'd sure appreciate it… Congrats again… Right… Good talking to you."

The call ended. Roy stared down at the woman in the photo, taking in the hair, the round face, and the big eyes. No wonder she looked familiar. Innis Wilkinson was a Toft. A Toft working for the Blackwells. In her younger years she could have been Margarette's twin. But how in the world had the Blackwells come to employ a Toft, not to mention a murder suspect?

His hearty laugh echoed over the chatter of occupied cells. The Blackwells had a Toft working for them and were none the wiser. Granny Blackwell would roll in her grave if she knew – she'd think the Tofts had planted her there to gather confidential market secrets.

Roy pulled out a blank notepad from his desk drawer and wrote: "Innis Toft – ask Margarette."

Roy paced up and down the bakery, noting the vintage black-and-white photographs of elegantly dressed brides decorating the black-and-white striped walls. He leaned in closer to the first photograph and then walked over to the next. These women weren't from Coraloo as far as he knew – by the looks of the photographs, they were movie stars and royalty – but he recognized the room and the scrolling newel post one of the brides was resting her gloved hand upon. It was exactly like the one in front of him that led to the living quarters upstairs. He wondered if the space had once been home to a photographer.

Interesting.

He continued to walk the perimeter of the room, anxiously awaiting Margarette's arrival. A metal table and pair of chairs had been painted gold, adorned with a vase of green flowers Roy had never encountered before, and placed in front of the curtained storefront window. The owners of the pastry shop were newcomers – a brother and sister who claimed to have ancestral roots in Coraloo. As far as anyone knew they had yet to reveal which side of the feud they belonged to. It was quite possible they belonged to neither as a handful of families unrelated to the Tofts and Blackwells had settled in the valley below the hill in the town's early days, or at least that was what Margarette had explained.

He peeked around the store's stairwell, noticing a small door on the other side. It occurred to him that someone could be hiding a brewing operation in the basement. He'd have to keep an eye on this brother and sister combo.

Behind a display case of icing-topped cupcakes, fruit tarts, chocolate-dipped Madeleines, and other assorted sweets, a presentation of large cakes lined heavy wooden shelves at the back of the shop. Roy wondered about these cakes. How long had they been standing there? What were they made of to allow them to be on show for so long? What would a year-old cake even taste like?

He checked his watch, then looked over at the door. She was late. What if she'd forgotten? He knew better. She hadn't forgotten. He'd had to cancel dinner, explaining he had a lead on a case.

"You're working a case? In Coraloo?"

"Actually, I'm working two."

"Are you serious? That's so exciting! Wait… should I be afraid for your safety?"

Roy laughed. "Hardly, but you might be able to help me with something. We can talk about it tomorrow at the cake thing."

"Hey, stranger."

Roy spun around. He pulled her in close and kissed her on the forehead. "Hey yourself. Did you have a good day at school?"

"I won't until this festival's over. My students are bonkers!"

"They're not the only ones who've gone bonkers." He lowered his voice to a whisper. "I had to arrest Norvel for public intoxication and indecent exposure."

"What? *Norvel?* Gross!"

"He tried to show that grandmother I arrested at the market where he wanted to put his tattoo."

"All right, you win! You're definitely dealing with more craziness than I am." Margarette laughed.

It was good to see her laughing, looking more like herself – the way she was before the stress of wedding planning had taken over.

"Miss Toft?" A tall, elegant woman, her hair pulled back into a neat ponytail and a white apron attached to her thin waist, wiped a bit of flour off her chin with the back of her hand and smiled at the two.

"Yes," Margarette answered, approaching the counter. "I called about a tasting."

"Please, have a seat. I'll be right back with the cakes."

Roy pulled out the gold cafe chair, gently pushing it back in as Margarette sat. The woman disappeared behind a swinging door, then reappeared with a large tray of miniature cakes. If this was wedding planning, he'd happily do it every day, but Roy guessed that this didn't even scratch the surface of everything Margarette had been handling.

"Did any of your family see you come in?" Roy asked.

"I don't think so. Yours?"

"Hope not. Aunt Sorcha would have my head for this one."

They had agreed to purchase their wedding cake from the new bakery, Torte di Jami. Seeing as the ladies of both the Toft and Blackwell families had told their representative parties they would be making the wedding cake, Roy and Margarette had decided to go with neither. The Blackwells were talented at many things, but since the passing of Granny Blackwell cake constructing was not their strong point. It tasted good, but Roy had once nearly swallowed a toothpick sampling a slice. Margarette, on the other hand, said the Tofts had the opposite problem. They constructed some of the most beautiful cakes she had ever seen, but Eleanor Toft, known as the baker in the family, had a secret ingredient Margarette said was not altogether legal.

"You said you were working a couple of cases. That's so exciting!"

It was exciting, and he was glad she thought so. He wanted to ask her about Innis but decided he'd better ease his way into it, so he told her about the other case first.

"The recipe was stolen from the Historical Society."

"Wait… not *the* recipe."

He nodded.

"Do you think it was one of *the others*? Surely not someone local. Wait a minute… You don't think it was Pastor Donaldson, do you?"

"I've already spoken to him and a handful of others who all said the same thing… No drinking."

"But that doesn't make sense."

"You're telling me."

"And the other case?"

Roy knew that Margarette already had enough on her mind. But she had asked… "How much do you know about –?" he began.

The woman returned, setting in front of them a silver tray of simply decorated mini-cakes, pointing at each one. "We have lemon chiffon, red velvet, Italian crème, chocolate-hazelnut, pistachio, ginger rum, Bananas Foster, and key lime. These work best as a wedding cake."

"You mean you have *more* flavors?" Margarette asked.

The woman tucked her hands into the pockets of her skirt. "My brother can pretty much make whatever you like. I'm just here for a job. But these are his bestsellers."

"So business is good?"

"Excellent, actually." She pulled two cards out of her pocket, placing one in front of Roy and the other in front of Margarette. "You can mark the ones you like, and if something unique comes to mind, please don't hesitate to ask. He loves a challenge. Speaking of… I should get back to see if he could use a hand. So if you need anything, I'll be in the back."

She winked at Roy, then returned through the double doors.

"Do you know her?" Margarette asked.

171

"Not really. I haven't been able to keep up with all the new faces in town, but she seems nice. Why don't we invite her to the wedding? That will really stir the pot." Roy stuck his fork into a mini-cake neatly labeled with a triangular flag. Lemon. Lemon was always his favorite. The icing was smooth, not gritty, and the cake had a bit of a zing that lingered in his mouth.

Margarette stared at him. "Well, what do you think?"

"This is the one. This is it!"

"But you haven't tried any of the others."

"Doesn't matter. This is quite possibly the best cake I have ever tasted in my entire life!"

Margarette stuck her fork into the cake. She closed her eyes, chewed, and then swallowed. "Wow! It's so... The flavor is so... I don't know what to say. But it's not our cake."

"It's not?"

"Not yet... What if there's another flavor that's even more incredible and we miss out on it because we didn't even bother trying the others? He made us all these beautiful cakes. We can't let them go to waste."

"Good point." Roy stuck his fork into another cake and took a bite. He grinned, dropping his fork on the table and tossing his hands up in the air. "This is it. *This* is our cake. It's like banana pudding, but it's a cake. It's so good." All thoughts of the lemon cake disappeared.

Margarette followed his nudging. She made a face. "Nope. It's yummy, but it's not our wedding cake."

He tried again and again, his belly filling and his mind a little foggy from all of the sugar. There was no way he would be able to eat dinner.

"How about this one?" he said, holding up a fork of red cake.

"No red velvet. It'll look like someone murdered the cake."

Roy made a face and flicked the cake off his fork. There was one left. "All right," he said. "You go first this time."

Margarette stuck her fork in, lifting out a cake of brilliant green. With her mouth full, she garbled, "I don't know if the sugar is getting to me, but this... *This*..." She pulled the cake closer and took another bite, then another.

"Didn't your mother ever teach you to share?" He pulled the cake away from her and stabbed a hunk with his fork.

She pulled it back and took another bite. "Have you met my mother?"

He frowned. "Oh, right."

Roy swallowed the bite of cake. The creamy icing melted in his mouth, the lime evoking images of summers spent wading through creeks. "*This* is the one."

Margarette forked another bite of cake. "Yes. This *is* the one."

A sureness fell over Roy. A sense of accomplishment and contribution to their forthcoming nuptials. "Is this how you feel every time you check something off that list of yours?"

She wiped a splotch of icing off her cheek. "Full? No."

"So what else can I do? I want to help."

"You can tell me about that other case. Is it something I can help *you* with?" she asked, scraping up the remains of the key lime cake. She had held tight to the wedding plans and now was changing the subject.

"You have a cousin, Innis."

Margarette lifted her eyes. "How did *you* know she was my cousin? I only just found that out myself. And what does she have to do with the case?"

"I spoke with her the other day."

A looked passed over Margarette's face that he could not quite interpret. "You did? And she said she was my cousin?" She breathed in heavily, then exhaled.

"No… Bill Shepherd told me."

"So the case is about her? You've got my full attention, Roy Blackwell."

"What can you tell me about her?"

"Honestly, I really don't know anything about her." She changed the subject again, forking the remaining bite of red velvet. "Let's talk about something more interesting… like cake! So the lime cake it is. I'll tell her we've made up our minds. Nothing too fancy; we'll keep it plain. Sound good?"

"Sure. So this cousin of yours –"

"Honestly, Roy, you probably know as much as I do… if not more."

Margarette had said she wanted to be honest about the dress, but why did he feel as though she wasn't being honest about Innis? The Tofts knew everything about everyone, especially those in their family. It was highly unlikely that he knew more about Innis Wilkinson than Margarette. Roy had an unsettling suspicion the Tofts were hiding something about Innis Wilkinson. And so was Margarette.

CHAPTER 20

Margarette stepped into the Coraloo Flea Market for the third time that month, thoughts of the Bella Fottasi, her wasted phone call, and the Blackwell dress preoccupying her. She had told Roy it smelled, and then for some reason she had emphatically told him she was going to wear it. So that was that: she would wear it. She had to. Margarette sighed. At least she could check the cake off her list; thankfully Coraloo's local shops did not have a year-long waiting list like the dress shop in the city.

She took a deep breath and reminded herself the Blackwell ladies were about to become family – before long this would all be over and she would be one of them. *One of them. No longer a Toft.* For a moment she felt unsettled, oddly unsure – not about Roy of course, but about leaving the family, as Toft-y as they were. They were still her family. Surely they wouldn't disown her. She'd still be able to sit at Sylvia's and attend the morning service, wouldn't she? There was no sign outside that forbade Blackwells from entering the salon, but she wouldn't put it past the ladies to encourage Sylvia to have one installed.

Margarette had told her mother the Blackwells were throwing a household shower, to which her mother had made a snide comment about the Blackwells not knowing what one would need in a house because none of them lived in one. Then her tone had suddenly shifted and delight spread across her face as she announced she would throw Margarette a *personal shower*. At first Margarette had cringed at the idea of the Toft ladies gifting her with intimates, but there was no stopping a Toft, so she agreed.

Anna Sue Toft had decorated the room in a smattering of pinks and golds, elegant next to the dark hardwoods of Margarette's childhood home, taking on a romantic, vintage boudoir feel. Margarette loved it. Her mother couldn't have planned it more perfectly.

The women – cousins, aunts, and great-aunts – sat in a circle beside the fireplace, Sinatra playing in the background. The ladies were dressed for tea except for Sylvia, who was experimenting with a new look – dreadlocks. A wedding portrait of Margarette's mother and father hung above the stone fireplace. Above the portrait hung the family crest – a red shield held up by two crown-wearing long-eared hares, one on each side, and at the center of the crest, a large dahlia with the phrase "Audentes fortuna iuvat" scrolled beneath. Fortune favors the bold. A few of the Toft boys had the crest tattooed on their biceps. Sylvia had it tattooed on her lower back. It was what Margarette wanted – the marriage, not the tattoo. A long-lasting, for better or worse, for Blackwell or for Toft kind of marriage.

The finger foods, crepes, tartlets, fresh fruits, and pastries added to the morning. To Margarette's relief Anna Sue had foregone any games. Margarette had always found games a little tedious; this was one thing she and Roy did not have in common. Having been a bachelor for so long he had developed a routine of playing cards at the tavern with his mother before she passed. He continued to occasionally play with Charlie Price and Roy's cousin Stephen. Margarette figured she really should consider learning a game or two.

The gift wrappings were as spectacular as the event itself. Oh, how Margarette wished the wedding would go off as smoothly. She had to hand it to her mother. Under different circumstances – that is, if she were marrying a Toft – Margarette would have been thrilled to have her help sort out all the wedding details.

Margarette carefully untied the ribbon from around the first package. She lifted the lid and folded the tissue back.

"Really, Mother?" Margarette held the familiar lacy negligee by its two skimpy straps.

Anna Sue winked at her. "It's the one we saw in the city."

The cousins giggled, the aunts declared it lovely, and one of the great-aunts made an inappropriate comment about Roy. Margarette had been to enough showers to know what was expected, so she smiled and nodded graciously.

The next two gifts were much the same, skimpy and lacy, with explanations like: "That one's not for sleeping", "Does it come with an instruction manual?", and "How would one even put it on?"

Anna Sue stepped to her side. "This one's from Aunt Pearl."

Aunt Pearl sat hunched over, her hands shaking. "Aunt Pearl..." Anna Sue raised her voice. "Aunt Pearl! Meggy's opening your gift."

Aunt Pearl whispered something to the woman beside her. The woman's face soured, but then she forced a smile. She looked up at Margarette as if to speak, then shook her head.

"Did you tell her about the cucumber patch?" Aunt Pearl asked, loud enough for Margarette to hear. "They'll die," the old woman said to the cousin beside her. "Every single one of them."

Of all the Toft superstitions this one was the worst. Margarette didn't need to be told about the cucumber patch. She'd heard about it since the day she'd turned twelve – as if hearing it on your twelfth birthday was some sort of Toft rite of passage. Not that it mattered. None of the Toft ladies grew anything in their gardens that was even vaguely edible. But of course Margarette would never say such a thing to a woman who wholeheartedly believed that if she walked through a cucumber patch before her wedding night she would ruin the entire crop. Where did they come up with this stuff?

"Did you tell her?" the old woman asked again.

Anna Sue jumped in. "Aunt Pearl, she's opening your gift. Don't you want to watch?"

Margarette proceeded to untie the package, then lift the lid off the box. She stared at the contents, forgetting to smile. Had Aunt

Pearl gifted her a bundle of blue tulle? She lifted the item out of the box, realizing that what she held in her hands was some sort of long, sheer nightgown. It smelled of mothballs and crinkled as she moved it.

The ladies gasped, shaking their heads as if fighting back the tears. Margarette was confused, but the other women in attendance knew exactly what Margarette had been gifted:

"I heard she was going to give it to her."

"It's gorgeous!"

"Will you look at that?"

"Does Aunt Pearl know she's marrying a Blackwell?"

Margarette found her smile. "Thank you, Aunt Pearl."

"Did she open it?" the aunt asked.

"She did," the woman beside her answered.

"I wore it on my wedding night. You can wear it on yours. Thomas will like it."

Another round of whispers filled the living room:

"She doesn't know."

"Should we tell her?"

"Heavens no! It would kill her."

"Maybe we should take it back. Sylvia may want to wear it one day."

Margarette crammed the nightgown back in the box, trying not to think about the last time it had been worn, or the fact that Aunt Pearl had mentioned the man Margarette had once intended to marry... her ex-fiancé Thomas.

"Does anyone want another petit four?" her mother asked, deliberately changing the subject. Margarette would thank her later.

"Did someone get her a broom?" another aunt asked.

Every Toft knew that a new house meant a new broom. It was bad luck to bring the old dirt into a new house.

"It's not that kind of shower, Aunt Celia," Sylvia said, twisting at one of her attempted dreads.

178

Margarette inhaled the scents of the Coraloo Flea Market once again: spices, lavender, leather, and cedarwood. At the center of the market, standing on a very tall ladder changing a lightbulb in one of the tinkling chandeliers, was the woman with the scissors around her neck. Innis Wilkinson.

It was as if she had suddenly taken up residence in Margarette's life. One day she was just an anonymous woman pushing a cleaning cart up the hill and the next she was a family member – Margarette's cousin – whose identity as a Toft seemed to be common knowledge to everyone but her; even Roy seemed to know all about her. She'd not had time to process all she'd heard about Innis at Sylvia's when Roy had brought it up. Normally a mysterious family member would have piqued her interest and sent her on a scavenger hunt for missing links and holes in her own family history. But she didn't want to go down that road. Maybe she was afraid of what he'd have said – a coincidental piece to the puzzle demonstrating just how alike Innis and Margarette actually were. For a moment she imagined herself with her clipping scissors tied around her neck with a piece of Aunt Sorcha's homemade ribbon.

Margarette waved at the woman who looked as much a Toft as any of the other women in the family, but Innis did not wave back. She supposed that strangeness ran in families, like wrinkles and strong fingernails. Maybe bad decisions did, too. Was she so very different from Innis? The ladies said Innis had married the wrong man – a clear warning to Margarette to avoid the same fate. In their minds she should have married Thomas; she had made the wrong decision there, and marrying Roy would confirm their suspicions and mark her as another "Innis": a Toft who had married badly. But Margarette had known in her heart of hearts that Thomas was not "the one". Not like Roy Blackwell; he was the right fit, she was sure of it.

Margarette glanced back up at Innis – busy, focused, and for some reason distant from the rest of the family. Maybe she and Innis were more alike than she'd wanted to admit.

Clover had said to meet out back. Margarette pushed through the rear doors and found herself looking at rows of campervans, RVs, and trailers: big ones, small ones, roundish ones, and one painted oddly like a rooster. These were the Blackwells' homes. The rooster appeared as if it hadn't been lived in for months. Wreaths of wilted flowers lay on the top and tall blades of grass were doing their best to hide the wheels of the moveable home. But the other mobile dwellings were well maintained like a quaint, coiffed village on the top of the hill.

"Hey there," she called to a small boy carrying a live chicken nearly twice his size. "I'm here for the shower. Do you know where I'm supposed to go?"

"Nah, I took a bath yesterday. Mom says once a day's enough, but sometimes I have to do it more. I'm going to give Sprinkles a bath. Wanna watch? You can hold him down for me while I spray him off with the water hose."

"Have you ever given Sprinkles a bath before?"

"No, but he smells real bad. And I thought if he smelled better Mom wouldn't make us eat him for dinner."

"Oh... Well –"

"Margarette!"

She whipped around to see Clover walking toward her. She was partly relieved, though curious to see how the whole chicken-bathing event would turn out.

"We're out back, next to the garden. Did you walk here?"

Margarette had, in fact, chosen to walk, as it was a beautiful rain-free day. The sky was bright and blue with a spattering of puffed white clouds. The early afternoon was cool in the shade and warm in the sun, as summer steadily made its way to Coraloo.

"I did. Thank you for doing this. I feel like you've all given me so much." Images of her wearing the Blackwell dress flashed into Margarette's mind. "I mean with the blessing and all."

"If there's one thing you need to learn it's that the Blackwells celebrate everything."

She followed Clover past the rolling homes to a massive and oddly ornate garden surrounded by an orchard of apples, apricots, and plums. Long tables, like the ones she had seen at the blessing, lay beneath a pergola of gauzy white.

Margarette's stomach churned and her heart raced. She suddenly felt unwell, anxious maybe. Where was Roy's book when she needed it? She was immediately overtaken by the greetings and warm hugs of the Blackwell women, which added to the unwelcome nausea and onset of nerves. She found herself in a sea of smiling Blackwells, and all of the older ones looked the same. She tried hard to keep face for the sake of these women who had lovingly gifted her a family heirloom that she wanted to throw off the other side of the hill in the hope that it blew away to some foreign country, where it would be sacrificed to the god of ugliness – the one Margarette had foolishly professed she would wear. She felt alone… suddenly a stranger at her own party, even though they had blessed her, rubbed her feet, and fixed her hair. They knew her, but she hardly knew them. A stack of presents sat atop a table off to one side – most likely towels, possibly a toaster, and a few other new things she didn't really need but would be happy to replace in her cottage. But judging by the size of the gifts, there was certainly no broom. Thankfully, the Blackwells didn't seem to care about things like new brooms.

Margarette felt faint and a bit wobbly. Maybe she needed to eat.

She had never made it to this point in her engagement to Thomas. In fact, she hadn't even opened her notebook. She'd called the wedding off two days after he'd proposed.

"Give it time," her mother had said. "Love is an emotion. It's not reality."

But Margarette had known better. As handsome and successful as he was, he wasn't the right fit.

The Blackwell ladies talked of life and love, of marriage, and of how most of them had birthed their wedding night "miracles" nine months after they'd said, "I do". Then, somewhere between her fifth and sixth bite of cake – which wasn't nearly as bad as Roy had said it would be – one of the aunts brought up Margarette's uncanny resemblance to the market's cleaning lady.

What is so fascinating about this woman that everyone suddenly wants to talk about her?

181

"I've heard stories about her," Aunt Moira said. "Townsfolk said she was a real looker in her early years. Good thing she didn't make a play for any of our men."

"I'm glad she didn't snag *my* Blackwell," another aunt proclaimed.

"She thinks we don't know she's a Toft… but we know," Aunt Moira said.

There was a brief pause and a glance at Margarette. Was it a glance of pity? Or a glance that said, "We'll let you stay, too."

"Poor thing's family disowned her when her father ran off."

The Tofts had disowned Innis? The cousins had failed to share that well-kept family secret. The Tofts were throwing Margarette parties and forcing their way into the wedding plans, yet they were still hoping she'd marry someone else. What would happen when she actually did marry Roy? Would she be ostracized from her family just as Innis had been before her? The Tofts were kooky, for sure, but she couldn't imagine life without them.

"She's lost something up top," someone else said. "I feel sorry for her. There are tales about her. Strange tales."

The question came out of her mouth before she could stop it. "What kind of tales?"

The women stared at her, as if she should have already known the answer to her own question. She couldn't very well own up to the fact that she had only just learned Innis was a relation and that her soon-to-be husband was interrogating Margarette for information about Innis that she didn't have. So she sat there fidgeting, twisting the engagement ring back and forth on her finger, still in shock that she – the historian – hadn't even realized she and Innis were related.

"She vanished. Disappeared for years," one of them said. "And when she came back she wasn't the same. Wouldn't talk to nobody…"

But Roy had talked to her.

"Something happened to that woman," someone else added. "Something the Tofts are keeping to themselves."

Margarette shifted in her seat, feeling torn between family loyalty and curiosity.

"Anyone for more cake?" Clover asked.

Margarette was grateful for the change of subject.

A slew of Blackwell hands went up. The shower – and the cake – carried on around Margarette, but she wasn't there – her mind lost somewhere between her scissor-toting, wrongly married, Toft-disowned cousin, and the fact that in less than two weeks she was going to be a Blackwell, yet she didn't have the dress she wanted to wear. Was there possibly another reason she hadn't found the dress? Was she holding back? Had she intentionally put it off? No… that couldn't be it.

And then there was the uncomfortable ordinariness of the shower, as if the Blackwells were trying to accommodate her Toft-ish-ness. She needed the oddness – the quirkiness of the blessing and nearly everything else the Blackwells did – to take her away from reality. This was too familiar. Too normal.

A horrid sense of doubt swept over Margarette. Her heart raced. She felt dizzy. She needed to go. To leave. To think. To rest.

Margarette leaned over to Clover, who was busy writing down the last item she had opened along with the name of the gifter. "I don't feel well."

"Oh! Can I get you something? Water?"

Yes, water. That might help. She nodded, then everything went dark.

From some distant place, she heard, "Fetch Roy!"

Then a different voice asking, "Do you think she's pregnant?"

And another, "I told you we weren't feeding her enough."

Margarette could have opened her eyes if she'd wanted to. But she didn't. She wanted to sleep, to hide for just a few minutes until the voices in her head and the worried chatter around her ceased.

Roy had promised he would be there to help her carry the shower gifts back down the hill. They'd planned to sort through them together. He had wanted to see everything she'd received at the Toft shower, too, but Margarette had refused.

The market had run its course for the day. The vendors had packed up and the stores had closed, creating a quiet Sunday afternoon emptiness in the market. Roy secretly hoped to catch a glimpse of Wilkin, but instead he saw Innis climbing down the ladder, shaking slightly. Having once seen a kid hospitalized from a fall, Roy jogged over to the ladder and held it tight until Innis was safely at the bottom.

"Thank you," she said.

He looked closely at her. She didn't seem nearly as aged as he had first assumed. She lowered her head and looked away.

He saw his chance to get the answers he wanted, but she spoke first.

"Do you have any more questions for me, Constable Blackwell?"

There was something different about her. Was it confidence? Was she posturing after their last brief conversation? Or was she hiding the information he sought, something that might shed light on the mysterious file of Wilkin Wilkinson?

He tried to remember what he'd wanted to ask her, but the words would not form.

"Well then, if there's nothing more…" Innis pushed her cart and began to walk away.

"Mrs Wilkinson!"

She stopped and turned back. "Mr Blackwell, is there something you need? I have things to attend to."

The doors at the back of the market burst open. One of Roy's aunts was running toward him, arms flailing. He never quite knew what to make of his aunts. For all he knew they were just trying to make him stop talking to Innis.

"It looks like there are things you need to attend to as well." Innis began to push her cart away again.

"Wait! Do you know Margarette?" Why had he asked that? Margarette had said she didn't know Innis well. Did he think she'd lied? She wouldn't… But Innis was part of her family.

"No, I don't. Should I?"

Roy was confused. "Margarette Toft. You're family."

She looked up at him with a hard stare. "I'm not a Toft, Mr Blackwell. I'm a Wilkinson. Do you understand?"

He didn't, not really. But there was something in her tone. Was it animosity? Resentment?

"We're getting married, Margarette and I," he said.

"Congratulations." She turned back toward the cart.

"Her family doesn't approve." He paused, wondering whether the next part would be a step too far. "Is that what happened to you, Mrs Wilkinson? Is that why you don't talk to the family... because you married Wilkin?"

The question was in there somewhere, but he couldn't quite get it out. Did the Tofts know Wilkin was a murderer?

She stared over at the Blackwell woman running toward them. "What do you want, Mr Blackwell? I don't have time to discuss my relationship, or lack thereof, with my family."

Roy was already on shaky ground, but he wanted to gain her trust in case he had the opportunity to speak with her again. "I was wondering if you would mind talking to her... to Margarette." His stomach knotted again. This could go terribly wrong. "There's an event next weekend, sort of a ladies' night. I thought it might be nice for you to stop in, as a friendly face... to give her a word of encouragement." What was he thinking? Surely Margarette would wonder why Innis Wilkinson had suddenly shown up at her night-before party.

She eyed him curiously. "I usually don't carry on in that way, Mr Blackwell. And I assume that my... family... will be there?"

Of course they'd be there. He dodged the question. "You've been married awhile, haven't you?" He hadn't known where he was going with the conversation when he'd started out, but he was quite pleased with the way it was ending.

"I have, yes. Marriage is important to me, Mr Blackwell."

"She could use someone to talk to... someone who understands."

Innis looked back at the woman who had finally made her way over to Roy, hands on her thighs, out of breath, and trying to speak.

"I'll think about it, Mr Blackwell," Innis said. "Tend to your family for now." With that she pushed her empty cart away.

"Just take a deep breath," Roy said, turning to his aunt. "What are you trying to tell me?"

185

"Oh, Lord help us! She's gone! Oh, such a young woman! Such a young bride! Oh, Roy! Oh, Roy!" The woman fell on him, hands over her eyes, weeping.

Bride. Gone. Margarette?

"Has something happened to Margarette? What's happened? Where is she?"

"Oh, she's gone! Without even having a proper funeral!"

His heart dropped. His stomach came up into his throat. "No... I have to see her! This can't be right. Where is she?"

The woman pointed to the open double doors. "In the garden."

Roy sprinted back to the Blackwell compound and into the garden, where Margarette was sitting up in a chair, a younger Blackwell massaging her shoulders while another placed cold rags on her forehead.

She looked up. "Roy? What are you doing here?"

His chest tightened and he forced out the words, "I thought you were dead."

CHAPTER 21

May 11, 1976

Innis Toft walked proudly, her arm linked with Jean-Michel's. She wore a yellow sundress of her own design, made especially for their first official date, with the scissors, sharpened that morning, gleaming around her neck. The Heaken Beaver Festival was in its second week. On the stage where Jean-Michel had performed earlier in the week a reenactment of the town's controversial and highly debated founding was coming to a close with the portrayal of an epic tavern brawl that started over a pair of shoes.

To her right a line of locals waited to try their arm at Throw the Shoe in the Cider – a traditional festival game in homage to the Blackwell family, most of whom had left the town long ago, though a few remained as high-ranking employees – mostly management but also a few designers – at the shoe factory. The rest were a nomadic clan of artisans, traveling from town to town, settling for a year or two to sell their wares before moving on. The few who remained must have been too preoccupied with the failing factory to dispute the Tofts' dramatic interpretation of the town's founding, as the performance ended with a Toft standing with one foot on a Blackwell's head, waving a pair of shoes victoriously in the air.

Innis didn't care about the age-old feud. Her mother had only been a Toft by marriage, and when the family forgot her Innis had chosen to forget them as well. She could hear the whispers as they walked by:

"Look at the seamstress with that actor."

"You know who she is, don't you? That's the dressmaker's daughter."

"Young Innis? You don't say!"

"Whatever happened to her mother?"

"She died."

"How sad."

"Yes, very sad."

"But look at her now."

"She's glowing."

"They're a good match."

"Yes, a fine match."

"You know her mother made that famous actress's dress, don't you?"

"Her mother would be so proud if she could see her now."

"Turns out she's a Toft after all."

Innis was unable to hide her smile. For the first time in years the town noticed her... The Tofts noticed her. Her *family* noticed her. It was as if she'd stepped out of the darkness and into the light of Coraloo. She highly doubted the onlookers really knew her mother. But now they knew *her*. Not that it mattered. She was going away – away to see the world. With him. With Jean-Michel – perfect, exotic, talented, successful, handsome Jean-Michel. And she was never coming back.

The crowd erupted with applause under the red-and-white bunting as the actors left the stage.

Jean-Michel leaned in close to her; she could feel his breath on her ear. "I'm better than they are."

Captivated by his presence, she simply replied, "I know."

The mayor of Coraloo, Lawrence Hennigan, stepped into the center of the stage. "And now it's time to crown our Heaken Beaver Queen. If all the eligible ladies would please make their way onto the stage."

Innis stood still, watching as the town's unwed ladies followed his cue... those whose skirts she had hemmed and buttons she had repaired... those she'd watched outside the ice cream parlor... those she saw, but who never saw her.

As if he'd heard her thoughts, Jean-Michel kissed her on the back of her hand and said, "Let them see my girl shine!"

My girl... She was his girl.

He escorted her up onto the stage and twirled her around, to the applause of those gathered. Then he walked over to the center of the platform, bowed, and waved, casting a theatrical eye out over the onlookers before whisking himself off the stage. The crowd erupted into cheers once again.

His girl.

One after another the girls approached the microphone and stated their names. Innis's eyes were on Jean-Michel. He blew her a kiss. The women to each side of Innis accepted his gesture as if the endearment had been meant for them. A collective swoon swept through the ladies in the audience, with the exception of a few Toft cousins Innis had not seen since childhood, eyeing her with clear jealousy.

Jean-Michel nodded approvingly. Innis glowed in the spotlight, proudly stepping toward the microphone. "My name is Innis Toft…" Her voice reverberated, carrying across the onlookers and over to the panel of judges – the priest, the constable, and the former Heaken Beaver Queen.

Innis's eyes remained on Jean-Michel, but his seemed to be focused on a pair of reading glasses hanging from the bag of the unsuspecting postman.

She needed to say more… to tell the audience something interesting about her life, her hobbies, her dreams, as the other contestants had… but there was nothing interesting to say. She blinked and glanced over at the postman. The glasses were gone, and as she looked back so was Jean-Michel. Had he left her? Had he brought her this far just to leave her?

But then he reappeared, emerging from the crowd with his eyes firmly fixed on her. He mouthed something to her, but she didn't understand, nor did she care. He had returned to take her to faraway places.

She smiled and continued. "I'm the seamstress." She had said it with such pride that one might have thought she had said, "I'm the queen."

The crowd murmured and the judges scribbled down notes.

The other ladies introduced themselves, including Ava Poteet, the innkeeper at the Lord Odenbon Hotel, and Freya Falside, the librarian who was not only dating Ava's twin brother but until recently had been told she was most likely to win. The prize-giving was customarily a simple procedure – a mere formality – as it was usually common knowledge beforehand who would wear the Heaken Beaver crown. But Innis and her actor had changed everything. There was a moment of silence, a tallying of the vote.

The mayor returned to the microphone, tapping it for clarity. "Is this thing on?"

He cleared his throat as the women posed, hands on hips, shoulders slightly askew, chins titled upward to hear the verdict. Innis attempted to follow their lead.

"Ladies and townspeople," said the mayor. "I present to you this year's Heaken Beaver Queen… Innis Toft!"

Innis gasped as the crowd cheered. She buried her head in her hands and desperately fought back the tears. She had watched this moment from her shop window for so many years, knowing it would be both pointless and humiliating to put herself forward on that stage. Who was she? The seamstress? The daughter of the dressmaker the town had forgotten?

She breathed in the smells of the festival and turned around to receive her crown, only to look up and see none other than Wilkin Wilkinson, son of the pageant's sponsor, holding the rhinestone-encrusted antlers. He brushed a stray hair behind her ear and placed the crown tenderly on her head. She shivered, wishing she had thought to bring a sweater. It suddenly seemed cool for May, and Wilkin seemed older – not the boy who had sharpened her scissors but the man who had promised to return them to her.

"Thank you, Wilkin." She kissed him on the cheek, mystified by her new revelation. She had known Wilkin since she was a young girl and had never seen him like this before… Maybe it was the way of the festival…

A two-fingered whistle broke the spell. Dazed, she looked out into the crowd to see Jean-Michel standing there.

His girl.

Wilkin carefully removed his shoes, one at a time, placing them side by side on the stage. The town gasped. Innis felt her heart momentarily stop. Surely Wilkin wasn't about to do what the removal of his shoes traditionally suggested. But it was happening, right here in the middle of Coraloo, in front of everyone, while she stood center stage in her antlered crown. He put his left hand inside his pocket. She studied the crowd. They sensed it too.

He removed his hand and opened it up to show her the ring. "Can I be yours, Innis Toft?"

She had waited for this moment her whole life... to be asked, but not by Wilkin Wilkinson, the scissor sharpener. No matter that he had promised to protect the scissors... *her* scissors. She was not Wilkin's girl. She was *his* girl.

She opened her hand and showed Wilkin the rhinestone button – a gift, a treasure – casting a glance at Jean-Michel, whose arms were crossed defiantly, his face red.

His girl.

She smiled sweetly at her longtime acquaintance. "I'm so, so sorry, Wilkin. I've already found mine."

CHAPTER 22

Roy had walked her home from the bridal shower – Margarette hadn't said a word – and then carried the gifts inside. She had asked to be alone, saying she wasn't feeling well, but despite his temptation to run home and consult the book to diagnose her Roy knew it was something else. After repeated reassurances that she would be "fine", Roy walked home and left her to recuperate, distracting himself by trying to locate an elusive leak in his bike tire.

She had fainted. It could have been the heat, but Roy knew it was probably more to do with the stress of satisfying mothers, grandmothers, aunts, Blackwells, and Tofts. Something was on her mind... something she didn't want to talk about. He wanted to give her the space she needed, but at the same time he was desperate to make certain she hadn't actually come down with... He tried to not let his mind go there. He had to stop thinking that every ache, fever, or flutter was the beginning of the end. He had to focus on what he knew to be true: she needed rest. That was all.

He pulled the pliable black inner tube from the outer bicycle tire, then wiped his hands on his father's denim work apron. He glanced back at his own bicycle, mounted securely on the wall where he had left it. Maybe he should go for a ride to clear his mind. *No, not today.* He wasn't ready. Riding would only conjure reminders of the time he should have spent with his father. He carefully checked the rim strip on the interior of the bicycle rim. That's where the problem was – worn out.

He'd decided to put the Wilkinson case on hold until he heard back from his college roommate. What else could he do? The excitement he had felt was dwindling as the evidence he needed refused to surface. Who was this case really about anyway – Wilkin or Roy? Wilkin posed no threat to the public as far as he could tell – the file had been stuffed away in a drawer – until Roy stumbled upon it… He hadn't been looking for an unsolved case; all he'd wanted was a bit of excitement, a bit of change. But the other case had found him.

His thoughts moved to the mystery involving the recipe. He was sure he had questioned nearly everyone in town by now. Roy laughed, imagining the incarcerated drunks filing into the morning service. It was then that an epiphany struck. Roy set down the rim. Why hadn't he connected the dots before? Everyone he had seen publicly intoxicated attended the morning service. As an added bonus Margarette would be there. He could go check on her and make sure she was all right.

The morning service parishioners strolled into the stone church, greeting one another with hugs and handshakes. Roy wasn't surprised to see their shocked faces. Was it because he was a Blackwell and had never attended the morning service before or because he was out of uniform? He wasn't opposed to organized religion; he just had never really seen the need.

Roy wriggled into the wooden seat and arched his back. He hoped Margarette would see him, not knowing where she usually sat.

An elbow jabbed him in the ribs. He looked up at the woman beside him, determined to get his attention. "We voted last month to pad the pews. It was shot down, seventy-five to seventy-six. The young ones want to preserve the nostalgia or some nonsense like that. I say stuff and fluff 'em… Just pad the pews!"

Roy had to agree. Padding would be a nice addition. How did people manage to sit for so long on the bottom-numbing planks of wood? He noticed Bert Thompson sitting alone on the other side of the church. It was the first time Roy had seen him out in public since Bert's wife had passed – odd, since Bert was a known agoraphobic. Roy tried to catch his eye to give him a nod, an attempt to say hello, but Bert kept his focus forward.

Three rows back he saw Claudette Twittlebottom, and behind her Norvel Poteet. He'd yet to question Claudette, but he might as well.

She seemed a little too observant for his liking, as though she knew everything about everyone in Coraloo. He sensed he wouldn't have any trouble getting a word or two out of her. The Fox-McGogginses were sitting at the back. Roy couldn't dismiss the possibility that Earl had stolen the recipe himself, selling the stilled beverage to take out the shapeshifters or whatever it was he called them. Directly in front of the McGogginses sat the couple from the market.

This place was the only link that connected them. It had to be someone in the church selling moonshine. He made a note to question Claudette and kept a roaming eye out for anyone passing containers of the contraband under the pews.

The pitcher of communion wine was placed at the front of the table, ready and waiting. Margarette had arrived. Roy smiled as he recalled how he'd had to intervene in church affairs several years ago to resolve what came to be known as the "Great Morning Service Communion Wine Debate". It was how Margarette had ended up with the job. Not only had the Tofts laid claim to the morning wine recipe, but they had also decided that since Margarette was of such a good, upstanding character, and a schoolteacher to boot, she should be the one entrusted with making the wine. Prior to this it had been a battle every time the ladies of the committee gathered to discuss the matter. The serving pastor at the time ultimately had to call in Roy, as the discussion had become less a matter of the sanctity of the blood of Christ and more the fear of seven bloody-nosed senior parishioners should the debate become any more heated.

"But Edna's always made the wine," someone argued.

"Edna got Grandpa drunk!" another exclaimed.

"You're supposed to sip it, not gulp it!" the other shot back.

"I say we just forget the wine and drink grape juice. It's what Jesus drank, you know."

"Jesus didn't drink grape juice. The Bible says he drank wine. W-I-N-E. Wine!"

"Is it sugar free?"

"I'm not drinking anything with preservatives in it."

"A little preserving never hurt anyone."

"Looks like you could use a bit more preserving yourself given the size of those crow's feet."

"I'll show you who needs preserving!"

A woman, standing at the back of the room yelled, "Maybe Effie should bring it!"

The women all shot a glance back at Effie, who innocently shifted her gaze to the ceiling.

Edna spoke up. "Effie, the last time you brought the wine, the church smelled like grape bubblegum for an entire week. And there's no need to talk in the third person. You're not the queen."

Effie crossed her arms. "It was grape soda. Grape is grape. It all goes down the same way."

Roy watched as the ladies' group bantered back and forth about the Lord's Supper. No doubt the Lord would have had something clever to say about it all; he just wished he knew what exactly.

Edna was now on her feet, waving her hands in Effie's face.

Roy stepped into the center of the committee, holding back a wry smile. "Ladies, if you can't settle this yourself I'm going to be forced to arrest you all." He suddenly had images of the entire committee of elderly ladies stuffed into the two cells, their arms hanging out as they banged the wine pitcher against the bars, singing "Onward Christian Soldiers".

The ladies fell silent for a moment, and Roy smugly thought that he had gotten through to them and they could all go home.

But then another voice chipped in: "I think we should handle this the old way. We settle it in the ring!"

To his surprise, the ladies seemed to be in agreement for once, nodding their approval of the age-old idea. They would settle the three-day debate with boxing gloves.

To Roy's knowledge the ring hadn't been used to settle a conflict in years, not since the church bell debacle of the mid-seventies, and he had no intention of allowing today to be the day the practice was resurrected.

But the ladies were not to be deterred. The topic of debate switched from the wine to the win. Who would fight first? Did anyone have a pair of gloves Hilde could borrow? When would they do it?

"Ladies!" Roy raised his voice to intervene once again. "I'm not going to let you descend into fisticuffs over which of you should make the communion wine…" He paused. Truth told he wasn't sure the ladies could even lift the gloves, with the exception of Hilde. "There has to be another solution."

"Darn right there's a solution… excuse my language," Edna said. "You all let me make the Toft wine the way it's always been done."

"That's all we need, Edna. Do you want to get the whole morning service intoxicated?"

"Jesus didn't drink wine, anyway."

"It says right here in the Word that he did!"

"It's interpreted wrong."

"Are you saying my Bible is wrong?"

"I'm saying you're reading it wrong."

"Are you suggesting I can't read?"

"If the shoe fits…"

"Are you calling me a Blackwell?"

"Ladies!" Roy shouted. "I've had enough!"

"Of course you have. You're a Blackwell!" said Edna.

All the ladies nodded in agreement for the second time.

"Maybe if Edna wasn't so blind and could read the recipe she wouldn't have gotten Grandpa drunk. That's all I'm sayin'," Effie stated.

Roy contemplated the situation. Edna's eyesight was apparently fading, and she'd let the wine ferment for longer than it should have. Before, the brew had walked a thin line between wine and juice, but that wasn't the case on the day Grandpa had made his way up to the table three times.

"So why not have someone else make the wine?" Roy asked. "Someone in your family. Someone who's not on the committee." He wanted to say "someone younger" but was afraid the ladies might start throwing right hooks his way if he did.

Roy was all too familiar with family recipes. The Blackwells had their own carefully guarded wine recipe for communion. He didn't know who made it, but one thing was certain: one sip was enough. If he ever ran out of what was in the jug above his desk he could probably use it to remove the fingerprint ink instead.

"We do have a schoolteacher," one of them suggested.

"We also have three attorneys, an architect, and a doctor."

"Don't forget Sylvia. She's an entrepreneur."

"Oh, Lord! Don't let Sylvia make the wine!"

"I'm not suggesting any of them," Edna said. "I'm suggesting Meggy."

In the end, thanks to Roy's intervention, they had settled it without anyone landing a blow. All parties were happy except for Margarette. Roy had barely known her then; she'd been just another resident of Coraloo. Roy spotted her at the back of the church. His heart leaped. He gave her a little wave. She smiled and slowly made her way down the aisle, saying hello to family members, hugging students past and present, and giving a wave to friends as she went. Everyone loved her. She could have had any of the fellas in the room if she'd wanted.

Margarette sat down in the empty space on his right but didn't have time to speak, as the choir stood, prompting the rest of the congregants to do the same. Margarette stood and reached for one of the books tucked into the seatback in front of them. Roy followed her cue. Then she started to sing, only she didn't need to look at the words or the notes on the pages in front of her. It was as if she had opened the hymnal for his benefit, which was helpful seeing as he didn't know a single word of the choral hymn.

Margarette had once told him she couldn't sing. Roy had argued that everyone can sing, but some people just weren't very good at it.

197

They had laughed about it, and he had reassured her that she was being too hard on herself. But as he stood beside her Roy realized the truth: Margarette Toft couldn't carry a tune in a bucket... and he loved it. Not that he was an expert on all things musical, but he'd sung tenor in the high school choir and spent a year in the marching band before dropping out, much to his parents' disappointment. He listened to her singing passionately, out of tune and off-key, as if she truly meant every word that came out of her mouth. He tried to sing too, but his throat had become strangely sore, possibly from the hundred-year-old dust that settled between the cracks in the stone floor, or maybe... The headache suddenly returned. He rubbed his temples.

Roy looked around at the people in front of him and to his sides, all gathered together in this one place, all of whom he knew by name. He wished one of them could offer him some relief... divine healing... a miracle tonic. Perhaps that was what had drawn each of them here – a need for healing of one sort or another. Maybe just being together, despite all their differences, was a source of comfort.

The truth was, they all knew and counted on him to be the constable – their constable. It was his duty to keep them safe. Safe from thieves and murderers. Who was he kidding? Wilkin Wilkinson presented no real threat; he'd been distracted by the Wilkinson file, that much was true, but at what cost? Maybe that's what was bothering Margarette; he'd been too distant.

One by one, unprompted, the congregants filed up to the altar. Roy followed Margarette's lead. From somewhere behind him he heard a voice say, "I hope the constable doesn't drink it all."

He wanted to laugh or even smile, but the throbbing in his head seemed to worsen.

In front of him he heard another say, "This is her best batch yet."

"I bet this is how Jesus made it."

This time Roy did laugh out loud – a chuckle that echoed against the wooden-beamed rafters. The line stopped moving and everyone stared. Margarette grinned. As embarrassed as he was, he would have done it again if it made her smile like that. He approached the altar and dipped what looked like a piece of a saltine cracker into a wine glass filled with the Toft wine, as he had seen other parishioners in front of him do.

On the way back to his seat Roy caught sight of Norvel, who took the cracker and pretended to dip it in the wine before eating it. *So Norvel Poteet didn't partake?* How could he have thought that a man who wouldn't even taste a drop of communion wine might possibly be making moonshine in his garden shed? Roy conclusively decided he could cross Norvel off his lists of suspects.

Pastor Donaldson spoke on freedom from fear and bondage, freedom from jealousy, freedom from stress, and – one Roy knew good and well the pastor had slipped in just for the Tofts – freedom from rivalries. There were a few groans to this point. If a person could be freed from it, the pastor covered it.

Eventually he dismissed them and Margarette turned to leave.

"Margarette –"

She turned back, her eyes weary, her skin lacking its usual youthful glow. He had been right; she wasn't well. Something was wrong.

And then she spoke. "Are we doing the right thing, Roy?"

The question hit him harder than Hilde and her boxing glove could have.

"What do you mean?" he asked. But he knew what she meant.

"Us. The families. It seems so…" she lowered her voice to a whisper as the morning service-goers exited the building, leaving them alone in the second row, "forced."

"What are you saying?" His jaw tightened. He wanted to go back in time, to change whatever could be changed to make things different, to bring them back to the way they were… when it was Margarette and Roy. Just Margarette and Roy.

She stared at him, but he couldn't read her. Was she sad, upset, mad, frustrated?

"Is it me? Have I done something?"

She looked confused, as if she were sorting it all out in her mind.

"No, not at all!" She paused, as if once again processing what she was saying as she said it. "I love you, Roy Blackwell."

He exhaled the breath he didn't realize he had been holding and took her hands in his. The church was practically empty now, with the exception of a few clusters here and there. He would talk to Claudette later.

"Then what is it? Whatever it is, I'll fix it. I'll make it better. I'll take care of you. Let me help."

She breathed in heavily, then sighed. "I know, but I'm tired, Roy. I'm tired of all the *things*. It's too much. I can't sort it all out. I forget who I'm supposed to be half the time. Sometimes Toft, sometimes Blackwell. Please tell me this is going to work. It's going to work, right?"

She'd said she loved him, and that was all he needed. "Of course it's… *we're* going to work. Just a few more days and it will all be over. We'll be married and there'll be nothing anyone can say about it."

"But will it truly be over?"

At that moment Anna Sue Toft popped up beside Margarette decked out in her Sunday best, complete with an oversized hat and a feather that blew away from her mouth when she spoke. "Is everything all right? It looks a little intense over here."

"We're fine, Mom."

Are we? Roy wondered.

"Good to see you in the morning service, Roy. I take it you'll be worshipping with us from now on?"

He hadn't thought about it, and looked to Margarette for an answer. She shrugged.

"How silly of me," her mother prattled on. "Of course you will. Meggy makes the communion wine. Heaven help us if we had to decide who would take it on next. She makes the best the church has ever had, you know. Everyone says so, don't they, Meggy? I guess I shouldn't boast. It is Sunday, after all."

Roy cleared his throat again. He was definitely coming down with something… Maybe it was the same thing Margarette had.

"Maybe we should discuss this over lunch," Roy suggested, looking solely at Margarette. "We could grab a bite at the festival. The Taste of Coraloo begins today."

Anna Sue glanced uncertainly at Margarette. "Sorry, Roy, but we

200

kind of have a little pre-wedding family event to attend."

So there was still going to be a wedding. A wave of relief washed over him.

Margarette's face contorted. "We do?"

"Of course, Meggy, don't you remember?" Anna Sue brushed the feather away from her face again. "And Roy, I wouldn't worry too much about the dress. She'll find one… eventually. It's a bit of bad luck to have waited this long, but I'm sure one of your aunts has a spell or something they can cast over the whole thing."

Roy looked at his bride-to-be; he wouldn't let Anna Sue's taunt faze him. Margarette hadn't told her mother about the Blackwell dress. Probably a wise decision.

Margarette's cheeks flushed. "I'm not feeling much like lunch or a pre-wedding event, Mom. I think I'll go home and lie down. There's still so much to do… It's the last week of school and I'm behind on grading the presentations. And I still have to get everything together for the reception –"

Roy took her hand. "What can I do? There has to be something."

She placed her other hand on his shoulder. "I've got this," she said with a weak smile.

He wanted to help her. He needed to help her. But before he could offer again a familiar voice called to him.

"Roy!"

He looked back to see Pastor Donaldson heading his way.

It wasn't exactly perfect timing, but he did have a few more questions to ask about some of the church parishioners.

Pastor Donaldson extended his hand to Roy. "Good to have you here this morning. Should I get used to this?"

"You should indeed," Anna Sue cut in, propping her hands up on her hips. "If Roy's going to be a Toft…"

The room seemed to fall still, the moment frozen in time. "We'll see," he replied.

A Toft. He hadn't thought of it that way. Margarette had often said she couldn't wait to be part of the Blackwells and take his name. But it also worked the other way. He may not have been taking her name, but he was going to be part of the Toft family. What would it be like attending Toft family functions as "the enemy from the hill"? Was that how Margarette felt? She had done everything she could to try to fit in, willingly taking in every aspect of the Blackwell traditions – including a dress she couldn't stand.

The dress. His mind shifted again to the Wilkinson case, suddenly remembering the photograph he had seen of a wedding dress in the file. It had clearly been taken right outside the evidence room. A thought struck him: maybe if he found the dress he could close the case once and for all.

Roy unlocked the archives. He'd been down in the basement more times than he could count, but he'd never seen a dress. The back wall was stacked with labeled boxes: "decorations", "old uniforms", "books". He stepped back, wondering if he was missing something.

It has to be here.

He rubbed the back of his neck. What would his former pre-law self have done at this point?

Look at it from a different angle.

Only this case didn't seem to have another angle. He tilted his head, giving the tower of boxes, in desperate need of a good sort through, one more look. Maybe he could fill his time clearing out the archives. He read each and every box label – most of which had been marked out and then rewritten in ball point pen or black permanent marker – thinking it would be much easier if one of them clearly stated "Wedding dress inside!"

A different angle.

He ran his hand over each box, deciphering what had once been written but later deemed unimportant. He grinned. There it was... or had been. Scratched out under the word "Uniforms" was the word "Evidence".

A surge of excitement rushed through his tired body.

Roy dislodged the box and set it down on the floor, lifting the lid.

He frowned at the sight of the neatly folded stacks of blue uniforms inside. He wondered whether the Historical Society had any use for them, or maybe the theater department. If Jasper and Everett – the volunteer deputies who'd been serving as long as Roy had – knew about them they'd be begging to wear the old uniforms.

He carefully lifted out the first set, leaving it folded. As he was going in for the second Roy saw what he'd been looking for – a glimpse of white and a soft sheen that clearly contrasted with the dark wool of the old uniforms.

He set the other uniforms aside and held up the dress. Then he quickly set it back down. Something else had caught his eye – a creased and yellowed flyer for a performance by something called the Acteurs Agissant Acting Troupe in a modern-day retelling of *Great Expectations*, featuring the debut performance of a man named Jean-Michel.

Roy could hear the shaky, metallic ring of the rotary phone through the cracks in the ceiling. He placed the dress and the advertisement back in the box, and, bounding up the stairs, made his way back to the first floor.

"Hello, Coraloo Police." He felt another rush of excitement. "No, it's all right that you called… Did you say you found something? Could you repeat that?"

Roy reached for a piece of paper and a pen. He wrote the name "Jean-Michel" and the word "missing".

"An actor… I saw that in the file. And the timeline adds up… France? Are you sure?"

Why would Wilkin Wilkinson have spent seven years living in France?

"My thoughts exactly. Innocent men don't run or hide away in France."

Roy tried to make sense of these new shards of evidence. Even if Wilkin wasn't guilty of murder he was guilty of something. Roy was sure of it. But that wasn't all; it turned out his old roommate Henry had more to add.

"An alias? Are you sure?"

There was another piece to the Wilkinson puzzle and a new suspect to boot. He might not have just one murderer on his hands, but two. He needed to talk to Wilkin, and now he knew exactly where to find him.

CHAPTER 23

May 25, 1976

Innis Toft sat on a stool in the back room surrounded by yards of purple satin. If she was to travel the country with the actors she would need a costume. She had no desire to stay in Coraloo. No desire to spend her life in the shadow of a father who had abandoned her and a town that disapproved. No desire to carry on the forgotten legacy of her mother. She wanted adventure and a fresh start. And more than anything, she wanted to spend the rest of her days with the man who had wooed her with a single rhinestone button: her Jean-Michel.

The bell on the door clanged. She looked up to find him standing in front of her, a diamond ring perched between his thumb and forefinger, the stone glistening under the light. She started to speak, to answer his unspoken request, but he placed a finger over her lips and the ring in her hand. She slipped it on. It was loose, with a dent on the side, and it could have used a good clean. For a moment she couldn't help but wonder whether he'd acquired it the same way she had seen him acquire other things. *But what does it matter?* she thought, as she threw her arms around his neck.

The bell on the door clanged again.

Wilkin Wilkinson entered and defiantly faced Jean-Michel. "I'll fight you for her, actor! Two o'clock on Tuesday. I'll see you in the ring."

Jean-Michel placed his hands confidently on his hips. "I will not fight you." He took a step closer to Wilkin. "O war, thou son of hell." His eyes were fierce, his arms raised. "Whom angry heavens do make their minister." He clutched his hands to his chest. "Throw in the frozen bosoms of our part. Hot coals of vengeance! Let no soldier fly." He flapped his arms wildly. "He that is truly dedicate to war hath no self-love; nor he that loves himself hath not essentially, but by circumstance, the name of valor."

Innis swooned. Jean-Michel bowed.

But while his interpretation of Shakespeare's *Henry VI* had captivated Innis, Wilkin reminded Jean-Michel to bring his boxing gloves.

Businesses closed up early and students were dismissed from classes before lunch. The mayor ordered the boxing ring assembled in the center of town. The tavern advertised half-price ciders and rumor had it Father Tweedie was taking bets. It had been years since such a challenge had been issued, but Wilkin was not only a man of tradition but a man of honor. He would handle this as a man, and in the way of Coraloo.

Wilkin waited in the center of the ring, shuffling back and forth. He threw a jab with his left and a hook with his right, while Jean-Michel sat in the corner on a wooden stool, watching.

Innis handed Jean-Michel a pair of gloves. They had belonged to her father, but he had never used them.

Jean-Michel stood, throwing off the fringed green cloak Innis had made specially for the occasion. The crowd cheered. He bowed dramatically to those standing around him and blew a kiss at Innis.

The mayor brought the two men together. "Touch gloves. Keep it clean, men."

Wilkin extended his right glove.

Jean-Michel turned to face the audience. "To love or have loved, that is enough." He looked deeply into the eyes of Wilkin. Then, switching from Hugo to Emerson, he added: "Peace cannot be achieved through violence; it can only be attained through understanding."

Wilkin pulled his arm back and knocked Jean-Michel to the ground.

"Point, Wilkinson!" the mayor shouted.

The crowd groaned.

Jean-Michel stumbled to his feet, wobbling back and forth. "It's not the size of the dog –"

Before he could finish his interpretation of Twain, Wilkin hit him again.

"Point two, Wilkinson!"

Jean-Michel fumbled to his feet again, then dropped dramatically to the ground. "I cannot fight anymore. I have injured myself. It is my leg. We shall continue this another day."

The town doctor, a young man in thick glasses with a stethoscope around his neck, began to examine Jean-Michel, but the actor refused public treatment. "I am a man of modesty, Physician."

Two young men lifted the actor onto a stretcher and proceeded to lower him into the crowd, where a few offered to pray over him and others offered to administer a tonic.

Innis was left standing alongside the doctor, who was frantically looking for his stethoscope, as she watched the love of her life being carried away.

She turned to leave, but Wilkin halted her.

"Innis Toft, I have loved you since the first time I saw you. I will fight for you for the rest of my life. May I be yours?"

She shivered. Her heart raced in a way that almost made her uncomfortable – in a way that frightened her. He was the scissor sharpener. He couldn't take her places or make her swoon. He didn't wear silks or sparkle when he walked. He couldn't be the one, her heart's desire. It wasn't possible, was it?

She pushed away the thought and the truth behind the filched stethoscope. Jean-Michel hadn't officially asked her to marry him; he had given her a ring – somebody else's ring. Avoiding his gaze, she clutched the scissors around her neck, remembering Wilkin's promise to protect them.

"I think I'm already spoken for, Wilkin."

Chapter 24

Margarette sat in The Rightful Hare with her head in her hands, fighting to keep her eyes open. The pub, stylish and modern with red leather seating and black wooden tables, was one of the newer businesses in town – a response to the older, long-established tavern across the street, the famed Beaver's Beard. The twenty-four-armed, three-tiered brass chandeliers – complete with tiny white shades to conceal the bulbs – dripped with large, bulbous crystals. Brass candlesticks adorned each table and the menu – a heavy book with a gold tassel – outlined the creations of three gourmet chefs. The former soda shop was both the newest and the most expensive addition to Coraloo. And it belonged to the Tofts.

Rumor had it that several months ago a tourist had been talking to the barman at The Beaver's Beard, inquiring about the Blackwells' claim to fame.

The barman had explained, "Mungo Blackwell is a legend... a town hero... one of a kind."

To which Margarette's uncle, Tolliver Toft, had slammed his ale down on the table and declared, "Enough is enough!"

It was time for the Tofts to gather elsewhere. Thus, The Rightful Hare had been established directly across the street from The Beaver's Beard.

It had been a long week, with only one more day to wrap up the school year and turn in the final grades. Margarette was fighting sinus pain in her face, exhausted from staring up at the ceiling for nights on end unable to fall asleep, her mind awhirl with worry – about her grading, her students, and, most of all, the impending wedding. No matter how much she tried to quieten the nagging fears inside her, willing herself to sleep and forget it all for a few hours, she couldn't. Of course she wanted to marry Roy, but she didn't want to lose her family by doing so. Her mind spun. If only she could touch base with Roy, spend some time with him just *being*. Like they used to, before the wedding planning and feuding families had taken over. She'd hardly even seen her fiancé in recent days, occupied as she was with Toft dinners and cocktail parties where family members made last-ditch efforts to introduce her to out-of-town guests who just happened to be visiting and who were "closer to her age". She knew what they were up to. Maybe she didn't care about the fallout. She cared about Roy. That should be all that mattered, right? *If only he had a different name...* Would she care as much if his last name were Poteet, Hennigan, or Smith? or... Butcher? *But then he wouldn't be Roy.*

Sylvia had called, insisting Margarette attend her night-before party at The Rightful Hare. Margarette had resisted, especially since it was a school night, but Sylvia had persisted: *"Oh, come on, Meggy! I have it all planned. It'll be good for you."*

Margarette knew Sylvia would never let her have a moment of peace if she didn't go and so she had agreed.

She lifted her eyes to an enormous painting of a rabbit with a sword kicking a shoe down a hill. She wished she had something to kick down a hill – a shoe would do, or, better yet, that dress... After all, she was marked already, so what did she have to lose? At any rate, it would give her an excuse to leave the tavern. *Excuse me everyone; I just need to go outside and kick something.* She smiled at the thought.

Sylvia took a seat at the high-top table looking surprisingly normal. Gone were the dreadlocks and her make-up was refreshingly minimal. "Cheer up! It's going to be okay."

She smelled of fried chicken, and Margarette thought she'd spotted a chunk stuck in Sylvia's teeth.

"This night is all about *you*," Sylvia said. "Let me get you something to drink." This night was supposed to be a last soirée with the ladies before she married, though it was actually two nights before and was quickly becoming a "make Margarette not feel like such a slug party".

Margarette knew it was just another excuse for the Toft ladies to have a night out and a final chance for them to try to change her mind.

Margarette was about to say no thanks, but she was thirsty. "Lime and soda?"

"Sure thing. Tolliver has everything set up for you... DJ starts in an hour. Come on! Let's have some fun!" Sylvia started moving in a mashup of what appeared to be a shimmy and a twist. "You can be tired in the morning."

Margarette laughed. "I have to be a grown-up in the morning. I think a few sixth-graders would notice if I went missing."

Sylvia glanced to her left, most likely scoping the pub for single men. "Choices are slim tonight, so you'll have to save me a dance. Promise?"

"Maybe."

"Listen," Sylvia sighed. "This'll be the last time I mention it, but if I don't get it off my chest I'll never forgive myself."

"Why not? Go ahead."

"Meggy, you've got to forget all about the Blackwell. He's not the one for you. You're young – sort of. Look at yourself. Don't settle... There's always The Butcher."

Margarette rolled her eyes. Couldn't at least one person in the family be on her side?

Were the Tofts really so shallow to think that she would drop someone as perfect as Roy just because he happened to have the "wrong" name? She thought about him when she took her walk, crossing the footbridge over the river to and from her cottage. She thought about him as she graded papers. She'd thought about him as she lit a fire, intending to burn the wedding notebook. And she was thinking about him now. She needed him. She missed him. She wondered if he was across the street at The Beaver's Beard. Maybe she should walk across the street and talk to him. Maybe they could hold off on the wedding until she sorted herself out.

"Meggy!" Sylvia yelled, pointing frantically at some poor soul dancing by himself in the crowd of invited single women Margarette didn't know – most likely comprised of every non-Blackwell woman in town. The remainder, a hodgepodge of aunts, were huddled in the corner over what looked like a heated game of Rook. There were a few tourists dotted around taking selfies in front of the hare, and a handful of men brave enough to mingle among the Toft revelry.

Toft night-before parties usually had very little to do with the bride and everything to do with a bunch of women getting out of their monogrammed, cookie-cutter lives to make fools of themselves just so they had an excuse to visit the spa the next day. Margarette was quite certain she could leave and no one would notice.

Sylvia was occupied with a tourist, most likely drumming up business for the salon judging by the way she was touching the lady's hair and studying her skin. Margarette figured Sylvia had forgotten all about her lime and soda, but she was still thirsty, so she pushed her way to the bar.

"Lima and soda, please."

The barman wiped his hands on a white cloth and smiled at Margarette. "This your shindig?"

"It was supposed to be. How'd you guess?"

"The tiara."

"Right."

Margarette had forgotten that Sylvia had placed the jeweled piece on her head. It was actually beautiful, an antique that had belonged to a long-gone family member. She lifted it, smoothing out a few disheveled hairs, and set it down on the counter.

"It looked good on you," he said with a wink. "I'll get you that soda. Lime, right?"

She nodded. He'd winked at her. Why had he winked?

Margarette shifted on her stool uncomfortably. There was a time when she would have embraced such a wink, returning it with a half-smile and a fake giggle. That more or less summarized how she had come to be with Thomas. She often wondered what he was doing and how his marriage was working out. Two weeks after Margarette had called it off she'd questioned her decision. But so had he. He'd taken the money they'd set aside for their honeymoon and flown to Aruba, where he'd met the love of his life… Monique.

An eerie quietness descended in The Rightful Hare, as if the pub itself had heard her heart, her wonderings about another man. Had it been so, this quiet would not have been borne out of worry, but of delight. So great was the Tofts' dislike for Roy that even at her own party several of the aunts had been unable to hold back from attempting to sway her into the arms of William Butcher Jr once again.

> "He looks just like that superhero – you know, the one with the glasses – don't you think?"
> Margarette had no idea.
> "He has an apprentice you know."
> She'd already heard.
> "And that house of his. It's so grand, so elegant."
> "Well, I guess nothing beats living in the mortuary with a pile of dead bodies." She hadn't meant to say it out loud, but it had just come out.

Margarette took a few sips of her soda, turned on the barstool ready to say a few hellos and a few goodbyes, and faced the reason for the silence: Innis Wilkinson was standing in front of her.

Innis, who wore scissors around her neck; Margarette, who kept clippers in her purse. Innis, with her blonde curls tied up in a black bow, adding a youthful edge to her older appearance; Margarette, whose curls hung full and cropped. Innis, who had married the wrong man; Margarette, who was beginning to wonder if she was about to do the same. Innis, shunned by her family; Margarette...

She glanced over at the table of aunts. Her mother had joined them.

"May I sit?" Innis asked.

"Sure."

The music started up again, along with the dancing and general milling about of entertainment-hungry tourists.

Innis said something, her voice faint. Margarette leaned in. Innis smelled of perfume – a floral with a hint of spice – oddly, not how Margarette had imagined the cleaning lady would smell. She supposed that she'd expected her to smell like blue window cleaning spray or lemon dusting polish.

"I'm sorry, would you mind saying that again?"

"I have something for you." Innis extended her hand, her fist closed.

Margarette extended hers. Innis unclenched her fist and dropped the tiny item into Margarette's palm. She turned the item over, examining it and trying to discern the meaning of the small rhinestone button.

"Thank you. It's nice."

"I have two things to tell you."

"Okay."

The woman beside her was a family outcast, pushing her cleaning cart in the shadows of controversy and gossip. What Margarette knew of the woman's history was based on fragments from salon chatter. But she couldn't shake the suspicion that somehow her life and Innis's were on parallel tracks. Innis was the woman who had married the wrong man. The woman who could have had it all. There was something about her. Something that drew Margarette to Innis. And at this moment she was probably the most relatable person in the room. Margarette saw herself in this woman – a reflection of what could be.

Innis grabbed Margarette's hands and looked earnestly into her eyes. There was something familiar there, something kind, something… family. "Never marry a mortician."

A *mortician*? Had she heard correctly?

Margarette pulled her hands away, the statement hitting a bit too close to home. Had Innis overheard the family pushing her toward William Butcher Jr? Had she noticed Margarette casting an accidental glance his way?

"I'm sorry… did you say mortician?"

"You can't trust them. They're deceivers – watching even when you can't see them."

"Right, but… how did you…?" Margarette fumbled over her response. Then she laughed. "Don't worry. There are no morticians in my future."

"Are you sure?"

"Of course I'm sure."

Innis nodded over at the whispering women. "They're not."

"I know."

"So are *you* sure?"

"About morticians or my marriage?"

"Both."

"Do you have all night? This could take a while."

"I was invited here to talk to you. He'll protect you."

He?

"Roy? Roy invited you here?"

Margarette didn't know whether to be upset or thankful that Roy had dived head first into Toft affairs. But one thing was for sure – she was definitely intrigued.

"Can I buy you something to eat?" Margarette offered.

The woman smiled. "That would be lovely."

Margarette motioned for the server to bring a menu over just as one of Roy's sidekicks burst through the double wooden doors.

"Mrs Wilkinson! There's been a brawl! You need to fetch your husband from the jail!"

Innis Wilkinson adjusted her cardigan. "I'm sorry I couldn't visit longer. Let's do this again sometime. And please thank your fiancé for inviting me." She quickly stood and proceeded toward the exit.

"Never marry a mortician." The first piece of advice, but there should have been something else. A second thing. Margarette had to know the second thing.

She laid some money on the counter and took off after Innis, only to be stopped at the door by Sorcha Blackwell.

CHAPTER 25

Roy had waited all week for this. But where was Wilkin? He glanced at his watch and yawned. It was getting late. Not too late for The Beaver's Beard and its slew of regulars and tourists, but late for Roy. The plan had been for the ladies to hang out on the other side of the square at their night-before party, while Charlie, at the insistence of his wife, had suggested the men do the same – even though she was opting to stay home with baby Agnes. A typical night for Roy at The Beard was a bite to eat and a game of cards, and that was the end of it. Charlie had said a relaxing night out sounded good to him, so he'd agreed to hang out for a few hours to appease Velveteen. Roy didn't mind having a bit of company while he waited. If he was going to have a shot at talking to Wilkin, this was where he'd find him.

He yawned again, inhaling the familiar yeasty tang in the air and wondering if Margarette had found time to rest. The tufted green cushions on the tavern stools had worn thin and the plaid banner hanging over the bar was dingy with dust. Mungo Blackwell and his Heaken beaver hung above the large stone open-hearth fireplace, already lit for the cool spring night.

Laughter echoed around him through the cedar-beamed rafters, along with a hearty cheer from a win at a hand of cards somewhere in the back. The pleasant murmur of conversation filled the air. At the center of the open two-story building, a large light fixture fashioned from antlers hung from a bronze chain. The bottles of ciders, ales, and beverages of other persuasion glittered and sparkled, catching the light behind the well-trained barmen, who tended as much as they talked.

Glancing around the tavern, Roy saw a few faces he didn't recognize – tourists most likely. But Coraloo was growing. Newcomers were doing their best to settle above storefronts and in rundown cottages, willing to pay to have them refurbished to their personalized specifications. The newcomers would become locals before long, just as Charlie Price had.

A waiter walked past with a tray of nachos. The Beaver's Beard was known for its deer meat nachos – hand-cut chips piled high with venison. Customers could fancy them up any way they wanted from this point – go upmarket with the figs and goat cheese, or keep it traditional with some cheese dip and jalapeños. Roy had his own combination: topped with fried sweet potatoes and ranch dressing. Margarette much preferred the traditional fare, and only tourists ever ordered the gourmet options. He and his mother had spent many a weekend night partnering in a hand of euchre, taking down a pewter platter of the infamous entree. As it wasn't currently deer season, it looked as if the tourist who'd ordered the platter was going to be disappointed with their meatless nachos.

Roy gave another yawn. He should be in bed by now. What time was it anyway? Nine? Ten? He and Margarette were supposed to be getting married the day after tomorrow but they hadn't had a full conversation since Monday morning. Four long days. He'd been given no instructions other than to be there.

"Just show up!" she'd said. "I've got everything handled."

That was over a week ago. Before the Blackwell shower. Before she'd fainted. Before she'd become distant, asking him whether they were doing the right thing. Before he'd ever wondered the same thing himself.

Roy stood to leave. It was late and he had no further reason to be at The Beard. These men would understand if he called it a night. To Roy's left, his cousin Stephen was deep in conversation with Charlie Price about their wives' book club, and whether or not their weekly meet-up at the tavern for deer meet nachos and Blackwell cider also constituted a book club if their conversation lent its way to what the other was currently reading.

"It can't be a book club," Charlie argued. "There aren't any pastries."

"But did we or did we not just spend the last half hour going on about C.S. Lewis?"

"Do you think the ladies have theological discussions about the central truths of Christianity?"

"Probably not. I think they mainly talk about muffins."

"Muffins?" Stephen laughed. "I know for a fact they talk about a lot more than muffins."

"See, I just made my point. You need muffins to have a book club."

"Are muffins a pastry or a bread?"

"I don't know. Want another cider?"

"Yep."

Roy listened in on their conversation as he waited for his bill. He had a couple of questions of his own… about truths, not the muffins. He'd been thinking a lot about that kind of thing lately, getting as much from Charlie and Stephen as they went back and forth about spiritual themes in modern fiction than he'd ever gotten from any Blackwell service. He had a few questions that might settle his uneasiness, but he figured now wasn't really the time.

To Roy's right, Jasper and Everett were casing the tavern for conspiracy theorists.

"I know a flat-earther when I see one, Jasper."

"You can't tell that by looking at someone."

"I can spot 'em a mile away."

Jasper pointed his bony finger toward a man standing on the second floor. "What about him? Does he believe the Earth is flat, Everett?"

"No, but he's seen Big Foot."

"How'd you figure that one?"

"I was with him when he saw the big feller just the other day."

"Hey, Earl!" Jasper shouted, waving Earl Fox-McGoggins over to the bar.

"Hey there, Roy." Earl leaned in so close Roy could smell the melted cheese on his breath. "Have you found the you-know-who that did the you-know-what?"

Roy shook his head. "Nope." He didn't need reminding that a month had gone by and his only hunch had turned out to be the postman, who, he'd discovered, wouldn't even partake of the communion wine.

"Something strange is going on around here." Earl tapped the colander on his head. "You might want to think about getting yourself one of these." Earl backed away slowly, looking from side to side as if to make sure he wasn't being watched. Truth was, Earl was always being watched. For many townspeople, the antics of the Fox-McGogginses were prime entertainment.

"Festival always brings in the crazies," a voice mumbled from the far end of the tavern bar.

Roy caught sight of Wilkin Wilkinson out of the corner of his eye – a recluse, sitting by himself. The unsolved file suddenly masked any thoughts of wedding doubts.

"I think it brings *out* the crazies," Roy laughed, easing his way into conversation. "Cells sit empty for a year, then the festival gets going and I start hauling them in." He didn't know whether half a dozen qualified as "hauling them in", but a little exaggeration never hurt.

"Every year." Wilkin laughed under his breath, then took another sip of his cider. His two gray braids hung down from beneath his fedora, just stopping short of his cider. Wilkin kept his head down, his eyes on his drink.

What makes a man drink alone? Guilt? Murder?

Roy had his own guilt, his own regrets, but they'd never brought him to The Beard. He'd rather be out on his bike, but then he would remember... and he couldn't bring himself to ride alone.

Seeing an opportunity opening up with Wilkin, he stepped closer.

"Excuse me, fellas," he said to Stephen and Charlie as he wandered away.

His leg burned. It had to be the sciatica; he'd read about it that morning in the book. He'd made a cayenne pepper patch to see if it would work and brewed a cup of green tea. The anti-inflammatory properties would surely help. Dr Toft had said it was nothing serious – just something that came with age. Sugar could cause it to flare up, apparently, so it must have been the cake. He rubbed the side of his leg and hobbled over to Wilkin.

Roy scooted up onto the bar stool beside Wilkin. "I'm not sure we've officially met." He extended his hand. "Roy Blackwell."

Wilkin returned the gesture. "I know who you are."

"Have you been down to the festival? Four weeks a year... never gets old."

Wilkin remained silent.

"You're married to Innis, right? I ran into her at the market last week."

Wilkin motioned for the barman to bring him another cider.

"It's on me," Roy said, lifting his mug. "Here's to truth and marriage."

Wilkin slammed his mug on the counter. "Leave my wife alone. No more questions! We'll stay out of your way, and you stay out of ours."

Roy decided it was now or never. He might as well come out with it. "Actually, I have a few questions for you, about your wife and a certain actor."

Wilkin jumped to his feet, cider spilling across the dark mahogany counter. He pulled his fist back and swung.

Roy dodged the blow. "What was that for?"

Wilkin swung again. This time his fist connected with Roy's jaw. Roy reached for his arm, but Wilkin kept swinging. Everett and Jasper jumped into action, but they were no match for Wilkin.

Roy tried again, "Just calm down, Mr Wilkinson; I only wanted to talk. Let's go down to the station and sort this out like civilized men, shall we? Can you do that?"

"Nope," Wilkin said, leaning back to take another swing.

He missed, but Roy didn't. He caught him just right, laying Wilkin flat out on his back.

Wilkin laughed, knocking the fedora – and the braids – off his head, exposing a haircut that was high and tight. "That was a good one. All right... I'll talk to you."

If Roy had actually had a drink, he'd have thought he'd had too many at this point. *Wilkin Wilkinson wears a wig?*

"Too late," he said. "Let's go"

"We'll get him, boss," Everett said, pulling up the backside of his pants.

"On three, Everett," Jasper said, squatting down next to Wilkin. "One, two –"

"Get off me, you idiots!" Wilkin roared, shoving the pigtails and fedora back on his head.

Roy extended a hand and helped the man to his feet. "Come on. How about you sleep it off? Then we'll talk."

He led Wilkin out of The Beaver's Beard and into the cool night air of Coraloo.

Across the way The Rightful Hare was aglow, the thump and bump of music pouring out the open door. Margarette was in there, and if Innis had done as he'd asked, she was in there, too.

"Jasper, run across the street and fetch Mrs Wilkinson," he said.

At the center of the festival, fallen calm for the night, a team of men under the waving arm of Mayor Hennigan and his megaphone was erecting the boxing ring. Earl Fox-McGoggins stood in front of it, most likely to keep any young ones from trying to use it as a trampoline and ladies' groups from using it to settle debates.

Roy thought they'd gotten rid of that thing years ago. Either way, they were clearly expecting someone to fight.

CHAPTER 26

May 30, 1976

Innis Toft had sketchbooks full of wedding dresses – unusual styles and adaptions of her mother's original gowns. Her favorite she had drawn when she was nine. Now it was time to choose the one that suited her best. It had to be a one of a kind. Simple, but stunning. It would tell her story with every thread and tuck.

She had seen little of Wilkin Wilkinson and even less of her Jean-Michel over the past week. He and his troupe had been keeping odd hours – staying awake in the evenings and sleeping during the day. They appeared only for performances and autograph signings, occasionally popping into her shop for a repair.

During one of his visits Innis had asked him if she should set a date.

He'd grabbed her hands and said, "In a word, I was too cowardly to do what I knew to be right, as I had been too cowardly to avoid doing what I knew to be wrong."

She didn't quite know how the Dickens quote answered the question, but he hadn't said no, so she'd set a date. Word of the intended event spread quickly through Coraloo, setting the town in motion for what was destined to be the closest thing to a royal wedding the townspeople would ever see. She'd booked the church and was inviting everyone who walked into her shop. Innis Toft and Jean-Michel – she'd never bothered to ask his last name – would be married before the festival's end.

She stared at her dress, the final product, and decided that one more fitting wouldn't hurt. She carefully removed the scissors from around her neck and set them down by the cash register. She stepped into the back and slipped on the gown – a perfect fit as she'd known it would be.

The bell over the door clanged.

"Just a minute!" she called out.

"It is I!"

My Jean-Michel.

Innis rushed to the front, but not before she had wrapped a yardage of purple satin around her dress. It was bad luck for the groom to see the bride before the wedding day, and if he saw the dress before they stood together at the altar… well, the marriage might as well not even happen.

He leaned over the counter, his eyes sparkling like the rhinestone buttons he wore. "You are part of my existence, part of myself. You have been in every line I have ever read since I first came here." She was beginning to wonder if he could speak anything other than Dickens or if he was so immersed in the character of Pip he was actually confusing her for Estella. She pushed the thought aside.

"Oh, Jean-Michel. Tomorrow I will be your bride! Then you can take me away on your adventures to far-off lands!"

"Tomorrow, you say?" he asked, as if studying the shop, taking in its wall of bridal portraits, the antique cash register, and the intricately carved newel post. "To-morrow, and to-morrow, and to-morrow, creeps in this petty pace from day to day."

Innis laughed playfully at his Shakespearean theatrics and pulled the purple satin tighter around her bridal gown. "The groom shouldn't see the bride's dress before she arrives at the altar. It's bad luck."

"Oh!" he shouted, pretending to faint and fall on the floor. "I am fortune's fool!"

She laughed again.

Jean-Michel stood up, shot a glance at the scissors, and bowed. "Good night, good night! Parting is such sweet sorrow. That I shall say good night till it be morrow."

It was only midday, but she knew what he meant.

Innis woke early the next morning to make the final adjustments to her gown. She'd done everything her mother would have, even wearing white silk gloves to avoid tainting it with the oils from her fingers. It was a masterpiece. It was entirely her – a reflection of her very soul.

She had gone up to the attic the night before to sort through the remnants of her mother's legacy. Among the treasures she had found pearls from the South Seas and Alençon lace from France.

She hung the dress at the back of the shop. Her mother would have been proud. She had a few hours before she needed to be at the church, but she could hardly stand the anticipation. She removed the scissors from around her neck to don the gown, suddenly remembering that it was scissor-sharpening day. How could she have forgotten such an important detail?

She closed up the shop, making sure the door was locked, and flipped the hanging sign to "Closed". Then she crossed the street and the footbridge to avoid Butcher's Memorial Parlor. She didn't need any morticians messing up her day – and peered in the ice cream shop, where she was greeted with waves and smiles. She still didn't know any of them, but everyone knew her. For once, everyone in Coraloo knew Innis Toft.

She arrived at Wilkinson's Hardware as she had every Saturday since she was a child, only to find the door locked and a "Closed" sign in the window. Her heart raced and her mind whirled. She had never gone more than a week without sharpening her scissors. What would she do? What would her mother have thought? The town elders had agreed to delay store opening times until after the wedding, but Wilkinson's had always been open, no matter what. Wilkin had always been waiting for her, ready to sharpen her scissors. Where could he be? She leaned in close to the window, peering through the glass, desperately hoping to see him. *There must be some mistake.* But the shop was dark and empty. Innis stepped away, feeling faint. She needed to see Wilkin; she relied on him to sharpen her scissors, to keep them safe... to keep *her* safe. He would fight for her... always.

Out of sorts and wildly distracted, Innis walked back directly past Butcher's Memorial Parlor. The sight of William Butcher stopped her short of her destination.

"Hello, Scissors," he said. "Are you ready for your big day? I hear you've found yourself a real catch. Quite talented…"

Scissors. They'd met before!

Shocked and frightened, she clutched the scissors. *Please don't ask to borrow them. Please don't ask to borrow them.* The day had already gone horribly wrong, and the last thing she needed was for the mortician to ask to borrow her scissors. *"Protect them from the morticians…"*

She couldn't move, frozen in fear.

The mortician kept talking. What was he saying?

Please don't ask to borrow my scissors. Please don't ask to borrow my scissors.

"Are you going to wear them down the aisle?"

She wanted to run, to hide. Where was Wilkin? He'd said he would always be there.

"I'd be happy to hold on to them for you."

What had he asked? Her brain was too confused with intertwined thoughts of Wilkin's proposal and images of Jean-Michel in his sparkly coat. Had she heard him correctly? Had he asked to borrow them?

She stared at the man, a young entrepreneur who'd apprenticed in the shop when they were young and found success in taking over the local funeral business as a man. She had seen him before – a long time ago, outside the ice cream parlor. She had heard him then, but not now. *Scissors.* What had he said?

"I'm sorry," she apologized. "Did you say you would be happy to borrow them?"

He looked confused.

It wasn't what he'd said at all. What had she done? And on her wedding day of all days.

"That's not a bad idea. I've wondered since the day we met what all the fuss was about. I'd love to borrow them sometime if you don't mind."

Innis gasped, gripping the scissors so tightly she could feel them digging into the palm of her hand. It had happened; the mortician wanted to borrow her scissors. Her mother had trusted her. The gypsy had warned her. She couldn't speak. Struggling to breathe, she ran back to her shop with William Butcher calling after her. She flung the door open and ran inside to hide, only to find that her wedding gown was gone.

CHAPTER 27

Wilkin Wilkinson sat down beside Roy's desk, using the contents in the clear jug to remove the fingerprinting ink from his hands.

"Don't drink it." Roy chuckled, then cleared his throat in response to Wilkin's silence. "Name?"

"You know my name."

Roy set down his pen and tapped the file in front of him. "I know a lot more than your name, Mr Wilkinson." Roy nodded at the pigtails and fedora. "But I'm not quite ready to get to that. So if you'll just cooperate, we can get this over with and see you back home with your wife."

Wilkin huffed, licked his finger, and gagged. "Are you trying to kill a man?"

Roy wanted to ask him the same question, but they hadn't got that far. "Name?"

"Wilkin... Robert... Wilkinson."

Roy wrote it down.

His fingers clean, Wilkin rested his cuffed hands on the desk and spoke. "You know, Blackwell, we're the same, you and I. Each caught up with a woman who's too good for us. The Tofts are a hard bunch to please. You've either got to be ridiculously rich or a gaudy halfwit for them to consider you good enough for their women. Lucky for her I was neither." He glanced over at the file. "So is that what this is about? Like I told them twenty years ago, I didn't do it."

Roy leaned back in his chair. "Then why'd you run?"

"I had to get away from this place for a while. You might want to consider it yourself if you go through with that wedding. You'll never be good enough for them. You want a good life with your bride? Run. France is lovely this time of year."

Roy thought momentarily about what Wilkin had said, then pulled himself back on track. "I'm not talking about France, Mr Wilkinson. I'm talking about the market. It looked like you had something heavy in that white bag."

Wilkson tipped his fedora. "Some things are best left unsaid."

"I don't think so. Here's what I know. This is my town…" He felt a sudden sense of ownership, a sense of pride in Coraloo and its people. "So it's my responsibility to keep it safe. And if I find there's a murderer running around, it's my job to take care of it."

"Where's your evidence, Blackwell? They couldn't find it then and you don't have it now. If you did you'd have hauled me in whenever you first started snooping around."

Roy thought quickly. "I have the dress."

Wilkin's face remained blank. "Now that's interesting. Wonder when that turned up."

"Why don't you start from the beginning, Mr Wilkinson? Then we'll talk about the dress."

Wilkin puffed out his cheeks and exhaled. "All right… It all started with a halfwit. An actor, if you will."

An actor. Roy knew that much.

"You see, Blackwell, I loved Innis Toft from the first moment I laid eyes on her. We were ten. She was the daughter of the dressmaker and my dad was her scissor sharpener… until I got old enough to do it for him. I saw her every Saturday for twenty years, but she never saw me. I loved her even when she didn't love me back. I only wanted her to be happy. I even went to the wedding."

"Whose wedding?"

"Innis and that actor's wedding. I can't remember his name. I don't want to."

Roy glanced down at his notes. "Jean-Michel. The victim's name was Jean-Michel."

Wilkin nodded. "You've done your research."

He had indeed. "So Innis was married before?" This made sense. A heartbroken lover.

227

A missing man. An accusation of murder.

"Jean-Whatever... the halfwit, that pocket-picking actor... he stole her dress. So I hunted him down. He wasn't hard to find. Those kinds of people have a smell... from his side business..." Wilkin passed a quick glance at the jug, "... if you know what I mean."

Roy had a pretty good idea. He'd been looking for one of those people himself.

"I had my eye on that actor from the first day he walked into her shop. At first I thought he might truly love her, but I know a thief with a side business when I smell one."

Roy momentarily considered asking Wilkin to help him sniff out the missing recipe.

"But she didn't see him the way I saw him. He fooled her, just like he fooled the whole town... as if the town needed any more upset. The shoe factory shut down not long after, and a lot of people were put out of work. It was all an act. That actor not only took half the trinkets and knickknacks in town; he took her heart so no one would see what they were up to. Disguises are more than a costume to cover what's on the outside. They often cover what's on the inside as well."

"That's a real nice story," Roy said, "but you haven't given me anything."

The door to the station flung open, Jasper entering with Innis by his side.

An anxious nervousness fell over Roy. He watched her enter, elegant and proud, with the scissors hanging around her neck. He stared at her. She was more beautiful than he'd realized.

"Mr Blackwell," Innis began, "I've come to retrieve my husband."

Wilkin's head hung low. "It's not what you think."

She laughed. "It never is, is it? Did you at least win?"

Wilkin attempted to lift his cuffed wrist. "Nope."

Innis turned to Roy. "Would it be possible for me to have a few moments alone with my husband?"

"Sure." Roy rolled his chair away from the desk and walked toward the cell. It had been a long week. He had half a mind to curl up in one of the cell beds and sleep for a couple of days. Instead, he tidied the bed and restacked the books for the second time that day.

The conversation between Innis and Wilkin was hushed and intense. She looked at her husband the way Margarette often looked at him. Occasionally, one of them would pass an awkward glance back at Roy before resuming the conversation.

Roy briefly made eye contact with Innis, blinked, and looked again, but she had returned to her conversation with Wilkin. From a distance he eyed her discreetly, her clothes clean, pressed, layered, but tattered – yet put together, somehow. Like Wilkin's wig, her shabby awkwardness appeared to be more of a costume than an accidental awkwardness. He recalled what his friend Henry had said on the phone about an alias.

Bewildered by the two of them, he shrugged his shoulders and sighed. Who were these people? They definitely weren't the people he thought he'd seen cleaning the market every day. He straightened the books again, then moved into the other cell and proceeded with his re-straightening.

Wilkin Wilkinson. The man was a drunk… wasn't he? Roy had seen him stumbling out of The Beaver's Beard on more than one occasion.

Roy turned quickly on hearing a giggle. Did Innis Wilkinson giggle? He'd never imagined her to giggle. A chortle perhaps, though he really couldn't imagine her laughing at all.

What were these two playing at? What were they hiding? Maybe it was nothing but a false accusation. Either way, Roy would get the answers he needed and then retire to his bikes for the night. They had a way of taking his mind off things, like his many ailments, and his worry over his upcoming wedding…

Roy pushed himself up from the cell bed, his knees crackling like dried-out elastic.

"All right, that's enough."

"I'll stay, but only for one night," Wilkin said, keeping his eyes on his wife.

"I think I should be the judge of that."

"And I'll tell you the rest," he said, glancing over at the file.

Innis extended her hand to Roy. "Thank you, Mr Blackwell."

"Actually, Mrs Wilkinson, I need to speak to you as well."

Wilkin pulled at the cuffs. "That's not the deal, Blackwell."

Roy ignored him. "Mrs Wilkinson what can you tell me –?"

"She doesn't need to be here," Wilkin growled.

Roy had no choice but to get straight to the point. "A man went missing over twenty years ago and your wife is a suspect."

Wilkin and Innis exchanged worried glances. "Would you mind if I took a closer look at those scissors, Mrs Wilkinson? Or should I call you by another name?"

At that moment the door to the Coraloo Municipal Building flung open again with Max Fox-McGoggins on the other side. "Constable! Constable! Come quick!"

"Calm down, Max. What is it?"

"They've done it! They've really done it! The ring is up and everyone's waiting!"

Roy had figured he would somehow be dragged into it. He'd seen them erecting the old ring but had assumed it was part of the festival's closing ceremony.

"Let me just finish up here. Then I'll come and check it out."

"No, you have to come now! They've called for you to fight. They want you to fight for Miss Toft!"

"What?"

"The elders voted. The ring is up –"

Fire burned in Roy's cheeks. "They've gone too far this time. If the Tofts want me to make a spectacle of myself… Well, I'm not going to do it." He had no doubt they'd selected some young person to take him out and make him look weak in front of Margarette.

Max tugged at his sleeve, pulling him momentarily from his anger. "But the Tofts didn't call for the fight. It was the Blackwells!"

CHAPTER 28

The strung lights illuminated the town square and the boxing ring beneath them. As had been deemed appropriate by all historical records dating up to the late seventies, the mayor stood at the contender's side. Roy paced the top of the boxing ring, attempting to calm the crowd. He'd seen the children reenact this particular piece of history down at the market, so he almost knew it by heart. Someone would actually have to want to fight him, and as far as he knew he didn't have an enemy in town.

Roy had run out, leaving Wilkin cuffed to the desk with Innis sitting by his side. He'd developed a bit of a suspicion about her, especially in relation to the scissors. Why keep them so close? What didn't she want anyone to know? Hopefully this nonsense would be over quickly so he could get back to the station.

"You all can go on home," he called out. "There's not going to be a fight."

The onlookers booed. Roy rubbed the back of his neck.

"Who among us has issued the challenge?" The mayor's voice rang out over the crowd – the Tofts on one side, the Blackwells on the other.

This can't be happening.

The town must have completely lost it if they thought he was going to stand up there and fight someone. It sounded like something one of Margarette's students would do. He looked at her sixth-graders, standing in a huddle, eyes wide, watching when they should have been in bed.

The sea of onlookers parted as Aunt Sorcha made her way toward the ring, climbing the side stairs with the aid of two Blackwell boys. Roy couldn't believe what he was seeing. *"The Tofts didn't call for the fight. It was the Blackwells."*

Roy tried to keep his anger down to a whisper as Aunt Sorcha stepped up to him. "What have you done?" he asked. "This is absurd! I'm not going to fight anyone."

"It's tradition, written in our history books. If any man can show just cause why this couple cannot lawfully be joined together in matrimony, let them fight now or forever hold their peace."

Roy would have laughed if he hadn't been so angry.

"I'm going to marry Margarette in two days. And no one is going to stop me."

"Not until you've shown those Tofts what you're made of. They'll never leave you alone. You have to show them, for the both of you."

"Aunt Sorcha, this is ridiculous! I'm not doing this."

She looked glum and disappointed. "Won't you do it for the family?"

The family.

Stephen's youngest son, Danger Blackwell – named after Pastor Donaldson, who delivered him in the middle of the flea market – climbed up into the ring, a pair of old boxing gloves in his hands. "We found these at the market. I think they'll fit." He handed the gloves to Roy. "Are you really going through with it, Roy? Are you?"

Roy's head throbbed and his palms felt sweaty. A million scenarios passed through his mind. What if he passed out? What if he was knocked unconscious and never woke up?

What if? What if? What if?

He looked across the sea of watchers, hoping to spot Margarette. She would know what to do. She always knew what to do.

The air whipped past him, bringing with it remnants of the day's Heaken Beaver Festival: a fragment of bunting, an empty popcorn box, and a pair of foam antlers.

"Roy," Danger persisted, "are you really going to fight? I can do it on your behalf if you want. I know all about the fights." He leaned in closer. "My mom says Blackwell history is my best subject."

This was insane. Maybe Wilkin was right. Maybe he did need to run off to France. But Roy was tired of running. He was tired of running from the things he enjoyed. Tired of hiding from his fears; tired of worrying that death was knocking on his door every minute of every day – the same death that had taken his father too soon. He couldn't do it anymore. He couldn't run. He had to face it.

"Are you ready?" Mayor Hennigan asked, arms raised to the crowd.

Those gathered cheered and waved beaver-emblazoned pennants in the air.

Ready?

Shadowy figures emerged from every direction of the town circle. This was actually happening. With all of its bizarre historical inaccuracies, it was happening.

The closer the men came the easier it was for Roy to identify them: Charlie Price and Stephen Blackwell, accompanied by a few cousins and an elderly uncle. He wasn't surprised to see the cousins or the uncle, but he'd thought Charlie and Stephen would have had more sense about them.

Norvel Poteet also emerged from the darkness along with a few of the town elders, all carrying old boxing gloves. He saw Earl Fox-McGoggins, Max Fox-McGoggins, Pastor Donaldson, Father Milligan, Tolliver Toft, and William Butcher Jr – Roy knew them all by name. He spoke to each of them almost daily. Surely Father Milligan had no reason to take up arms against him, unless he held a grudge from the time when he almost arrested the clergyman for pulling up Margarette's weeds.

The men climbed into the ring; Stephen stepped up in front of him. The other men, Max, and a few women he thought might be among *the others*, had lined up behind him. Roy swallowed hard. He had only been in one fight in his whole life – two if the run-in with Wilkin from earlier in the night counted; his jaw was still sore.

Stephen spoke first, eyes set on Roy. "Is she worth fighting for?"

He looked out into the audience for Margarette but couldn't see her. "I'd do anything for her."

"Then I have no reason to fight you."

Roy looked through the sea of spectators again. He would do anything... even die for her, which was most likely what would happen if a couple of these gentlemen got hold of him. It was a sacrificial love, a love that Pastor Donaldson had spoken to them about during their less than conventional pre-marital counseling session they'd had with him the day after the morning service in front of Coraloo Elementary. Roy had to admit that the pastor was an odd fellow at times, kept to himself. No one really knew much about him or where he came from. But he seemed to know what he was talking about. In the only free time it seemed Margarette had, the pastor had spoken about two becoming one, about selflessness, and loving each other beyond reason. He'd said it was a love of faith and forgiveness.

Perhaps that was the type of love that could bring him the freedom – from the fear, from the doubt, from the family – he so desperately needed. He thought he'd felt something like that love when he first slid the engagement ring into his pocket, willingly putting himself in a position to be battered and bruised by the responses of his family.

Stephen stepped aside.

Charlie stepped up next. "For what it's worth, I literally just found out about this and Velveteen really wanted me to do it." Charlie waved out into the crowd to where Velveteen sat in high heels and a black dress, wearing baby Agnes across her chest. "And I have no reason to fight you. I think that's what I was told to say." He stepped aside.

Roy shook his head. He'd always liked Charlie Price.

Roy's confidence rose. He felt strong, bold, proud. He felt brave... and oddly, he felt well.

One by one the men stepped up, refusing to play any further part in the tradition. Some apologized, and all, as was scripted by the Blackwell history, said, "I have no reason to fight you."

Those in the crowd obviously had their favorites, offering cheers and applause as each man approached the town constable.

Max Fox-McGoggins faced him, chin up, eyes squinted, gloves already tightened. "I'll fight you! Come on, Constable, I can take it! Do you know how many fights I get into at school every day? Just say it... Just say you'll fight me."

"All right, I'll fight you, but let me get these other fellas out of the way first. I'll save the toughest for last."

Roy gave him a wink; Max returned the gesture.

One after another – Blackwells, Tofts, and even *the others* who had gotten wind of the event and thought it would be fun to participate – refuted, by Blackwell tradition, their right to fight Roy for the hand of Margarette Toft.

By this time Roy was beginning to wonder whether anybody was actually going to fight him.

Thunder cracked in the distance. Roy looked up to see his next opponent, William Butcher Jr, facing him. *The Butcher.* The Tofts cheered, the Blackwells booed, and *the others* took pictures.

The Butcher turned to the crowd and bowed. "I'll fight you for her, Roy. I'll fight for her."

Fight or no fight, Margarette wasn't a prize to be won.

The wind picked up, bringing with it an odor that was strong, sharp, and sour.

The Butcher stepped closer so only Roy could hear. "I've wanted to make Margarette Toft mine since we were in high school. When she called off her first engagement I thought I had a chance. Then she found you. I've done everything in my power to pit the two of you against one a-brother…"

The Butcher closed his eyes, shook his head, then opened them. "One another." He continued, "It's easy when you can whisper into everyone's ear and they're none the wiser. I have an apprentice, you know… I made sure the Tofts knew. They like that sort of thing. Your Aunt Sorcha was more than happy to take my suggestion, too. This fight – it's tradition, right? The Blackwells like *that* sort of thing. And you… all you needed was a little distraction, something to keep you busy while I wooed the family. Poor Fox-McGoggins didn't even know he was playing along."

Roy couldn't stop the grin forming on his face. William Butcher Jr was smashed, and most likely unaware he was not only confessing to the theft of the stolen recipe but providing a motive. "Billy, I think we need to finish this conversation at the station."

"Are you going to arrest me, Roy? What for? Because I want your girl?'

"You stole the recipe."

"I didn't steal it. I took it back."

"William Butcher Jr, you're under arrest for theft and distilling without a license."

"Theft? That recipe was mine."

"Let's go –"

"No! That's not how this tradition works." The Butcher turned toward the crowd. "I will fight you, Roy Blackwell, for the hand of Margarette Toft."

"I'm not fighting you, Billy."

"Aww, come on, Roy! Let's give them a show!"

The wind suddenly picked up, blowing across Roy's face and through his hair. The people scrambled for their scattered items: hats, newspapers, umbrellas. Claudette Twittlebottom refilled her basket with fallen jams, and Norvel held tight to his postal bag. Children chased after their windswept foam antlers. And a mother held her baby tightly with one arm and a jar of Claudette's jam with the other. In the distance, Jasper and Everett were chasing a jar of jam rolling down the road.

The children watched him. He knew them, and they knew him: Roy Blackwell, constable of Coraloo. He didn't want them to know him any other way.

He turned back to face The Butcher. "I won't fight –"

But before he could finish his sentence William Butcher Jr had landed a right hook to Roy's shoulder, missing his jaw but sending him stumbling back. Roy held up his glove to say he was all right and to keep William at bay. This was childish, and William was obviously intoxicated by his own brew.

"Point, Butcher!" Mayor Hennigan called through the megaphone.

"Fight for her," William scowled, swinging again.

This time Roy ducked, sending the mortician floundering to the edge of the ring, pulling on the ropes and pushing himself off the mat.

"Come on, Blackwell. Fight me! Fight for her!"

Roy pulled off his glove with his teeth and flung it to the ground. "I'm not going to fight you, but I *am* going to arrest you."

The Butcher came at him again, but Roy caught him by the arm, pulling it behind his back. To his surprise, the Blackwells cheered. He grabbed The Butcher's other arm and proceeded to escort him out of the ring.

"William Butcher Jr, you're under arrest for theft and –"

"It's rightfully mine!" The Butcher wailed. "It belongs to my family!"

"You have the right to silence. You do not have to say anything, but it may harm your defense if you do not mention when questioned something which you later rely on in court. Anything you do say may be given in evidence."

"Evidence?" William shouted. "What evidence? Someone took it! Gone!"

"I think you need a good night's sleep. We can talk about it in the morning."

"Are you kidding me?" Max shouted from behind them. "I thought we were going to see a decent fight."

In the distance, Roy Blackwell heard Earl Fox-McGoggins say the sanest thing ever to escape the lips of a McGoggins: "You just saw one of the best fights you'll ever see – the kind where a man realizes what's important in life." And then, just when Roy thought for sure that Earl had been abducted by aliens and replaced with someone in possession of a little common sense, Earl added, "Max, have you got the wolfsbane in your pocket? It's a full moon tonight."

CHAPTER 29

Margarette had been watching from the back, long enough to see William Butcher Jr take a swing at Roy and miss. The Blackwells had cheered and the Tofts had broken out into a chant of "Butcher! Butcher! Butcher!" As if the festival hadn't made the town bonkers enough, her engagement to Roy had sent everyone over the edge.

She hadn't seen or thought about the ring since she was a little girl. Sure there had been empty threats about using it to settle minor disputes among citizens:

"It's my way or the ring!"

"Get your gloves; there's only one way this is going to end!"

However, the disagreements never made it that far; by the time the disgruntled parties petitioned the mayor and filed the necessary paperwork, the dispute had already been settled and the ring deemed too much trouble. But she shouldn't have been surprised to see the Blackwells and the Tofts resort to the public brawl – she figured someone started angling for the ring the minute their engagement went public.

She hadn't been able to handle it any longer. She couldn't bear to stay there while the families cheered and booed because of her. But Roy had stood there… fighting for her. She lay on her bed, curled up in her grandmother's quilt, the ring box empty on the bedside table. This wasn't how it was supposed to be. She wasn't supposed to be sad. In less than two days she was supposed be Mrs Roy Blackwell. *Blackwell.*

The only thing that seemed to be going as planned was the cake. Maybe they could just take the cake and run. She liked cake. A lot. The wedding notebook lay open, displaying images of ladies wearing white satin pillbox hats and tea-length dresses – no lace, no pearls. Simple. Elegant. And beside it was several years' worth of Blackwell study and research. Two dreams lay side by side. Would the realization of these dreams culminate in one disastrous moment?

Margarette hadn't known what she was getting herself into when she stepped into the first floor of the municipal building that day. Truth told, she'd never had a green thumb, so she couldn't be certain that Father Milligan was pulling up her flowers. Maybe it was her rebel curiosity that drew her in. Maybe it was because she knew the constable of Coraloo was a Blackwell. She had thought they would talk... that maybe he would inadvertently give her something to add to the notebook. But then he'd suggested the stakeout, and he'd wanted to see her again. And she'd wanted to see him. But not because he was a Blackwell. He was more than that. She should have trodden lightly, carefully weighing the risk. She should have thought it through. Had she imagined the family would suddenly be okay with it all? Had she thought she could just plant herself in the middle of a Blackwell life and have it all make sense? She'd told Roy is wasn't him... and she'd meant it. It certainly wasn't him. It was something beyond them both that she couldn't place. Something inside her that wondered whether, in all her planning, she had made a wrong turn. Because she had the notebooks. She had the lists. But she still did not have *the* dress.

She grabbed her pillow and threw it across the room.

"What kind of bride doesn't even have a dress? I'm getting married in two days!"

The huge box containing the Blackwell dress sat on the floor.

She stuck her tongue out at the notebook. *Take that, years of wedding planning! I do have a dress, and I'm going to wear it!*

Margarette lifted the lid, releasing the pungent aroma of aged perfumes. She inhaled, discerning the different accents of the fragrance: rose, lavender, and something spicy. Maybe she'd judged too harshly. She pulled the dress out and spread it out on the cottage's original wood flooring, taking note of the embellishments added by years of Blackwell brides. Then she noticed something else in the box, buried at the bottom beneath a layer of yellowed tissue paper. It was a hat, more like a fascinator, and it was so wide it took up the entire base of the box. It wasn't only wide, but tall, home to a menagerie of dried flora and paper mâché birds – handcrafted with the unconventional artistry of the Blackwells.

She stared at the muddle of creativity in front of her, then stepped up to pull her curtains shut. *Might as well try it on*, she figured. Margarette found the opening of the Blackwell dress and stepped inside. Knowing full well that it would never fit her curvy figure, she heaved the dress up over her bottom and stuffed an arm into each sleeve. Then she looked in the mirror. *Impossible*. She reached around the back and fidgeted with the zipper, inching it up with ease. Next she craned her arm up over her shoulder, reaching around her back to find it again, then slowly slid it up the rest of the way and stared at herself in the mirror. Against all the odds, the dress fit as if it had been made specifically for her. She didn't know whether to be pleased that she was wearing a dress that appeared to fit someone half her size or furious that she no longer had a legitimate excuse to dismiss the dress.

She glanced back down at the notebooks, then looked up into the mirror, catching sight of her blonde curls and pale skin. She stared hard, trying to find one genuine flaw with the Blackwell dress, but she couldn't. She smoothed down the front of the bodice, twisting round to the side to see the back.

It was time to stop playing dress-up. Time to put away the notebooks, face her reality, and stop trying to fulfill promises she had made to herself when she was sixteen, whether wedding or Blackwell-related. Couldn't she have had a normal hobby? A lot of people had hobbies: stamp collecting, birdwatching, fitness, fashion. Hers had always been the Blackwells. Only it wasn't just a hobby anymore. This was her life… her and Roy's life. She bit her lip, trying to keep her emotions in check. What had begun four weeks ago as an exciting adventure –. the planning of her and Roy's wedding – had become a whirlwind of competing Toft–Blackwell events designed to change her mind and her heart. She was exhausted. This wasn't how it was supposed to be…

Maybe she really was marked, and all of it was a sign. She tried to push away the comments and superstitions of her aunts and cousins. But what if they were right?

A roar of conversations rumbled outside her window. She stumbled over the folds of the gown to peek behind the curtain, watching the citizens of Coraloo returning to their homes. The fight was over.

Then came a knock at the door. She bundled up the bulk of the dress, undid the lock on the door, and peered outside.

Margarette quickly threw open the door. Roy was standing there, an ice bag held up to his face. She pulled him in, away from the crowd that was performing some sort of chant about pushing a mule up a hill.

"Roy! What happened?"

"I got hit with a shoe."

"A shoe? Someone threw a shoe at you?"

"Wilkin Wilkinson. I deserved it. I left him cuffed to the desk for two hours."

"Can I get you something for it? Does it hurt?"

"It's okay. The swelling should go down by the wedding."

The wedding.

She led him to the sofa. "Will it always be like this, with our families at each other's throats?"

"I'd be lying if I said no. They're both stubborn. Maybe we start a new clan... a clan of our own. A Toft–Blackwell clan. They'll be the peacemakers."

"So, constables... like you?"

He smiled. "Like me... and like you."

"I can't believe they wanted you to fight!"

"It wasn't much of a fight. The Butcher was plastered, so I arrested him."

"You arrested the mortician?"

"He's our thief... sort of." He tried to smile, but then a strange expression spread across his face. "What are you wearing?"

She flopped down beside him on the sofa. "It's the Blackwell dress, but you weren't supposed to see it until the wedding. I know it's a silly superstition, but do you really think things could get much worse?"

"It's awful."

Margarette tried not to cry. "It's all I have."

He forced a smile through the swelling. "I think I know where to get you a better one." He reached into his pocket. "Innis Wilkinson wanted me to give you this. She said you'd know what it is."

Margarette took the vintage-look card from Roy. She had one just like it.

"She said she got your message and could take care of it."

She flipped it over.

Impossible.

"Do you know what that is?"

"I... Yes, I do."

The name on the other side read: "Bella Fottasi".

CHAPTER 30

May 31, 1976

Innis Toft stood outside the church's wooden double doors. Someone had stolen her dress. She could not imagine who would do such a thing or how someone would go about it. She deduced it must have been an expert. Someone with talent, and someone no one would suspect.

The town constable had said there was no sign of a break-in – or a theft of any kind, for that matter. He questioned whether the dress had ever existed at all, and whether she had made the whole thing up. According to the constable her mother had gone crazy with fame. That was why her father had left them.

"One shouldn't get a big head, you know," he'd said. Then, seeing the way she was frantically ranting about her scissors, the officer had also suggested, "It's just pre-ceremony jitters. Maybe you should lie down for a bit before the service." He'd added that his wife was excited to see what Jean-Michel would be wearing and asked whether Innis had any spoilers in relation to the groom's attire that she would be willing to part with.

Innis had no idea what Jean-Michel would be wearing, but she knew he was on the other side of those doors, waiting to marry her.

With no gown of her own she'd had to return to the attic, where her mother's dress was boxed and buried under packages of prototypes and samples. The dress was her mother's first attempt at a wedding gown. It had lace sleeves that hung too long on Innis, like the rest of the dress. The high waist fell at Innis's hips, and the bodice drooped. This was not her dress, but she would make it work.

She gently touched the scissors. *Dull.* She needed Wilkin.

Tears fell down her face. She had let her mother down. She hadn't protected the scissors. She dabbed the tears away with a self-monogrammed handkerchief she had wrapped around a bouquet of Scottish thistle and pink heather – the thistle for unity and the heather for an extra bit of luck.

In a yellowed dress, slightly too big for her and desperately out of fashion, and with the scissors suspended by a red velveteen ribbon around her neck, Innis waited for the music to begin, the doors to fling open, and all of Coraloo to watch her walk down the aisle into the forever arms of the most spectacular man who had ever lived. She imagined them applauding and throwing rose petals at her. They'd gasp and be brought to tears to see her marrying Jean-Michel. They wouldn't notice the dress, but they would notice her. They would talk about this day forever. Her children and her children's children would hear stories of this great wonder. Their bridal portrait would hang in the community theater… or maybe on the second floor of the Coraloo Municipal Building. Mr and Mrs Jean…

He'd never told her his last name, unless Michel was his last name, which made no sense if he went around calling himself by his first and last name. Maybe he had told her and she just hadn't heard. Surely it was something fancy or French like Sauveterre, Rousseau, or Villeneuve. Innis tried to think, to imagine her new life.

Mr and Mrs Wilkin Wilkinson. No. That wasn't right… was it?

The organ blared and the doors opened, just has she had expected. Two young women she vaguely recognized stepped out in front of her. Innis figured they had decided to be her bridesmaids. She didn't know them, but she didn't care. All eyes were on her.

But as she moved down the aisle, looking from side to side to spot any familiar faces, including William Butcher, who was nowhere in sight, she noticed the whispers and the forced smiles. A few mouthed things she couldn't interpret, while another pointed frantically at the altar. Was it her dress? Because it wasn't her fault she didn't have a proper dress. She wanted to shout at the top of her lungs: "I'm not crazy! Somebody stole my dress!"

The bridesmaids parted in front of her, exposing a groom-less altar. Jean-Michel was not there.

She leaned in close to Reverend Ronald. "Excuse me, but where is my groom?"

He shrugged and shouted, "Has anyone seen the actor?"

At first she wondered if something terrible had happened, if Jean-Michel was all right. Maybe he'd been kidnapped or had fallen and been knocked unconscious.

Wilkin Wilkinson jumped to his feet from the bride's side of the aisle, his face red with anger. He raised his fist and shouted, "All hail the Heaken Beaver Queen!" and ran out of the church.

It was then that three things became clear. One: she would not be marrying Jean-Michel. Two: the kleptomaniac actor had stolen her dress. And three: the man she really wanted to marry had just run out the door.

She studied the faces in the crowd: those who felt sympathy for her, and those who thought they could relate to the pain and embarrassment they assumed she was feeling. They were wrong.

Innis dropped her bouquet onto the stone floor and walked back down the aisle, knowing her time to shine in Coraloo was over. They would never see her the same way again. In that moment she realized she had wanted to marry Jean-Michel more for them than for herself. She'd been seeking favor from the spectators. Granted, he was dazzling and adventurous, but he could never have given her the adventure she truly longed for: happiness. But now she was alone, for Wilkin had gone too, leaving her with nothing more than a drooping dress and a pair of scissors with dull blades.

CHAPTER 31

The only church in Coraloo was filled – the Blackwells on one side and the Tofts on the other. The Blackwells had attached garlands of fresh flowers to the end of each pew, creating a makeshift barrier that kept the families on their respective sides, which had been Margarette's idea to keep the families from crossing into each other's territory. Roy had done his part by appointing Everett and Jasper to stand guard, keeping watch for any unwanted shenanigans.

Roy stood at the front of the church watching, wearing his father's kilt and short coat, flanked by two gargantuan arrangements of long-stemmed white roses – the Toft contribution. Anna Sue Toft had insisted, having ordered them from a florist in the next town over two days after he and Margarette had announced their engagement. He had to hand it to her: not only did the flowers brighten the church but they gave off a pleasant aroma that masked its usual mustiness.

So far, so peaceful. In fact, everything seemed oddly quiet. Too quiet. Not a single person had said an ill word as far as he'd heard and there had been no attempts to throw food, bolts of ribbon, or small children – it hadn't been done before, but he wouldn't put it past them. He mostly wondered if they were up to something, if each family had some secret plot to halt the union of Blackwell and Toft. For the past week Velveteen had forbidden anyone with the last name of Blackwell to buy one of her macarons just in case. Roy had heard the ladies of the Blackwell book club had once taken up arms – or, more accurately, macarons – against Sylvia Toft. Unless one of the ladies had stuffed edible weapons in their handbags, the church should be secure.

Occasionally the Tofts would check their watches, waiting for the hand to point to 2:31. Margarette had explained to Roy that if a couple's pronouncement of marriage was made on the upswing of the clock the marriage would always be looking up. However, should the clock pass 3:00 for any reason, it was quite possible the Tofts would ask that the pronouncement be held off until 3:31, which would have them all sitting in the unpadded pews for yet another hour.

At the very back of the church, on the Toft side, sat Innis with the scissors around her neck and Wilkin in his wig and fedora. Roy had to hand it to those two. They had stayed married for who knew how long despite encountering a near miss on their wedding day, an accusation of murder, and long-term attempts to play dress-up in the shadows of real life disguised as a drunk and a scissors-wearing cleaning lady.

The organ blared a haunting tune that seemed extraordinarily out of place for such a happy day, but maybe that had been the Tofts' intention in their selection of tunes. Roy's groomsmen, Charlie and Stephen, joined him beside the altar.

Margarette stood behind the closed doors, trying hard to ignore whatever was poking her in the middle of her back. The organ boomed a droll hymn she was certain was of some sort of significance, and would no doubt be accompanied by some horrific event should it not be played at the exact right moment. Behind her she could hear the chatter of the crowd outside, mostly locals who were placing bets as to whether or not they would go through with their nuptials. The closing ceremony of the Heaken Beaver Festival had been put on hold for two hours as most of the town had made it clear they would rather wait outside the church to see if the wedding would actually take place.

Rumor had it an argument had broken out earlier in the day over what to throw at the bride and groom when, or if, they exited the church. Rice was suggested as a traditional choice, but someone had argued it made the birds explode, which led to the suggestion of birdseed, which was shot down as nobody wanted to see a swarm of birds relieving themselves over the crowd. Sylvia had reported the crowd would, in fact, be throwing nothing at the newlyweds, as most of them doubted either of the families would allow the ceremony to come to completion.

Instead, the bystanders would pretend to throw whatever it was they felt worked best: pretend confetti, rice, birdseed, or macarons.

The violin-playing children exited stage left. Then the organist raised her hands and dropped them onto the keys, the pipes humming as the doors at the back of the church opened. Margarette's heart pumped wildly, though she no longer felt worried about the expectations of the two families. She wasn't afraid of superstition, or that Roy wasn't the right fit. Truth and love had won her over, and with Roy by her side none of it mattered anymore.

She stood off to the side, a bouquet of peace lilies in her hands – her own choice. It wasn't what every Toft bride carried, but according to her mother they were a fine choice: a symbol of peace and good luck.

The bridesmaids, Clover and Velveteen, who held Agnes in her arms, stood side by side. Their procession began with gasps and exclamations of praise from the Tofts:

"How lovely!"

"Look at those dresses!"

"They even make the red-headed one look good."

"I hear Anna Sue picked them out herself."

"Such good taste."

There were also comments from the Blackwells:

"Who picked that color?"

"What did they do? Order them off the internet?"

"I bet her mother picked them out."

"How unflattering."

Margarette could not work out how the ladies were walking in the tight-fitting gowns. In fact, their walk was more of a shuffle, and the gigantic bow on the one-shouldered olive-green dress seemed to be giving Clover fits as it persistently swished into her face.

The door closed behind the bridesmaids. The sound of bagpipes filled the air.

Margarette took a deep breath. *Dear Lord, please don't let them kill each other.*

The doors swung open again and the guests stood for the bride.

Margarette Toft began her walk down the aisle wearing the Blackwell dress. Someone on the Toft side gasped, and it was later claimed that two of the aunts had fainted.

"What is that? Toilet paper?"

"I knew she had bad taste, but that's not even a dress."

"Aren't brides supposed to be beautiful?"

Margarette kept walking, head forward and eyes on Roy, appearing not to notice the cantankerous chatter taking place to her right. The dress rattled and swished as she walked, with an occasional jingle. When she'd tried it on, Margarette realized that bells had been sewn into the hem. On the inside she'd added a tiny earring – a flowerpot with a blooming tulip, a piece of her grandmother that she wanted to leave behind with the dress. Her something "grew". Call it superstition, call it whatever. The beliefs of the Tofts would always be a part of her. And now they were part of the Blackwell dress. The dress was borrowed… and old, so she had crossed those off right away. And her something new: a change in heart, a freedom from the bondage of indecisiveness – making that wrong decision, making a mistake, missing a blessing.

On the right-hand side of the church the response was completely different. One of the Blackwells actually applauded. Another tossed granola and dried blueberries at her, and someone else said, "She's the loveliest Blackwell I've ever seen!" At this point a handbag narrowly missed Margarette as it flew over from somewhere on the Toft side, followed by a shout of "She's not a Blackwell yet!"

Margarette tossed the offending uncle a look, having no trouble holding a hard teacher stare that said, "If you don't let me get down this aisle, so help me I will stuff that handbag down your throat." Then she smiled sweetly and returned her focus to the man waiting for her at the front of the church. She never wanted to take her eyes off him again.

Roy watched her, smiling as if he knew something no one else in the church did. He was speechless, not because of the moment or due to her bridal beauty, but most likely because she was wearing the ugliest dress he had ever seen in his life. She wasn't even sure he'd be able to find her beneath all that mess of taffeta, lace, dried flowers, beading, and other nonsense taking place underneath.

He made a disgusted face and writhed a little. Margarette bit her lip, trying not to laugh.

When she made it to the altar, she passed her bouquet to Velveteen and took Roy's hand.

He looked into her eyes and whispered, "I can't believe you actually wore it. It has a kind of smell."

"I know."

Margarette could see the Tofts anxiously checking the time out of the corner of her eye. She looked up at Pastor Donaldson and discreetly motioned with her hand for them to speed things up, knowing that half the family was hoping by some phenomenon the wedding would be delayed and the Toft–Blackwell marriage would fall apart, leaving Margarette free to marry the mortician – as despite his recent imprisonment he still had an apprentice – all because the official pronouncement of husband and wife had been made on the fall of the clock rather than the upswing.

The pastor began. "Dearly beloved…"

A resonating honk blew from the pipes, startling the onlookers and waking a few sleeping babies, including Agnes Price, who was ready for a feed. The organist startled herself awake and motioned with her hand for the pastor to continue.

Roy and Margarette had originally planned to say their own vows; they had envisioned themselves talking about their union, putting an end to the age-old family feud. Margarette had imagined the Toft and Blackwell elders giving a standing ovation as she waxed on about the healing power of love. But the busyness of recent weeks meant that she'd had no time to prepare; and Roy had been too preoccupied with the unexpected rise in crime to think straight. So they had decided to do it by the book. The ceremony continued, the sun casting rainbows of color as it shone through the stained glass. In the un-air-conditioned church, the temperature rose. Both sides broke out their handheld paper fans, furiously flapping them back and forth. Margarette occasionally looked back to see one of the older aunts casting an evil eye at an older aunt on the other side.

For years the town officials had tried to call peace meetings, but after multiple failed attempts at keeping the families from feuding the officials had decided to let them live their separate lives. Then Roy and Margarette had happened, and the families could hardly hold back after more than a hundred years of feuding.

They were nearing three o'clock, and it was becoming clear the families couldn't be in one room together much longer.

"Roy, do you take Margarette?"

"Yes," Roy replied.

"And Margarette, do you take Roy?"

"Yes," Margarette responded.

There was supposed to have been so much more to this day, taking their first communion as man and wife, lighting a unity candle, listening to a song performed by her sixth-grade students. So many elements, carefully clipped and placed in the book outlining her dream wedding.

"I now pronounce you man and wife! Ladies and gentlemen, may I introduce to you... Roy and Margarette Blackwell!"

The Tofts rolled their eyes, forcing smiles and clapping half-heartedly. The Blackwells cheered, throwing their hats into the air.

The church bells chimed three o'clock. Margarette breathed a sigh of relief and Roy wiped the sweat from his brow. They had done it. They had successfully pulled off a Blackwell–Toft wedding. Or at least, so the families thought.

Little did they know that the official marriage had taken place the night before.

CHAPTER 32

The Night Before

Roy stood outside the doors of The Star on Doka Street, pacing back and forth.

Wilkin leaned against the door. "It's not like she's going to say no."

"What's taking her so long?"

"You've gotta let her do her magic."

Roy continued to pace, attempting to peek through the crack in the pulled velvet curtains that covered the inside of the cafe windows.

"Constable!" Wilkin called, halting Roy mid-stride.

"Where's the pastor?" Roy asked. "It's after ten. He'd said he'd be here –"

"Constable…"

"Hmmm?"

"Why'd you let me go?"

"Let you go?" Roy's mind wasn't on Wilkin. It was elsewhere… inside the cafe. "Oh, right… It was just something you said that got me thinking."

He looked over at Wilkin, who appeared calm and relaxed.

He'd learned a lot about Wilkin and Innis last night before Wilkin had hit him in the face with his boot for leaving him cuffed during the theatrics of the boxing fiasco.

"Innis told me all about that dress… I don't think she meant to, but she went on about it when I dropped off the scissors. She'd made that dress with bits and pieces of her life. It was as much a

part of Innis as the scissors. That dress was meant for her. Takes a special kind of woman to make a dress like that. One of a kind."

Roy nodded for Wilkin to go on.

"I knew he took it when the coward stood her up. So I went after him, like I said, but he was nowhere to be seen. I caught up with that troupe of his in the next town over, but they hadn't seen him either. Said he'd joined up with them when they pulled into Coraloo. Swore he was a local. I threatened to kill him if I found the halfwit – I wouldn't have... I don't hunt, and besides that I'm a vegetarian."

Roy was about to inquire a little further into that, but he let it go. He was learning a lot about the Wilkinsons.

"But I'll tell you one thing," Wilkin continued. "I'd have fought him to the death if he'd even laid so much a painted fingernail on those scissors."

Roy believed him, bypassing the fact that Wilkin had been willing to take the man's life over a pair of scissors.

"You see, without the scissors you cannot make the dress. You have to get rid of the excess – the parts that are no longer needed – to expose the good. Sometimes we have a hard time letting go of the excess... the fear and the uncertainty. But if we allow ourselves to be trimmed – pruned, so to speak – we can grow. Do you see where I'm going with this, Blackwell?"

Roy was almost sure he did.

"Then the next day they tried to arrest me for the boy's disappearance. I told them I wanted to find him as much as they did.

"Innis and I tried to live a quiet life, but the detectives were crawling all over the place looking for that actor. It seems the rest of the actors disappeared, too. Moved on to take advantage of some other town, I'd guess.

"We could have lived anywhere – Paris, London, New York – and we did, for a while. With Innis's skills and her mother's legacy she was in high demand. But Coraloo was the only home she'd ever known. That's when we decided to do our own little bit of acting. We came back and put on our own show. The people around here have always been distracted by a good show. We'd be the people they thought we were. Seems like we got so deep into it we forgot who we once were. If you act crazy enough, people will begin to believe it."

So it was all an act… their life, and their perception of it.

But Roy just couldn't wrap his mind around the fake personalities. "I don't understand. You're saying it's all an act with you and Innis. Are you even married?"

"Weren't you listening? We are happily married. That we didn't hide. You have to look for the truth, Blackwell, in others and in yourself. That's when you'll know who you really are and what you were really created to be."

Roy was lost for words. All of it was a lie. So, were they really crazy or not? Sane people just didn't run around pretending to be someone else.

The next thought hit him hard. Who was he trying to be?

"What's that saying, Blackwell? 'The truth will set you free.' You've given me a bit of freedom tonight."

Freedom. Roy needed that freedom.

"Maybe we can talk more about that another time," Wilkin suggested. "Lies can be lonely, but as for the rest of the town knowing our game, we'd prefer to keep it this way, if you know what I mean."

Roy understood. Wilkin wanted him to keep quiet about their ruse.

"I guess I do have one more question." Roy scratched his head. This somehow seemed too personal. "Everyone in Coraloo knows you fake the limp, so why do it?"

"Well, that's the funny thing. I believe you have it backwards. I don't fake the limp. I fake the ability to walk upright. You should always walk upright. Stand proud and stay sharp. Nobody likes a dull constable, you know. You have the whole town watching

you; they see you for who you are, and from what I've seen, that's
something to be proud of."

"Are you ready, Constable?"

"Ready?"

Wilkin nodded to his right, where Pastor Donaldson was walking up to meet them.

"Sorry I'm late," Pastor Donaldson said, out of breath. "Are you ready, Roy?"

He was. "Yes, sir."

"Are the girls inside?"

Wilkin nodded.

"Shall we?"

The pastor pulled the door open. "After you…"

Roy stepped inside The Star. *Their place.* The hanging star lights had been dimmed, casting a warm glow across the room. At the front of the cafe, before the glistening jars, stood Margarette wearing Innis's dress, the original Bella Fottasi – simple, elegant, and authentically vintage.

Innis Toft was waiting by her side, the famous scissors still strung around her neck. Last night Roy had learned the origin of the alias – Bella Fottasi – a scrambling of letters from the name of Innis's mother, Isabella Toft. Innis had held on to her property in Coraloo, and as it was under the name Toft at the municipal building no one questioned to which Toft it belonged. The shop had remained empty for several years until their return, when for reasons of anonymity the pair thought it best to rent out the commercial space and flat above, which currently housed a lovely Italian cake shop – owned by a brother and sister, who Innis came to understand were the children of her father's fourth wife – who had wandered into the flea market one day looking for their half-sister. She'd leased the space to them under two conditions: they didn't pay and they kept her secret. The basement, however, with its exterior exit at the back, was the perfect place to live, design, order materials, and manage her team of seamstresses in France. And while the cleaning carts made great transportation devices for large dresses, there had been one time when she'd forgotten to remove a dress she had still been working on from the cart and Wilkin had run it back home.

Roy walked up to Margarette, taking her hands in his.

She turned to Innis. "I don't even know how to thank you."

Innis gave a gentle smile. "It fits you perfectly."

Despite its years in the evidence closet of the municipal building, it had held up well, and only needed a little tweaking and a minor repair or two from the designer. Lace-capped sleeves with a sweetheart neckline, it fell beautifully at the ankles. Innis was right. It was perfect: simple, unique, vintage.

Roy leaned in closer. "Isn't it bad luck for the groom to see the bride before the wedding?"

"Probably, but I'm willing to risk it."

"How was your day?"

"Long… it couldn't end fast enough."

Pastor Donaldson walked over to join them. "So, how are we doing this?

Roy looked at his fiancée. "How *are* we doing this?"

She looked directly at the pastor. "Just keep it simple."

"All right, then. Will you Roy Blackwell take Margarette Toft to be yours? To love her, to care for her, in ailment and in health, for richer or poorer?"

In ailment. He was willing to risk it. Because he'd have her by his side, always.

"I do."

"And Margarette Toft, will you take Roy Blackwell to be yours? To love him, to care for him, in ailment, and in health, for richer or poorer?"

"Absolutely!"

"Is there anything else you'd like to say to one another?"

"Oh, yes!" Margarette exclaimed. She was the same Margarette he'd encountered that day on the first floor of the municipal building – confident, comfortable, and happy.

"Roy Blackwell, I can't do it all. The wedding, the school, and the family. I thought I could, but I can't. I can't do this... or anything in my life... alone. And you planned all of this. Here, in our place. You did all of this. And the dress. Roy, this is exactly what I wanted, and this is how I want our whole life to be. Our life in Coraloo. The life we'll build together. We can do this. I know we can. If Innis and Wilkin can do it, so can we, right?" She paused, taking in the star lights above her. "I love you, Roy Blackwell, and I am so happy to be yours."

Roy swallowed. Expressing emotion wasn't easy for him. "Margarette." He cleared his throat. "I was afraid... afraid of so many things. And for a minute I was afraid we would never make it here." He laughed, recalling the first time they'd brought the families together. "But I'm willing to let that go for you. I don't think our families will ever stop going at each other, but that doesn't matter. We can love them as they are..." He was losing his train of thought. He hadn't planned for any of this. But he really only had one thing to say. "I love you. I will always love you, Margarette, and I am happy to be yours."

"Well," Pastor Donaldson said, "I guess that about does it. By the power invested in me, I pronounce you husband and wife."

Roy leaned in and kissed his wife. He stayed there, in that moment, his lips on hers, never wanting to leave. It was their place – not necessarily the cafe, but the moment, a moment that didn't care about last names, superstitions, or traditions. It was a moment that belonged exclusively to Roy and Margarette.

Pastor Donaldson cleared his throat.

Roy pulled away from her with a smile. "We did it!"

She squeezed his hands. "We did!"

Off to the side, Wilkin yawned loud and wide. "Well, that was nice, but it's long past our bedtime. We'll be heading home."

"Soooo..." Pastor Donaldson said, "are you really going to do the whole thing over again tomorrow?"

Roy looked at his watch. It was well past midnight. "Not exactly."

The pastor looked over at Margarette. "You two are really going through with the official ceremony? Are you sure you know what you're doing?"

She laughed. "I think they'd be sorely disappointed if we didn't. This is this most talked-about wedding in the history of Coraloo… It's definitely one for my notebook."

"I guess you've got a whole new chapter to add, haven't you?" Roy added.

She rocked back on her red heels. "I have indeed."

"I don't mean to interrupt," the owner of The Star, a young woman donning a chef's coat, stepped in, "but if you're hungry I can see what we have out the back. It'd be leftovers."

Roy looked at his bride. "Are you hungry?"

"Starving!"

"I'll go and see what we have. Stay as long as you like. It's the least I can do for my favorite regulars."

Margarette twirled in Innis's dress, then stopped short. "Oh, Roy. I do hope she has pot roast!"

CHAPTER 33

After being showered with imaginary rice, birdseed, and macarons – they really weren't sure what was being tossed at them given that they couldn't see it – Roy and Margarette walked from their second wedding into the town square.

The heavy rains the town had seen over the past month had left the church grounds full of puddles. The Tofts refused to walk through the water and the Blackwells asked one another whether they should have worn rain boots. Earl Fox-McGoggins had offered to provide a marital canoe should the flood come, but Roy had thanked him and told him it wouldn't be necessary. A heavy cloud covered the sky, overshadowing the reception but creating an appropriate backdrop for the hung lighting, making for an ambience that was both cozy and romantic.

"Did we order this many cakes?" Roy asked.

"No." Margarette laughed, shifting awkwardly in the Blackwell dress.

In front of the bride and groom sat three cakes. In the center was a simple lime cake with buttercream frosting… exactly what they had ordered from Torte di Jami. The wise baker had gotten wind of the vast number of locals who had planned to wait outside the ceremony and had stayed up all night baking 300 miniature lime cakes as his gift to the bride and groom, as well as a bit of convenient advertising.

The mayor had suggested they occupy the square, using the boxing ring as ground zero. To the right of the lime cake was the Blackwell cake. They had been told the Blackwell cake was blackberry rum. It stood three tiers high, each separated by antique cake pillars and toothpicks. The icing was purple… and red, but was apparently almond buttercream. It sounded delicious to the happy couple, but it looked as though someone had attempted to melt the thing. One of the aunts said they'd been going for lavender and pink but just couldn't get the color to come out right. On the top was a one-armed bride. The aunts warned them to be careful as they thought the other arm might have fallen inside, while half of the groom had already sunk into the icing.

And on the left, the Toft cake. It was gorgeous, with white fondant roses cascading down all five tiers, wrapping around the bottom, and spilling onto the table in a semi-edible garden.

Roy leaned in. "Your side?"

"Yep. I'll give you five dollars if you taste it."

"That bad?" he laughed.

"Pretty on the outside but little to be desired on the inside."

"Well, the Blackwell cake may not look like much, but you've never tasted a cake so delicious."

"Even better than the lime cake?"

"Hmmm, maybe not…"

"Should we tell someone it's about to fall over?"

"Nope. It'll inevitably topple. Maybe we could have a countdown or something, see how long it takes. I give it less than an hour."

Over on the opposite end of the square, the talent show – the Heaken Beaver Festival's grand finale – was in full swing. Since the ceremony had ended, the town had been graced by the performances of a five-year-old juggling cans of tuna, Ms Brimble and Alfie reenacting a scene from *The Wizard of Oz*, and Max Fox-McGoggins reciting the first chapter of H.G. Wells's *The War of the Worlds* from memory, which was as impressive as the suit and tie he wore.

The sixth-grade student stood with his head down, hands resting one on top of the other. Then he looked up and gazed across the town. "No one would have believed in the last years of the nineteenth century that this world was being watched keenly and closely by intelligences greater than man's and yet as mortal as his own."

The audience sat there, captivated.

Margarette had told the school's headmaster that Max was a bright kid on more than one occasion. He simply needed a little wrangling now and then. At this particular moment Max was proving himself to be quite the actor as well.

"That as men busied themselves about their various concerns they were scrutinised and studied." At the word *studied* he paused, pretending to survey the onlookers with an imaginary magnifying glass. "Perhaps almost as narrowly as a man with a microscope might scrutinise the transient creatures that swarm and multiply in a drop of water."

This dramatic interpretation continued for more than an hour, and when Max was done the audience stood and applauded.

Roy felt rather sorry for the animal impersonator and flea charmer that followed, because by then most of the crowd had taken a mini-cake break.

Wilkin and Innis Wilkinson watched from the shadows, content in the life they'd chosen and the life they'd hidden. In her other life as Bella Fottasi, Innis was a quiet celebrity – like her mother before her – crafting gowns, unique to each client, and, by cutting away their excess, helping them realize who they were created to be: princesses, starlets, rock stars, and heiresses. She only had to meet them twice – once for the consultation and once for the fitting, usually as tourists just passing through Coraloo. Wilkin was happy to be by her side, playing his role among the Coraloo cast so she could play hers in the place she loved. Because he loved her. The two were entirely indifferent to the ignorance of feuding clans.

"Who invited Cousin Innis?" asked the Tofts.

"Who invited the cleaning lady?" asked the Blackwells.

Roy had learned a few things from the two of them – things about love, about family, and about finding his place in the world.

William Butcher Jr had found his place, too… at least until Roy could figure out what to do with him. The Butcher was currently serving time for theft… a lot of theft.

Roy had visited Butcher's Memorial Parlor after releasing Wilkin and locking The Butcher up to deconstruct the still he assumed Billy was using to intoxicate the town, only to find a back room of old caskets filled with paraphernalia – eyeglasses, pincushions, and a stethoscope – instead. William swore he knew nothing of it, claiming the items must have belonged to a family member. But Roy had already figured out the real reason no one had ever been able to find Jean-Michel. It was Innis and Wilkin who had first planted the thought in his mind… the thought that people aren't always what they seem, especially William Butcher Sr. It turned out Innis had every reason to fear morticians, especially those with a certain skill set in applying cosmetics, a severe case of kleptomania, and the ability to run both a thriving moonshining ring and a funeral parlor.

And the recipe, accidentally reacquired and repurposed in the form of Claudette Twittlebottom's Jubilee Jam, had been sold to more than half the town, including Pastor Danger Donaldson. She claimed to have no prior knowledge of its potency, nor how the recipe had found its way into her shop. As everyone else in town seemed to do when something unexplained came their way, she blamed it on the festival.

The sun set over the square, signaling the end of a successful festival completed by the most talked-about marriage in the history of Coraloo.

A tap on the shoulder turned Roy around. Before him stood Bert Thompson holding a hard leather suitcase. It was battered and covered with stickers relating to places he never would have thought to go: Suriname, Croatia, Zimbabwe, Trinidad.

"Going somewhere, Bert?"

"I'm good where I am, thanks, but I wanted to give you your wedding present." Bert handed Roy the well-worn piece of luggage. "It was ours… I mean, we used to travel before she got sick. I'd go on my own, but…" he glanced at the crowd around him. "It was easier with her. She made me forget everyone else was around. I'm doing better… I figured I'd better give you your present. I want you to have it. She'd want you to have it."

"Wow, so this was yours? Looks like you've been a lot of places."

Bert crossed his arms across his chest. "I wrote them all down if you want to talk about it sometime."

"Maybe over lunch?"

"Maybe." Bert squeezed his arms in tighter. "I should probably go. I'm taking it one day at a time."

"It was good to see you, Bert."

"Good to see you too, Constable."

Roy watched Bert walk away, maneuvering around the perimeter of the square to avoid as many people as possible.

Margarette stood off to one side, waiting. Bert said life had been easier with his wife around. Roy had a feeling life would be easier with Margarette as well.

She stepped toward him, eyeing the suitcase. "What was that all about?"

"This is our wedding present from Bert."

"It looks like it's been on an absolutely lovely adventure."

He looked at her, still wearing the Blackwell dress with the ridiculous – he didn't know what it was – on her head. A bird nest, maybe? He pulled her close to him as they looked out over the fading festival.

"Are you sure you're ready for all of this, Mrs Blackwell?"

She smiled, laying her head on his shoulder. "I am. I've never been more certain of anything in my life."

"Good. So how about we get out of town for a while and go for a ride? I hear central France is nice at this time of year."

CHAPTER 34

June 1, 1976

Despite remembering that the talent show had ended the Heaken Beaver Festival, complete with a mishap on the part of a beekeeper who was attempting to showcase his talent for hypnotizing a hive of bees, the citizens of Coraloo were unable to recall the whereabouts of either Innis Toft or Wilkin Wilkinson between the hours of 3 p.m. and 9:55 a.m.

The reverend had dismissed the witnesses after the abandoned wedding, asking they show their love to Innis in the best way possible – by leaving her alone to grieve. Most had gone straight from the church to the festival to watch the closing ceremony and talent show, while a few others had remembered there was to have been a reception after the ceremony and had snuck away to the church gardens to partake of cake and peanuts.

Wilkin was gone. His father had searched every part of town – up on the hill and below – but no one had seen him. And as for the actors, whom the town had immediately forgotten, they were gone too.

Innis went back to her shop, made sure the sign was turned to "Closed", turned out the lights, and went into her room to cry. But when she got there she didn't cry. Not one tear.

Instead, a new determination rose up inside her. She pulled her sketchbook out of the side table drawer and began to draw. First she drew a dress for her mother, then one for the lady at the pharmacy, then for the actresses from the community theater. She drew one for the mayor's first wife and then his second. She drew a dress for every woman whose face came to mind, designing each one so that it would fit her perfectly. She drew through the night, with the light of the moon shining down on her sketchbook, until she had run out of paper and was forced to use old receipts, wrappers, and anything else she could find to draw on.

Before she knew it the sun began to rise. She would make the dresses. She would reopen the shop and sell them downstairs just like her mother had done. And everyone would love them. They would love her.

But then she remembered she didn't need their love to feel happy. In those hours alone she had found herself. She had seen a creativity flow from her hands that could only come from the one who had created her. She suddenly felt loved in a way she had never felt before. She felt happy.

She covered her mouth to muffle the escaping cry, as if someone would hear her and discover that she had been up all night. Not that it mattered... not that anyone would care.

Innis gathered the papers together and tucked them under her arm. She needed to get away. She needed to get out of Coraloo, just for a little while, to figure out how to do what she truly longed to do. Then she would come back. Her blue hard-shell suitcase was already packed and sitting beside the door. She had envisioned it covered in travel stickers from the far-off places Jean-Michel would take her, but she had other plans now. The adventure would be her own.

She skipped down the stairs. She could get herself out of town before anyone saw her. It was a Sunday, but too early for the morning worshippers.

Innis was grabbing the rest of the cash beside the cash register when something caught her attention – her mother's rotary desk file. She had never paid it much attention before, though it was something her mother had used almost daily. It could prove useful for what she had in mind.

There was a sudden knock on the door.

Could it be Jean-Michel?

What would she say? Would she go with him, forgetting her change of heart? Forgetting the person she had found among the dresses of Coraloo, the individual bits of divinely created personality that had gone into each individual dress? No, she would not.

She looked up at the glass-paned door to see not Jean-Michel, but Wilkin Wilkinson. She opened the door, her heart fluttering and her stomach knotted. She flipped the sign to open and let him in.

Before he had stepped through the door, and before she'd had a chance to say what was on her heart, he asked, "Are the scissors safe?"

She placed her hand on the face she had seen every Saturday for as long as she could remember.

"They are now."

Until the day when she would oddly reappear, working as a cleaning lady for what had once been the Blackwell shoe factory, Innis Wilkinson was last seen that Sunday morning walking out of the courthouse on the arm of Wilkin Wilkinson.

Innis wore the scissors around her neck and the Heaken Beaver crown on her head. Wilkin wore a fedora and walked with a limp.

Reader's Guide

1. Wilkin says, "You see, without the scissors you cannot make the dress. You have to get rid of the excess – the parts that are no longer needed – to expose the good. Sometimes we have a hard time letting go of the excess… the fear and the uncertainty. But if we allow ourselves to be trimmed – pruned, so to speak – we can grow." Do you agree with Wilkin? How does this relate to the Toft superstition around clipping?

2. Take a minute to compare and contrast Innis and Margarette. Are they as alike as Margarette begins to assume?

3. There is a lot of playing pretend: the Blackwell children and their plays, Wilkin's limp, Jean-Michel's "acting", and Innis's disguise as the cleaning lady. Do you think there are others in the novel that are playing pretend?

4. Discuss Margarette – her sense of adventure, her eye for vintage, her notebooks of "clippings", and her fascination with the Blackwells. Can you relate to any part of her?

5. Discuss Roy's life before and after Margarette. What do you feel was ultimately driving his desire for more? Do you think he found the adventure he was seeking?

6. What parts of the novel did you find most humorous or relatable?

7. The cakes made by the Blackwells and the Tofts reflect a lot of who they are. In what way do you think this is true?

8. Did you like how the author handled the resolution of the story? Is there anything you would add or change for either Innis and Wilkin or Roy and Margarette?

9. "But Roy was tired of running. He was tired of running from the things he enjoyed. Tired of hiding from his fears; tired of worrying that death was knocking on his door every minute of every day. The same death that had taken his father too soon. He couldn't do it anymore. He couldn't run. He had to face it." Fear and overcoming that fear is a consistent theme for several of the characters. Discuss the fears of Margarette, Roy, Innis, Bert Thompson, and Anna Sue Toft. Do they overcome those fears? Are there fears (logical or irrational) in your life that you need to overcome?

10. The families seem to be identified by tradition and superstition. Do you have any unusual traditions in your family? Superstitions?

www.LaurenHBrandenburg.com